Dark Secrets

Dark Secrets

A Michael Moreland Story

Brad Lussier

RESOURCE *Publications* • Eugene, Oregon

DARK SECRETS
A Michael Moreland Story

Resource Publications
An Imprint of Wipf and Stock Publishers
199 W. 8th Ave., Suite 3
Eugene, OR 97401

www.wipfandstock.com

PAPERBACK ISBN: 979-8-3852-8203-6
HARDCOVER ISBN: 979-8-3852-8204-3
EBOOK ISBN: 979-8-3852-8205-0

VERSION NUMBER 04/17/26

Dark Secrets is a work of fiction. Names, characters, places, and incidents are either the product of the author's imagination or are used fictitiously. While the author enjoyed making some events and locations in the story historically accurate, he made up a lot of things, too. For example, Prohibition on Prince Edward Island was in effect from 1901 until 1948. In this book, however, it ended sometime before 1937.

Chapter 1

"Go Dadda?" Case gurgled past the spoon in his mouth. "Go Dadda?" he asked again. Inspired by his brother, Reed added his voice, and Case's solo plea became a duet as the boys' chant grew in urgency, "Go Dadda? Go Dadda?"

Over the last several weeks, the twins had learned to follow Michael's morning habits. After breakfast, as soon as he put on his coat and hat and picked up his attaché, they knew he would soon be leaving for his morning trip to Charlottetown. Always ready to join their father for a ride in his truck, the boys turned to Susan and back to Michael, continuing their cry, "Go Dadda? Go Dadda!"

Smiling at Susan while shaking his head, Michael turned back to the boys, stepped toward their highchairs, and bent down to look his sons in the eye.

"I'm sorry, boys. It's just a little too cold this morning," he said, adding a rub to both little heads, "but this afternoon, when it's warmer, we'll go for a ride. OK?"

Leaning forward over his cereal bowl and stretching his arms toward Michael, Case's chant grew louder, becoming less of a plea and more of a demand as he hit the highchair tray with his spoon. Not to be outdone, Reed matched his voice with Case's, and the chorus continued until Susan intervened.

Bending down to speak to them nose-to-nose, she said firmly, "Case? Reed? Daddy can't take you this morning. It's too cold for you. Now, you need to finish your breakfast, and then we'll go see Grandpa. You want to go see Grandpa, now, don't you?" she asked. "He'll be waiting," she coaxed.

"Guhpah?" Reed asked. Susan and Michael listened as Case added his voice. "Guhpah? Go Guhpah! Go Guhpah!" Their chorus continued as Susan followed Michael to the breezeway door.

"They call it the 'Terrible Twos' these days," Susan sighed. "I read about it in *Parents Magazine*. It's just a stage they're going through at this age when they want their own way. They're supposed to grow out of it."

"Are you sure?" Michael asked.

"Oh, yes," Susan answered. "But, they'll probably be growing out of it just as Christine is growing *into* it. We'd best be hanging on for the ride," she smiled.

"Well," it was 'Guhpah' to the rescue this time," Michael said, donning his hat and turning toward the door. "I have only one stop in Charlottetown today, the post office. I'll be back before long," he said, as he added a kiss to Susan's cheek.

The mail was sparse, but one letter posted to Michael from Suffolk, England, in early November of 1942 had finally found its way to Prince Edward Island more than a month later. Sadly, it brought no good news. Michael read the letter a second and third time as the early-morning snow gathered in wet flakes on the hood of his truck, where he had parked at the curb in front of the post office. Although no subsequent reading could change the news the letter brought, each gave Michael another moment to grieve over the sadness it contained. Clyde Wright's widow, Myrna, had posted it two weeks after she learned Clyde had been killed on a battlefield in North Africa.

Clyde and Michael's friendship was a natural consequence of the friendship their fathers shared. Bill Wright, faithful to his family name and heritage, worked in wood as his forebears had done for many decades before him. A man who was equally adept at turning balusters on a lathe or framing a timber barn, Bill owned other skills beyond woodworking, skills he had learned by necessity over many years. Michael's father and Clyde shared the respected title of "Barnyard Mechanic," a moniker earned by men whose skills extended beyond their training and years, men whose natural talent for solving problems regularly found ways to get things done. The men worked together from time to time, repairing anything from a plow for the fields to the tractor that pulled it. When one needed the other's help, their sons accompanied them, and Clyde and Michael made the most of their time together. "A matched pair of spanners, those two," Michael's father had called them. Michael smiled as he reminded himself that he'd had to trade the term *spanner* for *wrench* when he arrived in Canada.

Michael smiled again when he recalled one of the last episodes he and Clyde shared on their bicycles. Both had worked to save their shillings to buy the best used bike they could find. Loving speed over comfort, both boys had stripped off their bikes' fenders and anything else that added extra weight. With never enough time to satisfy their hunger for riding together, even rainy days found them on muddy trails, oblivious to the stripes of mud they wore up their backs for lack of the fenders they had so willingly sacrificed. As long as they could pedal faster and jump higher over the ramps they built on the trails that bordered the pastures near Clifton Manor, they were happy. Michael still bore a scar hidden in his hairline from the wound he earned when a brief airborne flight landed him on a stone wall, face-first.

Michael looked out the window beside him as he considered that he and Clyde would never again laugh together over their biking adventures. They would never laugh together about anything. Shortly after the war began, Clyde had joined the Royal Electrical and Mechanical Engineers and trained to maintain and repair tanks on the battlefields. He had been killed with four others during a Luftwaffe attack in Egypt well behind the front lines at El Alamein, where they had retreated to find a safe location to make their field repairs. Michael could hardly believe his friend was gone.

Clyde and Myrna had married just before Michael sailed for Prince Edward Island five years ago. "I remember their wedding day," Michael said aloud. "I'd never stood up for anyone before, and Clyde was a nervous groom, as I remember." Michael smiled. Just a year later, Clyde and Myrna's son was born. They named him Michael. Their daughter, Elizabeth, was born almost two years later.

"Why Clyde?" Michael asked again, just as he had asked several other times that morning. "He had a family, and for their sake, he'd trained to serve as far as possible from the front lines. What will they do without him now?"

Michael's thoughts turned to Susan, Case, Reed, and Christine, their six-week-old treasure. Christine had her mother's eyes and the sweetest, quiet little cry that already charmed even her older brothers. However, Michael's wistful smile disappeared as quickly as it had appeared when he thought of Myrna, now a young mother of two without her husband.

In the midst of his grief, guilt raised its ugly head to compromise any peace Michael might have known.

"What am I doing here on this side of the ocean when men my age from Britain and all over Canada are risking their lives on the battlefield? Even a young man like Luc Boucher went to war while I stayed here at home. Now Clyde has been killed while I've spent my days living in safety and comfort."

Michael started the truck but didn't drive toward home. His destination was St. Peter's Cathedral. Morning Prayer had ended a half hour earlier, but Michael needed to speak with Fr. Hunt. He didn't want to take his angst home to Susan and the children.

When Michael arrived, Fr. Hunt was just saying goodbye to a small group of men who were leaving the Vestry.

"I'll see you then," he said, as the men headed toward the exit, "at our next Vestry meeting in two weeks. We'll be discussing the new budget."

As the last of the men made their way out the door, Fr. Hunt turned to greet Michael.

"Well, if it isn't the new father of three, I see at the door," he laughed. "How is your newest, Christine? We have her christening set for Sunday. Is that what you've come to discuss this morning?"

"No, Father," Michael answered. "That will be a happy and blessed event. If you have a few minutes, I need your help with something grievous."

Michael's face told Fr. Hunt all he needed to know. He ushered Michael into his office and sat behind his desk, ready to listen.

Michael's story fell out of his mouth as if he were a boy again, talking to his friend, Clyde. Only when Fr. Hunt's wall clock rang the half hour did Michael realize he'd gone on so long. In the last minutes, though, Michael recounted no more fond memories. Instead, Fr. Hunt recognized an overwhelming sense of guilt.

"But why the guilt I'm hearing, Michael?" Fr. Hunt asked

Michael didn't need to think long.

"Because Clyde is dead," he began, "and I'm still here. He volunteered to defend King and country, while I've spent my days building a new home and welcoming three beautiful children. I'm healthy and able. I could have been there beside Clyde. Instead," he said, hanging his head and looking at the floor, "I've lived in safety and luxury here, thousands of miles from the dangers of this damnable war."

Fr. Hunt sat silently for a long moment and watched as Michael's anger subsided and turned to tears.

"I understand your grief, Michael. There's no way you could ever be prepared for the death of such a good friend, is there?"

Michael shook his head, swallowed, and offered a guttural, "No."

"And you're a man who solves problems and gets things done, aren't you?" Fr. Hunt asked.

Michael nodded again.

"And you care deeply for people, too, but this time you feel helpless when you think of Myrna and Clyde's children. There's nothing you can do, is there?" he asked.

Michael, still looking at the floor, shook his head, offering another quiet, "No."

"This is one sad situation you cannot fix, but I must advise you, you cannot blame yourself, either. As I remember, you once counseled two young men in your care who were considering joining the Royal Canadian Army. Isn't that correct?" Fr. Hunt asked.

"Yes," Michael admitted, "the Boucher brothers, Luc and Joseph."

"I also remember," Fr. Hunt began, "you did not try to dissuade them from enlisting, but you counseled them to consider that not all able-bodied men are called to serve on the battlefield. Some are called to remain at home, where their service includes caring for the homes and families of those who are serving abroad. You also said that men who remain at home stay there to ensure their country will be ready to receive those who return from war. Do you remember having that conversation with them?" he asked.

As Michael nodded, Fr. Hunt said, "You were telling those young men the truth, Michael. I've watched you care for people over the last five years, and that care continues with every new individual and family who finds safety, shelter, and employment at your hands. I don't believe our God expects anything more of you, Michael. He needs you saving lives *here*, not on the battlefield."

Michael raised his head to look at Fr. Hunt and mouthed a silent, "Thank you," as he stood, hat in hand, ready to return home. However, Fr. Hunt wasn't finished.

"Please, Michael, two things more, if you can stay a moment longer," he said as Michael took his seat again. Raising one finger, Fr. Hunt stood and took a violet clerical stole out of his bottom drawer and draped it around his neck.

He said, "I am not preparing for or suggesting a confession, Michael, but this stole offers the confidence of the Church over anything further that we may discuss."

Sitting again, Fr. Hunt, in a more serious voice, began, "I have no facts on which to base the suppositions I am about to offer, so please bear with me. In my experience, both in England and here in Canada, a decorated and knighted officer such as Sir Richard does not find his way across the ocean in the midst of a global conflict unless his service to the King requires the safety that only distance from the heat of battle can provide. Saying no more, I also cannot help but conclude that your service to Sir Richard is an immense help to him and to those who depend on his expertise while he remains at a safe distance from the Luftwaffe bombs in London."

After a moment while he settled his thoughts, he continued. "Considering the vital nature of the responsibilities I believe you and Sir Richard bear, my prayers for you and your families have taken on a curious nature. I have continued to receive a unique sense over the last six months or so, that you will discover, over time, that your work will have saved many hundreds, perhaps even thousands of lives, lives with faces you may never see."

Chapter 2

When Michael arrived at Hillside after leaving St. Peter's, the snow had stopped, and he parked the Ford flatbed in front of the garage. Brenda Kimmel was just coming out of the breezeway door.

As he got out of the truck, she said, "Good morning, Mr. Moreland. Mrs. Moreland is nursing Christine upstairs. Just a few minutes ago, Sir Richard delivered Case and Reed here after their playtime with him. You'll find them in the playpen in their bedroom. They seemed quite ready for a nap. I expect they'll be asleep in another few minutes."

"Thank you, Brenda," Michael answered. "I see you have your bicycle here for the ride home?"

"Yes," she laughed. "Since it's downhill all the way to Highfield's driveway, and, as you know, only a short pedal home from there, a few flakes of snow aren't enough to pose a problem. The snow is melting as fast as it hits the ground. I'll be back after supper to get the boys ready for bed."

When Michael went inside, he found that Susan had finished nursing Christine, and he was happy to take over the burping. Susan noticed something different about him as he held Christine more attentively than usual.

"What's happened, Michael?" she asked. "Don't tell me, 'Nothing', because I know you too well, and I can see that you are in pain. Please, tell me what has happened."

Without a word, he reached into his pocket and handed her the letter. After looking at the return address she turned to him and mouthed, "Oh, no."

He watched as she read each word. He saw her cover her mouth as she tried to stifle her groans. Minutes later, when she looked up from the letter, her tears joined his. She hurried to wrap her arms around his neck while he held Christine. It was a long moment before their tears subsided, and he said, "I need to see the boys." He handed Christine to her as he hurried to the boys' room. He had to see them before they fell asleep.

Twenty minutes later, he joined Susan again as she secured Christine in her cradle for her nap. Together, they sat on the side of their bed, her hand in his. Susan was the first to speak.

"You two were inseparable," she said. "I never remember you so happy as when you were with Clyde."

"We were a pair," he agreed, "a pair of matched spanners."

"I can't imagine what this must be like for Myrna and the children," Susan said. "I just can't imagine."

"Nor I," Michael agreed.

They sat silently for a long moment before Michael spoke again.

"I went to see Fr. Hunt. I had to tell him how badly I felt that it was Clyde who had served on the battlefield and died while I've lived here comfortably, thousands of miles away."

Sitting upright, Susan asked, "You're not thinking about volunteering, are you?"

"Not now," Michael answered, "but for an hour or so, I was almost ready to find a recruiter."

"What changed your mind?" Susan asked.

"Of course, you and our children were paramount in my mind, and I had to consider that I'm already committed to SIS. But Fr. Hunt said something else that helped, though I'm not sure I understand it yet," Michael answered.

"What was that?" she asked.

"He said something about the work your father and I do, and that it may save the lives of many souls, many that I may never see. He said that someday I will understand what that means, and meanwhile I need to make my peace about staying here, caring for the people here, and being ready to receive those who return from the war."

"Do you believe him?" Susan asked.

It was a moment before Michael answered, "Yes, but not entirely, yet. I don't understand what I could ever do to help people I'll never see. Just the same, he seemed quite convinced."

"What are you going to do now?" Susan asked.

"I need to tell your mother and father about Clyde. I'm sure they don't know yet. First, however, I need to pen a letter to Myrna, offering whatever comfort I can. Perhaps your father will be able to see that the letter gets to her by air mail."

"But hurry home afterwards, won't you?" Susan said. "The children and I need you here with us, OK?"

"Of course," he answered, "of course."

Michael went upstairs to his bedroom desk, a built-in rolltop hidden behind the double closet doors near the north bank of windows at the rear of the house. He sometimes worked late into the night, and, for Susan's sake, he had built the desk into the closet so that he could close the doors on his work whenever he finished for the day, keeping their master bedroom from becoming an office. A half hour later, he signed and sealed his letter and drove to Highfield. He found Sir Richard and Lady Moncrieff in the study.

"What's this serious look I see on your face?" asked Sir Richard.

"Yes," Lady Moncrieff agreed, "is something wrong?"

Handing them Myrna's letter, Michael said, "This letter says it all."

The Moncrieffs read the letter together and offered their sympathies.

"I never knew Clyde very well except as his father's son," Sir Richard said. "I know he meant a great deal to you."

"I remember one incident that required a bandage when one of you went airborne on a bicycle and encountered a stone wall, if I'm not mistaken," Lady Moncrieff said. "Neither of you seemed too concerned, as I recall."

"No," Michael smiled. "We were daredevils, and minor injuries came with that territory."

It was the first time Michael had smiled all day, and it felt good.

"Despite this sad news," Sir Richard began, "I received communiques from Washington and London concurrently today, both containing announcements you will find quite satisfying, I hope."

He reached for a folder on his desk and handed it to Michael. There were two documents inside, both press releases. One was from 10 Downing Street in London, while the other was from the White House in Washington, DC. Michael could hardly believe his eyes. Both documents were formal statements from the British and American governments concerning the atrocities and crimes against Jews occurring in Nazi-occupied territories in Europe. The documents were part of a Joint Declaration by Members of the United Nations, scheduled for announcement on December 17, 1942.

"Congratulations, Michael," Sir Richard began. "The man you recruited from the Nazis and who was formerly locked in a cell in Halifax, the man who, after flying with the RCAF and RAF, has since become an SIS agent, Ernst Hoffman, provided testimony and irrefutable photographic evidence of Nazi atrocities occurring in Europe to the United States OSS. That testimony in Washington last month, in concert with the evidence he had already provided to SIS, has resulted in the United Nations declaration next week. It will, no doubt, result in the rescues of thousands of innocent men, women, and children. Tomorrow morning's London *Times* and the *New York Times* will carry the entire story. While many will never know, some of us will never forget that Ernst went to Washington to testify because of you, Michael. Although your involvement may never be recorded by history, heaven and we will never forget it."

Michael was overwhelmed. Only an hour ago, Fr. Hunt had said something about hundreds and thousands of lives that would be saved. He hadn't understood Fr. Hunt's words then. He was beginning to comprehend them now.

Chapter 3

"Gerhardt!" Sir Richard called as he opened Highfield's front door to welcome Gerhardt Kimmel. "Breakfast awaits us in the dining room, but what is that you have there?" he asked, pointing to the loaf pan Gerhardt carried in his hands.

"It's a loaf of Greta's kuchen, of course," Gerhardt smiled, "warm from the oven. She remembered how much you enjoyed it the last time she sent some over."

"And I can't wait to sink my teeth into another slice," Sir Richard laughed. "Come," he said, "while the coffee is still hot."

Sir Richard had invited his neighbor to breakfast with him at Highfield every Friday morning since Gerhardt had been freed from the POW camp in Alberta almost two months ago. The stiffness of their first few meetings had since melted into a camaraderie that only two retired naval officers from World War I could understand. War had made them enemies for a time. The current conflict had made them friends.

Although young when he attained the rank of Rear Admiral, Sir Richard marveled that Gerhardt had been given command of a U-boat at the age of twenty-five. Gerhardt had never sailed on a battleship like the *HMS Revenge*, while Sir Richard had no experience aboard a submarine. The two could talk for hours about their lives at sea during the war. At one of their earliest meetings, they compared the vessels they captained.

"The *Revenge* was over 600 feet long and had a beam of 88 feet. Our crew numbered over 900, and the ship always felt crowded below decks," Sir Richard admitted. "I can't imagine what you endured in a U-boat, though."

"I commanded a U-31 type vessel, 212 feet in length and less than 20 feet at the beam. Our crew numbered 35, four officers and 31 enlisted men," Gerhardt said.

"And you've mentioned that the crew shared bunks and slept in shifts, but tell me," Sir Richard asked, "how often did your men see the sun?"

"We spent time on the surface almost every day to refresh our air supply," Gerhardt began, "for oxygen depletion and carbon dioxide build-up required us to surface after no more than 72 hours under water. We spent much more time on the surface than submerged, for two reasons. First, we could travel much faster on the surface, almost 17 knots. When we were submerged, we barely made 10. Furthermore, we needed to surface so that the diesel engines that propelled us on the surface could charge the batteries we used for propulsion when we were underwater."

"Of course," Sir Richard nodded.

"But, to answer your question about the sun, when we surfaced, only an officer and a few lookouts were required on deck for any length of time. Most of the crew didn't see the sun for days and days."

"I was given command when I was 41 years old," Sir Richard mused. "They thought I was ready, but I wasn't convinced. The responsibility felt immense."

"And I was a mere 25. By the end of the war, most men commanding U-boats were even younger than that," Gerhardt admitted.

The two men sat silently for a moment before Gerhardt spoke again.

"You were at Jutland," he said, "but did you serve beyond the North Sea?"

"No," Sir Richard answered.

"Then we never hunted each other," Gerhardt said. "My service was limited to the convoy routes of the North Atlantic and the coastal waters of France south of Britain."

Again, the men sat silently for another moment before Gerhardt spoke.

"Frankly, I was thankful we were captured," he said as he turned to look directly at Sir Richard.

"Thankful?" he asked.

"Yes," Gerhardt nodded. "When we were ordered to attack merchant vessels without warning, I found myself seeking ways to avoid engaging all but enemy warships. In time, some merchant ships were armed, while a number of British warships kept their guns under wraps, disguising themselves as civilian vessels. So, it sometimes became necessary to sail away from some potential confrontations to protect my crew. Still, I had no heart for sinking unarmed merchant vessels, especially those that might be carrying civilian passengers. I couldn't bear watching crewmen and innocent passengers drown. Their cries from the dark waters still haunt my dreams."

After a quiet moment, Sir Richard asked, "And your capture?"

"We encountered a merchant convoy off the British coast in the North Atlantic. When we surfaced to identify potential targets, two American destroyers sighted us. We submerged immediately, but with our position discovered, both destroyers dropped depth charges. The damage we suffered was sending us to the bottom, and I had to make a decision. We'd been submerged for more than two days, and our batteries were weak. We were suffering from a lack of sufficient oxygen, and I knew my crew could not continue without surfacing. When we surfaced, we took several hits from deck guns on both destroyers before we could hoist a white flag. Thankfully, we lost only two of my crew of forty. My war was over," Gerhardt said tiredly. "Still," he began again, "I have terrors that wake me at night."

Sir Richard nodded but waited silently for Gerhardt to go on.

"The first is the sound of the cries of so many merchant seamen and passengers who died in the ocean waters as their ships sank," he said quietly. "They were safe at one moment, but after I ordered the torpedoes, I had no means to save them. When a ship floundered, there would be many voices calling for help, some in languages I did not recognize. Within minutes, there were fewer cries as the weaker passengers, the women and the children, succumbed to the frigid waters. When those voices ceased, the men's voices grew desperate, crying out, pleading for rescue. Then, all fell into silence."

It was a long moment later before the tears came.

"We were men at war, you and I," Gerhardt said, "but no comparison can be made between us."

"What do you mean?" asked Sir Richard.

"You hunted and were hunted by your equals, men trained in warfare on the sea, battleship against battleship, fleet against fleet, on the open water. Your men aboard and your enemies at sea were officers and sailors at war."

"Yes," Sir Richard agreed.

"But we were predators at sea," he said, "hiding from the enemy. We rarely attacked those who could defend themselves. We hunted the unknowing, the defenseless, the innocent."

Sir Richard said nothing while Gerhardt continued.

"Oh, we had our own terrors on board. You see, we knew that three out of every four men who served aboard our U-boats would not return home from battle. But it was when we were imprisoned on the bottom, and depth charges were exploding around us, that our vessel suddenly felt like a coffin. The sea, at one moment an ally that hid us from the enemy, suddenly threatened to become a cold, unfeeling, watery grave. We could do nothing but wait in silence as our last minutes of life passed. When I gave the order to surface and surrender, I finally found a moment of peace. At last, I was assured that my men would now have better chances of surviving the war than any who set sail from Germany aboard another U-boat."

After a moment, while Gerhardt sat quietly to compose himself, he spoke again.

"I envy you for your memories."

"Envy me for my memories?" asked Sir Richard.

"Yes," Gerhardt said, "those that bring you neither guilt nor despair."

After another pause, Sir Richard rose to refill their coffee cups and cut two more slices of kuchen. When he returned to his seat, he said, "I'm glad."

"Glad?" Gerhardt asked. "For what, may I ask?"

"Glad you decided to save your crew's lives and all the other lives you spared before your final engagement with the enemy. I'm glad you and your crew survived and were able to return to your families. I'm glad you stayed in Canada to establish your home and raise your family. Mostly, though, I'm glad that we, who were once enemies, can now be friends and that our families have an opportunity to live together as closely as we do. And, Gerhardt," he said as he offered his hand, "I'm glad that we can look forward to the future together, for I believe that, in time, we shall learn that the best is yet to be."

Chapter 4

"It's their way, Anna," Lady Moncrieff said. "Our husbands feel the need to protect us, even if it's just from information."

"I understand, Angela," Anna Verrier said as she stirred her tea."

The two were sitting in the east sun parlor at Highfield, enjoying afternoon tea and the afternoon sun's shower of light on the snow-crested evergreens at the edge of the western sky.

"Of course," Lady Moncrieff continued, "their roles at the Secret Intelligence Service redouble their need for secrecy, but I have some information that, though it originated with them, is something that I need to share with you. I assure you, I have their full support in this matter."

"Angela," Anna began, "it sounds serious and almost sinister. Are we in some sort of danger?"

"Not at all," Lady Moncrieff laughed, "and I apologize for all the subterfuge the situation seems to require. Bear with me if you will as I explain.

With that, Lady Moncrieff refreshed her teacup and began anew.

"As I remember from our conversation some time ago, you told me of your escape from your captivity in Michigan, when you saw a young man, a stranger to you, running toward your captor. At the same moment, you were seeking refuge in a truck that had just delivered a load of hay. Is that correct?"

"Yes," Anna responded, "that's correct."

"And subsequently, on the train that delivered you home to Charlottetown, you thought you might have seen the same young man walk past you in the aisle?" she asked.

"That's right," Anna replied, "but I've always wondered if it was just my fears that imagined such a thing."

"Let me assure you, Anna, you were not imagining anything. I can tell you his name. You saw Ernst Hoffman."

"But it was Conrad Hoffman who kidnapped me," Anna said, confused.

"And it was his son who left Munich, Germany, years before, who hoped to track his father down in Michigan, whom you saw that day," Lady Moncrieff said.

"But Armand told me that the local authorities discovered Conrad Hoffman dead at a slough in the field behind the farmhouse. Did his son kill him that day?" Anna asked.

"No," Lady Moncrieff responded. "He didn't kill him. Conrad Hoffman collapsed and died moments after his son reached him."

"But why are we discussing this now, Angela? Conrad is dead, and his son is no one to any of us." Anna said.

"Ah, but he is, Anna. Let me tell you a fascinating story," Lady Moncrieff said as she sat back into the cushioned settee with her teacup.

Twenty minutes later, Anna summarized the story Lady Moncrieff had just recounted.

"So," Anna began, "I want to be sure I have this straight. Ernst Hoffman, Conrad Hoffman's son, who came here to Prince Edward Island as a Nazi spy and executed an attack on Highfield, was then captured in Halifax and jailed on espionage charges."

"Yes," Lady Moncrieff nodded.

"And after cooperating and helping the Royal Canadian Navy defend shipping in and out of Halifax for over a year, he escaped, abandoned his Nazi superiors, and joined the RCAF," Anna continued.

"That is correct, Anna," Lady Moncrieff nodded.

"And, after his aircraft was shot down in France, he joined the French resistance and subsequently became an SIS operative. He was called back to Canada and was here in Charlottetown recently with Sir Richard. Together, they traveled to Washington, DC, on SIS business. After returning to Highfield, his orders took him back to Europe to continue SIS work there. Correct?" Anna asked again.

"That is correct," nodded Lady Moncrieff.

"All right," Anna said, still confused, "but I ask again, what has all this to do with me?"

"There's one more part to the story," Lady Moncrieff answered. "Ernst Hoffman left Munich not long after his father joined the army at the start of the Great War. Neither Ernst nor his mother ever heard from his father again. Some years later, Ernst came to study in the United States before leaving for Canada in search of his father. Several years ago, after the current war began, his mother, Elke, escaped Munich in the midst of the Allied bombings and emigrated to Canada, where she found herself interned in a POW camp in Ontario, just for being German."

"All right," Anna said, her face begging for some kind of conclusion.

"With Richard's help, she was granted leave from that camp and recently came to live among the Highfield family here on Prince Edward Island."

Looking up from the cup in her hand, Anna asked, "Are you telling me that she is here now?"

"Yes," Lady Moncrieff said quietly.

"Conrad Hoffman's *wife* is here, at Highfield, *now*?" Anna asked again.

Lady Moncrieff nodded, "Yes. She lives next door with the Kimmels. She and Greta met when both were interned in Ontario."

"And she never spoke with her husband after he left during the last war?" Anna asked.

"No," Lady Moncrieff said, "never, and, according to Ernst, both he and his mother bear a litany of physical and emotional scars that Conrad Hoffman's abuse brought them over many years."

Looking toward the afternoon sun receding on the horizon, Anna said softly, "I'm not surprised."

A moment later, she turned to Lady Moncrieff to say, "She and I have a great deal in common. We're survivors of the same evil man's abuses, and, by some quirk of fate, we've become neighbors on Prince Edward Island. Would I be wrong to hope that she shares the same determination I have, the determination to leave the injuries I suffered from Conrad Hoffman behind?"

"No," Lady Moncrieff said. "You would be of one mind with her, Anna."

Anna was quiet for another moment before asking, "What does she know about *me*?"

"Nothing, Anna, nothing at all," Lady Moncrieff said as she leaned closer and took Anna's hand. "Ernst was very discreet. He told her only that his father had abducted a local woman at the time of his escape, and that he had kept her captive until his death. He also told her he had seen a woman running to hail the hay truck that had brought him to the farm that day, the day his father died."

Tears filled Anna's eyes as she said, "Yes, that was me. Conrad was running toward the field, and I saw a young man following him at a desperate pace. An older deliveryman in a hay truck was on his way back to Flint,

Michigan, and he kindly delivered me there, a few blocks away from the train depot."

Lady Moncrieff waited until Anna was able to compose herself.

"Last week, Anna, because Ernst's departure for Europe was imminent, I asked him for permission to inform you and his mother of these few details and to arrange for a suitable opportunity for you to meet one another, if you so desired," Lady Moncrieff said.

"And you haven't spoken about any of this to Elke? That is her name, isn't it?" Anna asked.

"Yes, Elke is her name, and no," Lady Moncrieff said, "I haven't spoken to her about you. She knows nothing more than that a woman exists somewhere on Prince Edward Island who was abducted, held captive, and cruelly treated by her husband for more than twenty years."

Anna took a moment to dry her eyes before saying, "Then, perhaps it's time we closed the doors on our past and celebrated our freedom. I will confess that it has taken me every day of these two years to stop looking over my shoulder and to finally sleep soundly through the night. Although I knew he was dead, the scars my body and mind carry have not fully healed. Who knows? Maybe sharing some time with another victim will help me escape any remaining night terrors. Maybe Elke will find a new bit of peace, too," Anna said.

"Then I'll speak with Elke, tell her your story, and if she is agreeable, we'll arrange an afternoon meeting later this week. How does that sound?" said Lady Moncrieff.

"I'll look forward to it," Anna said as her shoulders relaxed and a hint of a smile appeared on her face. "I'll look forward to it."

Chapter 5

Just two days later, Lady Moncrieff and Anna Verrier were seated in Highfield's library when Patrice ushered Elke Hoffman into the room. On the table in front of the sofa sat Lady Moncrieff's favorite tea service and a steaming pot of coffee next to a steaming pot of tea, both ready for serving. Patrice had her hands full with a tray of dessert plates, napkins, and silverware. Elke was carrying a covered cake plate.

As Anna and Lady Moncrieff stood, Elke said, "Greta and I were baking, so I brought some Lebkuchen, known here in Canada, I'm told, as German gingerbread. I hope it will be a welcome refreshment in the afternoon."

"How lovely," Lady Moncrieff laughed, "because I asked our kitchen to provide both tea and coffee. We'll be able to enjoy your Lebkuchen as you might have enjoyed it on the continent."

While Patrice made her exit and the ladies were standing, Lady Moncrieff made the introductions.

Turning to Anna, she began, "Anna Verrier from Charlottetown, Prince Edward Island, please meet Elke Hoffman, newly arrived at Highfield from Ontario."

The air in the room stood still as the two women looked at each other. For the briefest of moments, neither moved except to raise and offer a hand. Then, with their eyes still locked on each other, it happened. The momentary hesitation ended, and, in a simultaneous rush, they strode the remaining few steps toward each other and fell into a tearful embrace.

Lady Moncrieff could do nothing but watch as she retrieved her lace handkerchief. With no ice left to break, the women sat together on the sofa while Lady Moncrieff poured, Elke cut the pastry, and Anna delivered the dessert plates. As they took their first bites and sips, Anna shook her head and laughed.

"I thought I would have a thousand questions, but the past seems so irrelevant at the moment. Our history hardly matters now. Today and the future are so much more important," she said.

"Yes, I feel the same way," Elke said, "for I have no interest in our past, although I regret your years of suffering, Anna. I married mine, but you were forced violently into yours."

"Still, it is all in the past," Anna said. "My husband, my daughter, and my son were waiting for me after my escape. In many ways, we were able to pick up again where we left off."

"And your wounds?" Elke asked. "Please bear with me for such a question. I don't mean to seem impertinent, but I must assume you endured physical injuries."

Nodding, Anna began, "That is true, and I will probably always walk with a limp. I've suffered broken bones, but none that have not healed."

"Ernst and I," she began, "we had each other during Conrad's rages. We helped each other throughout those years. But you were alone, Anna. I am so sorry for what you had to endure."

"And Ernst is your only child?" Anna asked.

"Yes, my only, and he, a miracle of sorts for me," she said.

"How do you mean?" Anna said.

Elke paused, forming a difficult question. "I will guess," she began, "though I believe I already know your answer, that Conrad, for all the abuses you endured from him, never demanded the kind of intimacy any woman might expect at the hands of a man like him?" Elke asked.

"That's correct," Anna said, her voice full of surprise. "He never approached me in that way. But how would you know that?"

"Because my Ernst is somewhat of a miracle," Elke said as she looked down and shook her head. "It was only after our marriage that I discovered Conrad's true nature. He had to force himself to consummate our marriage. I could not understand what was wrong with me, or what I had done to offend him. You see, Conrad could not be enticed by a woman, *any* woman. Still, he felt a desperate need to show the world that he could father a child. Once we found I was with child, he never approached me again. Thankfully, you were never in danger of him forcing himself on you."

"Isn't it strange," Anna said, "because when he forced me to go with him and several other men during their escape from the POW camp, he defended me from an attack by another escapee."

"But there's a reason for that," Elke said, shaking her head.

"What reason?" Anna asked.

"By then, as I experienced many years previously, he considered you to be his property. I'm sorry to say that he wasn't defending *you*. He was giving a clear signal that no one could take what he considered *his*," Elke sighed.

Elke sat back, remaining quiet and distant for a long moment. When she spoke again, her voice had grown dark and sad.

"In time, I had to defend Ernst against his father's undue attentions. Conrad knew that I would never leave Ernst alone and undefended, so both of us became targets of his anger. That was when Ernst joined *Hitlerjugend*. There he found some respite from his father's attentions, but, sadly, he also fell under the influence of men who embraced other evils, men who were eager to indoctrinate the injured and the impressionable."

As Anna and Lady Moncrieff nodded in agreement, Elke suddenly brightened and said, "But we've rehearsed too much of the past. I prefer the present. You know something about my Ernst. You've heard about the man he has become since the old days, but I don't know anything about *your* children. Please, tell me everything!"

The ladies' conversation went on and on. After Anna and Lady Moncrieff listed the members of their family trees, Elke laughed to learn that Michael Moreland had at one time been the target of both Michelle's and Susan's attentions. Of course, Anna had pictures of Grayson, Michelle, and Logan, and Elke had already met Michael, Susan, Case, Reed, and Christine. All three women were happy to have things in common. All had sons serving the Allied cause in the war, on land, in the air, or at sea.

While the ladies were still enjoying each other's company, they could hear Sir Richard entertaining Case and Reed in his study next door. Not to be outdone, Susan, upon hearing the ladies' laughter as she passed by in the hall, stuck her head through the door with Christine in her arms. Of course, none of the women could resist an opportunity to hold the youngest Moreland for a few minutes. By then, Case and Reed discovered their mother and sister were ready to drive home to Hillside, and they made their appearance with Sir Richard close behind.

Before the afternoon ended, Anna and Elke enjoyed much more than an introduction. Their two sad and painful histories had been freed to become the beginnings of a brighter future.

Chapter 6

The London Ernst Hoffman saw in the air from the window of the Armstrong Whitworth Albemarle as it descended southeast toward the airfield at Biggin Hill was not the London he remembered. Evidence of Luftwaffe bombing raids was everywhere. Despite the destruction he saw for miles in every direction, the city was awakening with the early morning sun, and the streets were already teeming with life. As the aircraft prepared for landing, E.D. yawned, stretched his arms overhead, and reached for his bag. Within a few short minutes, the plane was on the ground, taxiing toward the hangar.

Waiting for him at the hangar door stood a man he had never met. E.D. recognized him only by the agreed uniform of the day—black topcoat and red muffler. As E.D. approached him, the tall, blond-haired man offered the agreed-upon welcome.

"Warm day, considering," he said.

Acknowledging the greeting his orders had dictated, E.D. responded, "Considering it's December."

With that, the men relaxed, shook hands, and Jan Mollenar led E.D. toward an unmarked RAF staff car waiting at the edge of the airfield.

"I'm not used to having a driver," Jan admitted. "My orders to meet you arrived by courier only this morning. I have to assume this level of security means you are an invaluable asset to the cause. I will do all I can to assist your mission."

"Thank you," E.D. answered. "I understand and appreciate your recent SIS commitment, which offers all the dangers but lacks some of the advantages known by those who enlisted some years ago and who once served in uniform. As you have undoubtedly been informed, the nature of my work requires a level of invisibility. While we are in London, I will need you to join me in that state."

"I understand," Jan answered, adding, "while we are in London?"

"We will be here for only a short time. I will need your help arranging transportation to further destinations in England and across the Channel," he said.

Once in the staff car, the men sat silently for the half-hour drive to the Hyde Park townhouse that had become Jan's home. Almost two years earlier, Jan had helped the Abrams family escape from Holland. After their subsequent travel to Canada, Jan was left to enjoy the townhouse alone. When the staff car left, Jan escorted E.D. to a comfortable bedroom on the second floor.

"The larder is well-stocked on the first floor, considering some of the scarcities we are facing," Jan said. "The bath is across the hall. Please make yourself comfortable. I'll put the kettle on downstairs."

E.D.'s travel bag held only essentials, and unpacking could wait. He tossed his bag onto the bed and went to the more immediate task of opening the envelope placed in his hand by an RAF officer who was waiting for him as he left the plane. His orders were sealed within.

As he finished reading the orders a second time, he heard a tea kettle whistling downstairs. He folded the orders, returned them to the envelope, and locked them in his attaché before going downstairs to find Jan.

Jan had prepared a light breakfast complete with E.D.'s choice of tea or coffee. E.D. followed the scent of fresh-brewed coffee to the kitchen, where Jan immediately filled his cup.

"I haven't had a cup of coffee in days," E.D. said. "Flying with the Brits always means tea. Thank you for doing the brewing," he smiled.

"I favor coffee as well," Jan laughed. "I put the tea kettle on, just in case."

"I'll confess I heard the whistle upstairs and winced," E.D. laughed, "so the coffee was a welcome surprise."

As they sat at the table, E.D. explained, "My orders come directly from MI9, the agency of the British War Office whose principal task is to aid the escape of Allied prisoners of war and to rescue downed airmen from Axis-occupied countries. Whereas MI9 works to extract these military personnel, I'll need your help to accomplish a contrary goal."

"A contrary goal?" Jan asked.

"Yes," E.D. answered. "While MI9 works to get our men safely *off* the continent and back to England, I need to find my way back *onto* the continent. I've been assigned to aid the underground cells near The Hague."

"Getting across the Channel and landing undetected is no easy task," Jan said. "Everything about it is dangerous."

"Understood," E.D. answered, "but there's nothing about any of our work that isn't dangerous. They've put us together on this operation for a reason. They consider you one of their best."

"I will do everything in my power to help you realize your goal," Jan said.

"Tell me," E.D. asked. "How did you get started in this business?"

"It's nothing I planned or sought on my own," Jan said. "It began in Leiden when I helped a Jewish couple escape the jail cells where they had been imprisoned for several weeks. They were desperate to locate their two children, a son and daughter whom they had been forced to abandon at the rail station weeks earlier. They had trained their children to walk toward the setting sun. By miracle after miracle, we were able to follow the children's trail through the Netherlands to the sea and then across the English Channel to Suffolk, England. When I arrived there with their parents, we found the children had already been sent to safety in Canada. The Abrams, Daniel and Deborah, were desperate to pursue the children, and I traveled with them as far as London, where they left me to realize my dream of studying at the Royal Academy. They found passage to Canada, where they were reunited with their son and daughter, Jacob and Naomi. I am grateful to be able to guard and keep their home while they remain abroad."

"That was quite a feat," E.D. said, "but you said you met them when they were in jail?"

"Yes," Jan replied. "When the Nazis shut down the university, I stayed in Leiden and found work in the city offices. I watched as local officials bowed to the Gestapo and helped round up Jews. As one of the younger men, I was assigned to work as a guard in the jail, a basement cellblock that was soon filled with Jewish prisoners. It was a horrible place, full of threats and fear. The Abrams were separated and living in darkness for most of each day. I visited them for brief moments on nights when we wouldn't be observed, offering them some small reason to hope that they would live to see each other and their children again." Jan closed his eyes and paused for a moment before saying, "Nightmares of those days still claim my sleep." After another moment, he said, "When the time was right, I was able to help Jacob and Deborah, escape."

"You took quite a risk," E.D. said.

Nodding, Jan answered, "I suppose I did, but I could do no other. It was my first of several escapes. Of course, I never thought I would risk returning to the Netherlands, but others there needed my help, and I could not refuse them."

"I understand," E.D. said quietly. "Some time ago, my plane, an RAF Vickers-Wellington bomber, was shot down near Strasbourg. When I offered my aid to the French resistance there, they put me to use immediately. Since then, I've spent my time out of uniform, hiding in plain sight. The horrors I've witnessed since then demand a response. I'll do whatever I can to see the Nazis defeated and the innocent spared."

"So, we're to find our way across the Channel to the Netherlands with The Hague as our destination?" Jan asked.

"Correct," E.D. nodded. "Where did you land after your last Channel crossing?"

"Hoek van Holland," Jan replied. "I'm sorry," he continued, "you may know it as 'Hook of Holland'. The Germans keep it heavily patrolled and defended, but I know some local fishermen who have met us offshore in the past and delivered us safely a short distance from one of several beaches the Nazis are less likely to patrol. Mind you, once we've made the initial crossing, it will fall to us to row ourselves to shore, where we'll land in darkness. Although nothing about the journey will be easy, I have confidence our Dutch allies will be ready to meet us and will serve us well."

"How soon can we expect to sail from England, then?" E.D. asked.

"The earliest would be two days," Jan answered, "but I would consider four days more likely. There are people on this side of the Channel who will need to contact those on the other side. Making those contacts depends on tides and weather. Meetings are done face-to-face, and that takes time."

"Understood," E.D. answered. "So, let's get started with what's left of the day and pursue our goal with all due haste. Allied lives and thousands of innocents, all potential Nazi victims, depend on us."

Chapter 7

At Highfield on a Sunday in mid-January, Michael and Sir Richard were enjoying a few quiet afternoon moments after a sumptuous dinner. Although Highfield missed Alida's kitchen skills since she and Philippe had moved to be with their daughter in St. John, Elke Hoffman had been honing her culinary skills at Highfield for several weeks. Today, following an appetizer of French onion soup, the menu included a roast round of beef, mashed potatoes with gravy, honey-roasted carrots, pickled beets, winter squash, and a German chocolate cake. When the Moncrieffs and the Morelands retired from the table, all were replete.

With dinner finished, Lady Moncrieff and Susan were content to take the children to the library for the boys' playtime before their naps. Christine was already asleep following her noon feeding.

Left to themselves in the dining room, the men's conversation turned to the battlefront news of the week.

"The Soviets have surrounded 22 divisions of the German Sixth Army at Stalingrad," Sir Richard said. "Over 175,000 German soldiers have been killed. Another 140,000 have been captured. Hitler's egotistical dream that he could successfully open a second front against the Soviets has now become his nightmare."

"According to President Roosevelt's State of the Union address in the newspaper last week," Michael said, "the United States has already committed one and a half million men overseas and is looking forward to an invasion in Europe. With Stalin approaching from the east and the Allies from the west and south, it appears Hitler will have his hands full."

"He won't be raising his hand in the air in that damnable salute to himself much longer," Sir Richard smiled. "Instead, he'll be wringing his hands in despair."

"You said something last week about German women being conscripted, didn't you?" Michael asked. "Have you learned anything more?"

"Oh, yes. It's another sign that Hitler is showing his desperation. German women between the ages of 17 and 50 are being conscripted to replace men in German factories. They need every possible man on the battlefield."

"So, this is another frantic move showing how close Germany may be to defeat," Michael said.

"Absolutely," Sir Richard agreed with a smile, "and I have some recent news of the war in Europe on my desk in the study."

"From your smile, I must conclude it's something good," Michael said.

"Oh, not just good, Michael. *Very* good," Sir Richard said with a grin. "Just two nights ago, the RAF conducted its first air raid over Berlin in fourteen months. Our bombers dropped over a thousand tons of bombs, sparking fires that could be seen for a hundred miles around. I hope some of those bombs fell in Hitler's neighborhood," he smiled.

"Have you any news from Nigel and Boyd?" Michael asked.

"There's not much to tell right now, and that makes their mother and me very happy," Sir Richard began. "After leaving the Indian Ocean, the *Formidable* had been in Rosyth for a refit. When the work was completed in November, she sailed for the Mediterranean to replace the *HMS Illustrious* in support of the invasion of North Africa. Nigel has finally realized his dream to fly some of the fastest fighters. After the Martlets he's been flying for several months, the *Formidable* now carries Supermarine Seafires—the Spitfire designed for the marine environment of the Fleet Air Arm. He's happy to leave the Fairey Swordfish and Albacores behind."

"And Boyd is still in British East Africa aboard the *Revenge*?" Michael asked.

"Correct. The *Revenge* continues to perform escort duties, sailing out of Kilindini Harbor in Mombasa," Sir Richard said.

"As I recall," Michael smiled, "Boyd was rather taken with a young lady, a Wren."

"Oh, yes," Sir Richard said, "her name is Kathleen, Kathleen Balfour. Her family is from Windermere."

"Is Balfour a familiar name to you?" Michael asked. "I'm familiar neither with the family name nor of Windermere."

"Well," Sir Richard began, "Windermere is in the Lake District in Cumbria, quite a lovely place where people retreat for recreation. As to the family name, Arthur Balfour was Prime Minister in the early part of the century, the author of the Balfour Declaration."

"The Balfour Declaration?" Michael asked.

"Yes," Sir Richard answered. "It was a declaration for the establishment of a national home for the Jewish people in Palestine. It was made in 1917."

"Given Hitler's unrelenting efforts to purge the German population of Jews, it seems that Prime Minister Balfour was a man ahead of his time," Michael said.

"Indeed," Sir Richard agreed, "a man of foresight and honor, and certainly beyond the realm of the Moncrieffs."

"What do you mean?" Michael asked.

"I mean that a family whose forebears once served as Prime Minister and who promulgated such a declaration may not be ready to approve a union with a family of mere Moncrieff status."

Michael recoiled at the phrase, *mere Moncrieff status.*

"I don't understand," he said.

Sir Richard began, "Kathleen Balfour would be the daughter of Robert Balfour, the 3rd Earl of Balfour. We Moncrieffs must gaze a long way up the social ladder to approach the Balfours."

Feeling ill at ease suddenly, Michael managed to ask, "So, you're saying that Boyd, because he's a Moncrieff, may not be considered worthy to marry into the Balfour family?"

"Perhaps," Sir Richard said. "I know how I felt when I dared to seek Angela's hand."

"How so?" Michael asked.

"I felt I might be overstepping my welcome. I knew she was willing to have me, but I was not at all sure her family was. Although I've met with some successes since, successes and honors that have raised my social status in the eyes of some, like many, I remain a loss to myself."

"Yet, Lady Moncrieff's family did accept you," Michael said.

"Yes, but still, I know I wasn't the one they would have chosen. In time, I became one they could *accept*," he said.

"Then is that why Lady Moncrieff helped to push Susan and me together?" Michael asked quietly.

"Push?" asked Sir Richard.

"Yes," Michael said. "She pushed us to confront the reasons we thought we weren't suited for each other. Susan thought she would someday suffer from epilepsy. I had neither social status nor wealth to offer. I felt I could never be accepted."

"As did I," Sir Richard confessed quietly.

"Yet, you accepted me into your family, granted your permission to marry your daughter, and someday to father your grandchildren. Is there any one of them you would deny today?" Michael asked.

Shaking his head and laughing to himself, Sir Richard declared, "Never in a hundred years."

"Then perhaps Boyd should follow his dream to marry Miss Balfour, despite what her forebears have been or done compared to what his have been and done," Michael said. "Perhaps Nigel will be able to do the same."

"I hope they will, Michael. Thank you," Sir Richard added, "I hope they will."

Sir Richard looked away again for a long moment, then looked down and shook his head.

"What is it, Richard?" Michael asked.

He answered, "It's just the past, one of those things I may never understand."

"How so?" Michael asked.

"Just thinking back," he said quietly. "She was a gold sovereign, shining in the sun. By comparison, I was a worn farthing in a poor man's pocket. Yet she saw something worth redeeming, I suppose."

"Angela?" Michael asked.

"Yes," Sir Richard said. "We came from such different stock, and I never knew what she could have seen in me. It wasn't just money. It was history. My family had no history to offer. I'd have given up, but she wore her father down. I knew I could never deserve her. I was the luckiest man in the world."

"Is that why she was able to get your promise to receive me if I came to you for Susan's hand?" Michael asked.

"Yes, Michael. At that time, you and Susan were just children. She could see things I could not. She had fought for our union, and I owed her that promise, just as I owed it to Susan and you," he said quietly. "I was a nobody when I met her. She taught me that there are no nobodies."

"But, your knighthood," Michael objected. "No one knighted by the King is a nobody," Michael said quietly.

"Oh, that," Sir Richard said, shaking his head. "You don't know that story, do you?" he asked quietly.

"I only know it was during the Great War, at sea, during the Battle of Jutland," Michael said.

"Yes, I was at Jutland, but if you read the history of that battle, you will find nothing of heroic note that included the *HMS Revenge*," he said quietly.

"Then what happened?" Michael asked.

Sir Richard paused a moment before saying, "I had met a young sailor on board, Able Seaman Stephen Clark. Some fifteen years earlier, his father, Christopher, had served with me as a Midshipman aboard the destroyer, *HMS Avon*. As part of his training, Christopher attended to and 'shadowed' the officers. I encountered him regularly aboard the *Avon*. He impressed me as a particularly attentive and caring young man. We parted when my orders took me to the *Revenge*."

Sir Richard paused for a moment then continued, "A year later, Midshipman Clark, while on holiday with his family, lost his life while rescuing a swimmer at a beach near Aldeburgh. He left his wife and only son, Stephen, behind."

"How sad," Michael said.

"Yes, and I didn't know anything about it until years later when an Able Seaman introduced himself to me aboard the *Revenge*. We passed on deck one morning when he snapped to attention, saluted, and spoke. "Sir, Commodore Moncrieff, sir," he said. "Permission to offer greetings from my mother, sir," he asked. At first, I was taken aback by his boldness at addressing an officer, but at the mention of his mother, I granted him the permission he sought. He said he had cited my name in a letter to his mother some weeks earlier. She recognized the name and told him that his father and I had served together. In our conversation, I learned of his father's tragic death."

Sir Richard hesitated for a moment as his thoughts traveled back more than twenty years.

"It was a cold, wet morning as we stood there on deck, and the seas were growing rougher by the moment. All at once, a gust of wind and a rogue wave hit us hard at starboard. We found ourselves awash as the frigid water crashed onto the deck and pulled us backward toward the sea. In no more than a second, another wave carried a Lieutenant Commander named Baird overboard and into the water far below. Without hesitation, Able Seaman Clark shouted, 'Man overboard', threw off his pea coat, and jumped overboard to rescue Baird. The waters were so icy, and the sea so rough that they might have perished in mere minutes. Thankfully, other sailors were on hand and able to lower a boat while Clark kept Baird's head above water. When the lifeboat finally reached them, the crew pulled Baird aboard. At that same instant, I saw Clark flounder from exhaustion, and I knew he was about to go under. No one else saw what I saw, but having learned that his mother had lost her husband to the sea, I couldn't let her lose her only son. I didn't have time to think. I leapt overboard and found Clark underwater. When we broke the surface, he lay limp in my arms, unconscious while I worked to keep us afloat. Thankfully, another boat was in the water by then, and they brought both of us to safety."

"Both Baird and Clark survived unharmed?" Michael asked.

"Yes," he said quietly, retrieving his handkerchief to dry his eyes.

Michael sensed that Sir Richard had more to say, and after an appropriate moment, he asked, "That's not the end of the story, though, is it?"

"No, it's not," Sir Richard said. "Both men were back in service within a week. The Admiral aboard the *Revenge* made a full report to the Admiralty Naval Staff in London. Clark was awarded the Conspicuous Gallantry medal for Baird's rescue. Upon our return to port, I was promoted to the rank of Rear Admiral for my part in Clark's rescue. As if that wasn't enough, the Admiralty referred its full report to King George, and at the war's end, I was knighted for 'Conspicuous Gallantry and Intrepidity in time of war at sea,'" Sir Richard said quietly.

Both men sat silently for a long moment before Michael broke the silence.

"Permission to speak freely, sir?" he asked with a smile.

Sir Richard had to answer with his own smile.

"Granted," he laughed.

"Thank you," Michael began. "On Sunday, Fr. Hunt quoted from John's gospel, 'Greater love has no man than this, that a man lay down his life for his friend.' You, sir, offered your life to save Able Seaman Clark. I submit that no sons or daughters on earth can boast a more noble lineage than those born to men who have proven their willingness to make such a sacrifice. Please consider carefully that both the Admiralty and King George honored you appropriately that day for the example you set for all senior officers serving in the Royal Navy."

Sir Richard had to shake his head and chuckle. "You have all but quoted His Majesty's commendation," he said.

"I'm sure the Clark family will always hold you in the highest regard," Michael began, "and when and if you have occasion to meet the Balfours, I believe they will as well."

Chapter 8

Within six weeks of arriving at Highfield after enduring nearly two years of incarceration and forced labor in the POW camp in Manitoba, Gerhardt Kimmel had gained nearly twenty pounds. Well on his way to full recovery from the physical and emotional scars he bore when he arrived on Prince Edward Island, he had begun to fill the void left by Philippe Henault nearly two months earlier. With his sons, Friedrich and Carl, at his side once again, the trio delighted Luc Boucher with the care they provided the farm buildings and the livestock.

"The Kimmels are used to doing everything by hand, so they've learned every shortcut to eliminate wasted energy. They carry something in and carry something out when working at every job. Almost every trip does double-duty. So, when Friedrich and Carl feed the cows, they arrive with not only a bale of hay, but also with the wheelbarrow and tools needed to muck out the stalls. While one finishes mucking, the other has already begun milking. It's like clockwork, and it's evident they love making everything more efficient," Luc boasted when reporting to Michael.

"German efficiency is known worldwide," Michael commented. "Will they be ready to work on firewood this afternoon?"

"Oh, they love the cordwood saw," Luc laughed. "They'd never seen what the PTO on a tractor could do. When I hooked it up to the cordwood saw, they were amazed."

"Then they'll love the wood splitter, too," Michael laughed.

"I hope so," Luc laughed. "With all the limbs the spring storms brought down and the thinning we've done around the cultivated fields, we've got fifteen or so cords to cut and split, more than we've ever needed here."

"Then we'll have some smaller stove-length wood to offer at the farmstand. Folks need stove wood no more than a foot long for their kitchen and parlor stoves," Michael said.

"We can handle that," Luc said. "By the way, Gerhardt had an interesting idea. He suggested we spread some manure on the gardens before we get a hard freeze. Mixing it with the mulch that comes out of the barns will feed the soil and protect it from run-off through the winter. When we clean the stalls we'll load the manure spreader at the same time, avoiding the need to make a pile we have to load a second time."

"That sounds like genius to me," Michael agreed. "When we plow in the spring, the soil will be seasoned and ready for planting. Let's do it." Turning toward his truck, Michael called over his shoulder, "I'm off to Freeman Ford to get some tune-up parts for the tractors and the trucks. I'll check in with you when I get back."

"Sounds good," Luc said as he waved and turned toward the barn.

Michael could hardly remember the last time he'd stopped to see Bill Stewart at the Parts Department at Freeman Ford. He had stocked up on the regular maintenance needs for oil changes and spark plugs in the spring, but the middle of winter brought the cold weather that sometimes made starting gasoline engines more difficult. If he got all the parts he needed today, he could spend a few hours each morning for the next couple of days getting the tractors and trucks in shape for the rest of the season.

As he drove to Charlottetown, he remembered some of his early visits to Freeman Ford more than four years ago. Bill Stewart had been more than helpful on a number of occasions, especially when Michael manufactured the cooling shroud for the flathead V-8 engine in his Ford flatbed truck. Bill's advice to seek a patent for his invention had helped make Michael a wealthy man.

Michael parked his truck under the Service Department sign and passed through the door toward the Parts Department counter inside.

"Well, if it isn't Michael Moreland," Bill laughed as he watched Michael walking toward him. "It's been a while," he said as he reached to shake Michael's hand.

"Yes, it has," said Michael. "How have you been, Bill?"

"Oh, I'm just the same," Bill said, "I never change. A little older maybe, but that's all."

"And a little thinner, too, I notice. And your wife?" Michael asked.

"Marge? Well, that's a different story," Bill said. "You know she's not been well for some time. Between the bursitis in her knees and the stomach problems she's had, I've cut my hours here in half. She does better when I'm with her more of the time. I'm thinking about hiring someone to help her at home when I'm here at work."

"I'm sorry to hear things have gotten this serious," Michael said. "Is there anything you need, or is there any way we can help?"

"Not that I can think of just now, Michael," he said, "but enough about my problems. What can we do for you today?"

"I've got a list," Michael said as he unfolded a page he retrieved from his attaché. "I think this is everything."

Taking one look at the list, Bill said, "Give me a few minutes to gather these parts for you. We keep maintenance items like this in stock. Feel free to visit the showroom while you wait, even though we haven't had a new car to sell for some time now."

"So, I understand," Michael said, "but that must keep you all the busier back here, stocking parts to take care of the older cars and trucks."

"That it does, Michael," he laughed, "that it does."

Michael took Bill's advice and made the stroll to the showroom, stopping to watch the mechanics at work in the repair bays on the way. Steve Freeman was sitting at his desk in the showroom when Michael arrived.

"Michael Moreland," Steve called as he stood, walked toward Michael, and offered his hand. "We haven't seen you here for some time."

"No," Michael laughed, "but every car, truck, and tractor at Highfield is a Ford we drove off this lot. They all need maintaining, so I'll remain a loyal customer as long as Bill keeps the shelves stocked."

"Yes, Bill," Steve said quietly as he turned to go to his desk.

Sensing something wasn't right, Michael followed and took a seat opposite Steve.

"What's wrong?" Michael asked.

As he sat down, Steve said, "Then I guess he hasn't told you."

"About his wife?" Michael asked.

"His wife?" Steve asked, puzzled. "Oh, Marge has her aches and pains. Everyone does at that age. No, it's not Marge," Steve said, shaking his head.

"But he just told me about her bursitis and stomach problems and how he's had to take some time off to care for her," said Michael.

"Yeah, that's what he tells everybody," Steve began. "But did you notice he's looking thinner? Oh, and if you look closely, you'll notice his lips, face, and even his fingernails have a blue tinge."

"I told him he looked thinner just now," Michael said. "What is it, Steve?"

"It's a kind of chronic pneumonia. He's susceptible to infections, probably due to the gassings during the war. From what he's said, men his age only have a few more years when it gets this serious," said Steve.

"And how long ago did it begin?" Michael asked.

"He's had his problems breathing since the war, but the doctors diagnosed the pneumonia five or more years ago," Steve replied, "but he's sure that doctors can't do anything for him now. Lately, he's been too fatigued to work full-time, so he only comes in every other day or so."

"Thank you for telling me. I'd never have known otherwise," Michael said.

Just then, Steve's telephone rang, and Michael rose from his seat with a nod and turned toward the hallway that led to the Parts Department.

Bill was returning from the warehouse when Michael got to the counter. Another employee was carrying two boxes that held Michael's order. As the other man returned to the garage, Bill looked down at Michael's invoice and said, "Everything's here, just as you listed it."

When Bill looked up from the invoice, Michael's eyes told him everything.

"Oh," he said. "So, Steve told you?"

Michael nodded and said, "I'm so sorry, Bill. I wish I could do something."

"Do something?" Bill asked. "Aw, Michael, c'mon. You've been doing something every month for almost four years."

Michael said nothing as Bill continued.

"I didn't know at first, maybe even for the first six months or so. But then it came to me. It had to be you, and all because I urged you to apply for a patent for your first invention. I was really afraid that someone else would file for it if you didn't act right away."

Michael said nothing but waited as Bill continued.

"It was only a few months after that when a check began to arrive from Quebec every month and then continued like clockwork. After the first few checks arrived, I bought Marge a new car, and we got some new furniture for the house. After that, though, when my cough got worse and I began to feel weaker, all that changed. I'd seen doctors for years after the war, and no one could offer any long-term answers. I began banking the checks to build up a nest egg. I knew I wouldn't always be here to take care of Marge," he said as he looked toward the floor.

When he looked up again, he continued, "I'm happy to tell you there's enough in that account to take care of Marge for at least the next twenty-five years. When you add my RCA pension, she'll be able to live like a queen, thanks to you. Don't worry about us, Michael. I must say, men the likes of you don't come along every day. We'll never be able to thank you enough."

"But, your doctors," Michael began, "are you sure they. . ."

Bill raised his hand, shook his head, and cut Michael off.

"No, Michael. They couldn't help my father; they won't be able to help me. It's pneumonia, and it gets worse over time. There might be a couple of years yet, but really, we'll be fine. We have our faith, and it's real, the same as yours. I'm not afraid, especially because I know Marge will have everything she needs. I have you to thank for that, Michael," he said as he stretched out his hand.

Michael took Bill's hand in both of his as Bill said, "Now don't be a stranger. I'll expect to see you in here again before too long,"

"You can count on it, Bill," Michael said, "you can count on it."

Chapter 9

After nearly a month in Scotland at Rosyth in the fall of 1942, the *HMS Formidable* had sailed for Scapa Flow. Sqn Ldr Nigel Moncrieff had reason to smile when they left port with twenty-four Grumman Martlets and six Supermarine Seafire fighters aboard, all gathered from other squadrons. With aircraft like these, Nigel was satisfied that the *Formidable* was fully equipped and ready to support the Allied invasion of French North Africa as part of *Operation Torch*. Thankfully, it now appeared the British invasion was imminent.

Successful in taking several Nazi Ju-88's out of the air and sinking the Nazi's U-331 in mid-November, the *Formidable* remained on patrol in the western Mediterranean, supporting other military operations and ready to defend Allied military convoys.

At the same time, Nigel's brother, Boyd, had spent almost two months at port in Durban, South Africa. Though based in Mombasa and charged with defending Allied Indian Ocean convoys, the *HMS Revenge* required her own refit, including several radar upgrades and several new anti-aircraft gunnery sets. The port at Durban was well stocked with the equipment, facilities, and personnel to get the refit done as efficiently as possible.

In any other circumstance, Durban, a port of unparalleled Allied strategic importance to Indian Ocean and Pacific campaigns, would have captured Boyd's interest for every waking moment. Durban was the temporary home to constant waves of supply ships, troopships, and battleships, but it was not the home of one Leading Wren Kathleen Balfour, who remained in Mombasa. After seeing her almost every other day while they were together in Mombasa, Boyd was at a loss when he suspected the *Revenge's* days in Durban might turn into weeks, or even months.

Fortunately, communications between the two African ports by both radio and the post were among the best Boyd could have imagined. The mail that took a week to travel by sea sometimes flew south from Mombasa and arrived in Durban after only two or three days. It was during his third week away from Kathleen when Boyd had reason to be concerned that something wasn't right.

He had never gone more than six or seven days without hearing from her, so after ten days, he began to worry. Although he had no reason to think she'd grown disinterested in their relationship, he had bouts when he feared the worst—that some other young officer had turned her head. He read and re-read all her most recent letters, looking for anything that revealed a change in her feelings for him, but found nothing. Although he continued to write daily now, still, it was another several days before a letter arrived from Mombasa. There was only one problem. His heart sank when the return address revealed the letter was not from Kathleen. It was from her friend, Cheryl Beatty.

Boyd took the letter to his quarters before he opened it. He wanted to be hopeful, but as he read, he could not help being alarmed. Cheryl had written,

Dear Boyd,

I am writing on Kathleen's behalf because she is not able to write for herself. She doesn't want to worry you, and she has asked me to send her love.

She has contracted malaria and is hospitalized with others who are suffering from the same malady. It has been over a week, and the doctor has yet to see any improvement in her condition. Still, he hopes her fever will break soon. Along with the fever, her symptoms are not unusual, but they are debilitating -chills, sweats, and extreme fatigue, along with a sick stomach and vomiting.

The doctor, content that Kathleen has no previous history of respiratory or intestinal illness, has told me he still has hopes she will make a full recovery. Because she remains feverish, she must remain under treatment and in quarantine until her fever breaks.

Since visitors are not permitted due to the risk of contagion, I am limited to rarely permitted telephone contact with the nursing staff. I will write to you again as soon as I have news from her doctor.

Until then, I will continue my prayers for her healing. I know you will join yours with mine.

Most sincerely,
Cheryl

Boyd was aware of the dangers of contracting malaria. Every enlisted man and officer had received training in how to avoid exposure to the disease. But he was also aware of the worst strains of malaria, the cerebral forms that could cause lasting physical and mental issues and, at its worst, even death. He knew that malaria affected not only the physical body but also had a way of affecting its victims' minds, leaving them fearful, unable to sleep, and prone to hallucinations. He prayed that Kathleen would receive adequate doses of quinacrine to aid in her recovery.

Despite all his training, knowledge, and work to maintain a positive attitude, he found nothing to comfort him. He lay on his bunk with his face in his pillow, starving himself of oxygen so he could imagine how desperately Kathleen felt, enduring the fever, cough, and breathlessness that malaria brought. His helplessness overcame him, and he succumbed to tears.

"I've only just found her," he whispered. "I can't be without her, I can't," he continued.

He thought back to the day they first met in Gosport, her knowing smile, and later the flash of her eyes, and the immediate magnetism that brought them together. Their reunion in Mombasa was magical, as were all those dream-like hours they'd spent together, her hand in his, their eyes meeting again and again, each peering into the other's heart.

"We were made for each other," Boyd half-sobbed. "I need her, and you know I've never needed anyone before. You can't take her away from me now."

At that moment, Kathleen lay semi-conscious on a cot in the Mombasa Hospital malaria ward among several dozen others. As an orderly mopped her brow with a cool water compress to reduce her fever, she looked up with fever-wearied eyes, unable to focus. "Boyd? Boyd?" she asked. "I'm afraid, Boyd. Hold me, Boyd."

"I'm sorry," the orderly said as he glanced at the chart at the foot of her bed. "I'm so sorry, Leading Wren Balfour, but Boyd is not here. However, I promise to direct him to you as soon as he arrives."

Almost two thousand miles away, Boyd still lay on his bunk with teary eyes, longing to hear Kathleen's voice as much as she yearned to hear his.

Chapter 10

Prince Edward Island, like most of Canada, was still reeling from the news of the Dieppe Raid of August 1942. Over six thousand infantrymen, mainly from Canada, were part of an amphibious and air attack on Dieppe, a German-occupied port in northern France.

Although located along a long cliff overlooking the English Channel and well within range of RAF fighters, the Luftwaffe proved more than a match for the RAF due to the support of heavy anti-aircraft fire from the ground. Despite the combined support of a regiment of 58 Churchill tanks on the ground, 220 RAF fighters and 250 RAF bombers in the air, along with 237 Royal Navy ships and landing craft, the Allied troops were unable to overwhelm the Nazi defenses. At the end of the day, the RAF had lost 106 aircraft to the Luftwaffe's 48. The Royal Navy lost 33 landing craft and a destroyer, the *HMS Berkeley*. The most significant losses, however, were numbered in human lives. Of the more than 6,000 infantrymen who landed on the beaches, 5,000 were Canadians. At the end of the day, 916 men had lost their lives, more than 2,400 were wounded, and more than 1,900 were captured and remained prisoners of war.

Thankfully for those on Prince Edward Island, none of the Canadian casualties at Dieppe came from PEI. By the end of 1942, however, 46 of PEI's own had been killed in action. The youngest were still in their teens, while the eldest was 49. Among these brave men were RCA doctors, RAF and RCAF pilots, RCN sailors, RCA artillerymen, infantrymen, and members of the PEI Highlanders and the Veteran Guard of Canada.

Although Prince Edward Island was the smallest province in Canada with a population of fewer than 100,000, its people had proven their support for the war effort at the enlistment offices. Nearly one out of ten of its population—men and women alike—continued to volunteer for active service during the war. During the same time at Highfield, Lady Moncrieff continued to lead women who were not available for service. Together, they remained active by supporting the Canadian Red Cross Society.

On one cold afternoon in the second week of January, Lady Moncrieff hosted a party of Highfield's women, joined by Elke Hoffman and Greta Kimmel in the east sunroom. Today, they were assembling food parcels for prisoners of war.

"It may be hard to believe," Lady Moncrieff began, "but I've just seen a report that the Canadian Red Cross Society currently sends out more than twenty thousand food parcels every week."

"All in bags like these that weigh over ten pounds when filled?" Brenda marveled. "That's amazing."

"And all with similar staples," Susan agreed, "like these tins of corned beef, milk powder, chocolate, dried fruit, biscuits, tea, and even soap."

"And cheese, pudding, margarine, and preserves," Ingrid added.

"Rationing here at home limits many families who don't enjoy the supply and variety of food that we at Highfield have from its gardens and livestock," Lois said.

"That is certainly true," Doris agreed. "Many folks depend on the farmstand which regularly has empty shelves before the end of the day, even in winter."

Patrice wore a quizzical look as she reached for a tin of corned beef.

"But there was a POW camp in Charlottetown in the last war, wasn't there?" she asked.

"Yes," Doris answered, "there was."

"So, did the Germans send food here for those prisoners?" Patrice asked.

"No," Doris answered. "They ate the same Canadian food, that we ate."

"But we're sending food for our soldiers now. Does that mean the Germans aren't feeding them?" she asked.

The discomfort in the room grew until Lady Moncrieff spoke.

"We really don't know how our men and women are faring as prisoners, but in the last war, their living conditions and their diets were often very poor," she said, "although officers usually enjoyed better quarters and better food."

"Are they mean to the prisoners? Do they hurt them?" Patrice asked.

"There were stories of mistreatment when the war ended, but we don't know about the current practices," Lady Moncrieff said. "However, I believe we can still assume that those of higher rank enjoy better treatment."

"Hugh will be glad to hear that," Patrice began, "because his father has been a prisoner for two years now. He was a commanding officer, so he'll be treated well, right?" she asked. Without a moment's pause, she continued, "Hugh's mother got a letter from his father, a letter that Hugh said the Red Cross collected and sent to Switzerland, then to Portugal, and finally to Scotland."

"Was that some time ago?" Lady Moncrieff asked.

"I think it was almost a year after he was captured. Hugh didn't say anything about any other letters," Patrice said.

"Well," Susan interjected, "as the war goes on, there will be more and more prisoners. We want to make sure that none of our soldiers ever has to worry about having enough to eat. Some may not need the meals we send, but other people, perhaps civilians, might. I'm sure that families living in the middle of the war zone will be happy for whatever the International Red Cross delivers."

"And these packages have everything," Brenda added. I'm so glad we can help in this way."

"As am I," Ingrid said, "and I've had another thought."

"Tell us, please," Elke said as she reached for the small bars of soap she needed for the remaining parcels in front of her.

"I wonder if we could send some parcels to Hugh's father. Since he's an officer, maybe the Germans will be sure to pass them on to him. What do you think?"

"A capital thought," Lady Moncrieff smiled. "Patrice, if you can get the particulars required to address the parcel, we can send one every week. Do you think Hugh can help you with that?"

With a smile that dispelled any worries she might have had earlier, Patrice nodded happily.

"He's out with Luc and Simon right now," she began, "hunting ducks and geese. When he gets back, I'll ask him straightaway."

When the end of their work for the afternoon was in sight, Doris excused herself and nodded to Patrice to follow. When the two returned from the kitchen, they brought not only a pot of hot chocolate, but also a pot of tea and a plate of fresh sugar cookies, each topped with a spoonful of peach preserves.

As the ladies filled their cups and served each other, it was clear their work was complete, but all looked forward to their conversation that would go on and on.

Chapter 11

Jacques Boucher and Michael had spent evenings for the last two weeks of January working on the *Lady M* in Highfield's boatshed. The cabin's mahogany required refinishing every season, a task that required stripping the old finish, bleaching, and varnishing every square inch. Before they could apply the spar varnish, however, any dark spots that remained after bleaching had to be treated with oxalic acid. Then they had to neutralize the acid with a baking soda-and-water rinse. Once thoroughly dry, the mahogany would be ready for its final sanding and the first of seven coats of varnish, each lightly sanded between coats.

Michael was reloading the woodstove in the rear corner of the boatshed when Jacques came through the door, stomped the snow from his boots, unwound the scarf from his neck, and took off his canvas work coat. The red of his flannel plaid shirt matched the red on his cheeks.

"I knew it would be warm in here when I got out of my truck and saw the snow melting off the roof and dripping to the ground," he laughed.

"I started this fire at noon today," Michael nodded, "and I've been back every hour or so to refill the firebox."

"Then there's a good chance that the mahogany is dry and warm enough for its first coat of varnish?" Jacques asked.

"Well, let's find out," Michael said as he picked up a rectangular leather case and started up the ladder at the *Lady M*'s stern.

"What have you got in that fancy leather case?" Jacques asked as he followed Michael up the ladder.

"It's called a moisture meter, brand new on the market. The McLeod's introduced me to theirs when they were finishing the woodwork at Hillside," Michael answered.

"So, a machine can tell us if the wood is dry enough?" Jacques asked.

"That's right," Michael smiled. "Take a look."

Jacques watched as Michael revealed what looked like a small wooden box that had a meter on its face, like a car speedometer. He plugged the machine into an extension cord and picked up what looked like a small two-tined fork with a wooden handle, connected to the box by another cord.

One look at Jacques's puzzled face brought Michael's explanation.

"Here's how it works," he said. "You push these two little pins into the wood, somewhere inconspicuous. The machine measures the water content in the wood by sending an electrical signal from one pin to another. We can see the results on the meter."

Jacques squinted his eyes and moved closer.

"It reads ten per cent by my eyes," he said.

"Just what I'd hoped," Michael smiled as he looked at the meter. "Anything below fifteen per cent is what we need. Time to open a can and get stirring."

"What'll they think of next?" Jacques mumbled as he shook his head and climbed down the ladder. Michael followed him to the workbench, where they opened a gallon of varnish, stirred it thoroughly, and divided it into two fresh paint cans. After they'd been working for twenty minutes or so, Jacques put his brush down and turned to Michael.

"I didn't tell you at the time," he began, "but when Ernst Hoffman was here a month or so ago, I couldn't help thinking about that day at the sawmill. It all came back to me like it was yesterday."

Michael rested his brush on the can lid, turned to Jacques, and nodded.

"I know a lot of water has gone over the dam since then," Jacques said, "and I understand, from what I've heard, that he's a changed man, but I still had to wrestle with my feelings."

Michael nodded again.

"But then I remembered the day when you and I met at the *Cask and Cork*, several years ago now," he said, looking down at the deck, "and I took a minute to breathe. I hurt some people that day, some older people, innocent people just trying to enjoy their lunch."

As Jacques looked up, Michael nodded, and Jacques continued, "And you put me in my place."

Neither spoke for a moment until Jacques said, "You owed me nothing, but you came and found me in the boatyard a day or so later, and you offered me a job when I really needed one. You didn't have to do that, but you did. And because of you, I met Doris and found a family of folks who never turn their backs on each other."

Michael nodded once more.

"So, all I'm saying is that I want to let Ernst Hoffman's past be the past. I owe him a second chance. You taught me that when you gave me one. So, I owe him his, and if I forget that again, I'd like you to remind me that we had this talk today, if you will," he said.

"Done," said Michael as he offered Jacques his hand.

As Jacques stepped forward to grasp Michael's hand, he laughed and said, "I still don't know how a man my size ended up face-down on the floor at the *Cask and Cork* with a little Brit on top, keeping me there until the constable arrived."

"You know," Michael said, "ever since that day, I've wondered the same thing, too!"

After a good laugh, the two went back to their work. When they finished a little after 8:30 that night, they agreed that the *Lady M* was beginning to look better than she had looked for a long time.

Chapter 12

Aboard the Dutch botter boat, *Anna Hoop*, a flat-bottomed V-hulled boat designed for sailing in the shallow waters of the Netherlands canals and estuaries, E.D. listened as Jan described the state of the Dutch underground in The Hague.

"The Abwehr has more than a hundred, perhaps even two hundred intelligence agents in the city. Probably half of those are executing Hitler's plans concerning the Netherlands, like charming the local authorities to adopt Nazi goals to identify and capture Jews. At the same time, they're being trained to aid the Wehrmacht in achieving Hitler's goal of defeating the British. With the Netherlands a short flight away from the British Isles, the Abwehr has concentrated its efforts on Hitler's dream of crossing the Channel and invading Britain. They've succeeded in landing several agents in England who maintain radio contact with the continent. Sadly, they have also had some success in charming some of our Allied agents to the Axis side. Later, though, a number of those agents proved to be *double* agents, who continued to work for the Allied cause," Jan said.

"So, it's almost impossible to know who we can trust," E.D. concluded.

"Exactly," Jan answered, "but it's even more complicated than that. Do you know the name Canaris? Admiral Canaris?"

"Yes," E.D. answered. "He's Hitler's man in charge of the Abwehr."

"Correct," Jan answered, "but we've learned his personal convictions force him to walk a tightrope. Through his network of agents, he has been known to find ways to help Jews escape. He has even invented missions and convinced some of his officers to lead Jewish prisoners to safety."

"So, again, it's almost impossible to know at any given moment who is a friend and who is a foe in The Hague," E.D. concluded.

"Yes," Jan answered, "so every time we land here, we need to determine who among our regular contacts remains trustworthy, find out who has left the fold, and determine who among our supposed enemies might prove to be a supporter of our cause."

"I've flown with the RAF, and I know what it is to crash in enemy territory," E.D. said. "I was lucky to be rescued by resistance fighters and hidden away when the Nazis came to search for me and the men with whom I flew. My goal for this mission is to locate Allied military personnel, particularly airmen whose planes have gone down. We don't want them captured and interrogated. I need to find them and lead them back to England," E.D. said.

"And I will do all I can to connect you to those who can find those airmen and help them get home safely," Jan promised.

At that moment, E.D. heard the captain of the *Anna Hoop*, Hans Visser, call out, "Hoek van Holland."

"Hoek van Holland," E.D. whispered to himself as the captain slowed the engine in the darkness, a little less than a half mile offshore. Hans smiled, pleased that not only the darkness, but also the rain and the west wind at their backs were in their favor. The Dutch coastline, only a few miles from Rotterdam, was littered with German shoreline outposts intent on intercepting any small craft ferrying Allied personnel to or from England. Over the past year, Hans had ferried dozens of passengers from these shores to England, but never before had he been called to deliver them to the Dutch coast. Now, two hours before dawn, the sound of the rain would help cover any noise the *Anna Hoop's* engine could make. The west wind would help drive the skiff to shore before daylight. As Hans and his crewmen lowered the skiff, E.D. and Jan prepared to board, and Hans offered his final farewell.

"Sterkte!" Hans said solemnly as he shook both Jan and E.D.'s hands. Giving the skiff one final push toward shore, the captain returned to start the *Anna Hoop's* engine and set a course south and west away from the coastline.

Neither Jan nor E.D. had ever known a darker sky. Leaving the oars in their locks, they let the wind have its way. It was half an hour later that the men saw a faint glow of lights on the coast. As they drew close enough to hear the surf hitting the beach, they noticed two sets of blinking lights on the coast, one to the north and one to the south, both blinking in a similar recognizable pattern.

"That may be them," E.D. heard Jan say over the noise of the wind.

"But I see two of them," E.D. said, "both offering the same signal."

"Yes," Jan answered. "When the Germans think they have broken our code, they send similar signals, hoping to intercept any Allied seacraft."

"But if they're both sending the same signal," E.D. asked, "how will we know which is which?"

"Hans radioed our people from the *Anna Hoop* with instructions to maintain the most recent code, but to go silent for one full minute before offering a second code, inverting the first. It will take both of us to watch the lights and detect any change in the signals."

"I'll take the one I see to the North," E.D. volunteered. "I'm seeing one long flash and two shorter flashes."

"Now count the seconds between the end of one cycle and the beginning of the next," Jan said.

Soon E.D. answered, "About fifteen seconds."

"Good," Jan replied, "that appears to match the signal I'm watching to the South. Now, we'll monitor our two signals. When the time between signals takes longer than fifteen seconds, we'll keep a count."

Both men peered into the darkness for another minute before Jan said, "There. The signal to the South clearly matches yours to the North. Now we'll watch and wait until one of them breaks the pattern and leaves 60 seconds between repetitions. Even without a timepiece in the dark, we should have no problem counting out the time."

Soon E.D. said, "Mine didn't repeat after 15 seconds; I'm still counting."

"All right," Jan said. "At 60 seconds, the pattern should resume."

The next time E.D. spoke, he said. "There it is. Exactly 60 seconds to my count."

"That verifies the new code," Jan said." We'll confirm one more cycle before we start rowing to the North."

And row they did. With Jan training his eyes on the signal light on shore, E.D. rowed with abandon. By now, the dawn's first light would ordinarily have begun making shadows on the beach, but the cloud cover protected them from discovery. When the skiff's bow hit the sand of the shoreline, three men came out of the darkness as one offered a hoarse whisper.

"Zwart of wit?"

Recognizing the coded question, "Black or white?" Jan answered, "Zwart, mijn vriend," and the two quickly shook hands. Moments later, the five men had dragged the skiff into a nearby fisherman's boatshed and were on their way through the darkness to a small house nearly a half mile inland.

Chapter 13

Breakfast had ended on a cold winter morning on the last day of January when Sir Richard retired to his study, picked up the telephone, and invited Michael to meet with him to hear some good news. Michael drove his flatbed over from Hillside within fifteen minutes, but before he could take his seat in Highfield's study, Sir Richard had already begun speaking.

"I believe historians will call January 1943 the beginning of the end for the Third Reich," he said as he leaned back in the leather chair behind his mahogany desk, his arms comfortably folded over his stomach.

"Then," Michael asked, "we have reason to be more hopeful than ever?"

"Yes," Sir Richard continued, "all the pieces on the board are poised for the endgame."

"There's good news then from the Allied forces in Europe?" Michael asked.

"Oh, not just Europe," Sir Richard smiled, "but also from the Mediterranean, North Africa, the Indian Ocean, and the Pacific theater."

"Say on," Michael smiled. "I want to hear all you can share."

"And you shall," he said, as he sat forward to reach for a folder on his desk. "I have it all here in *bullet* points," he smiled.

Michael had to shake his head at Sir Richard's choice of the word *bullet*.

"Hitler's mania, exhibited in his refusal to attend to the recommendations of any of his advisors, has made January 1943 a month for us to celebrate. First, his attack on his former Soviet ally has resulted in an overwhelming defeat of German forces at Stalingrad. As of the first of the month, 22 German divisions had been surrounded, over 170,000 killed, and another 135,000 taken prisoner. At the end of the month, another 90,000 German troops surrendered."

"I can't imagine the horror suffered by the German soldiers, and the grief of their families and loved ones," Michael said.

"Lives lost because of Hitler's unspeakable and maniacal inability to grasp reality," Sir Richard agreed, "but there's more. You may remember that last month, Hitler began conscripting women between the ages of 17 and 50 to work in factories so that more men could go to war?"

"Yes," Michael said.

"Well, now he is ordering all remaining men from the age of 16 to 65 into his labor pool, along with all women over the age of 17. The burden on German households with children and no parental support will wreak havoc on families. Now the children will have to fend for themselves," he said.

"So, the whole population has to suspect that their country is in dire straits," Michael said.

"Yes," Sir Richard nodded, and it's showing up in some subtle ways. For the first time, the newspapers, instead of boasting of constant military successes, are hinting at what's really happening. Even the radio broadcasts have left the usual marches and cheerful interludes behind. Recognizing the realities of the losses on the battlefields, they've turned to music that some call *mournful*."

"Has the RAF had any recent successes on the continent?" Michael asked.

"Yes, they have, and the Americans have joined us there. You'll remember that in November of last year, the RAF bombed Berlin, dropping over 1,000 tons of bombs. Just two weeks ago, on January 16, the RAF bombed Berlin again, the heaviest attack ever. A few days later, the Soviets finally succeeded in ending the Nazi siege of Leningrad, which Germany had enforced for more than a year and a half."

"And the Americans you mentioned?" Michael asked.

"Yes, I got ahead of myself," Sir Richard said. "About a week ago, after the Luftwaffe attacked a school on the outskirts of London, killing forty-one children and six teachers, the United States Air Force, with more than 90 B-17 and B-24 heavy bombers, targeted Germany's main military port and the naval yards where the Kriegsmarine builds its U-boats. The Luftwaffe, desperately defending the Wehrmacht elsewhere, couldn't offer any defense against the attack. The US aircraft, after dropping their bombs, flew away unscathed."

"Remarkable," Michael said. "And in North Africa, the Pacific, the Mediterranean, and the Indian Ocean?"

There are hopeful signs in all four," Sir Richard went on. "In North Africa, the British 8th Army under General Montgomery captured Tripoli at the end of the month, freeing Libya from Italy's control for the first time since 1912. Meanwhile, Australian and US forces recaptured New Guinea from Japanese control. The Allies are currently forcing the last of the Japanese forces from Guadalcanal in the Solomon Islands. In the western Mediterranean, where Nigel is aboard the *Formidable*, the Allies have control. While the Royal Navy continues to support the invasions in North Africa, I predict an Allied invasion of Italy soon. The Indian Ocean has remained relatively quiet since the earlier attacks on Ceylon last year. Boyd will remain safe aboard the *Revenge* on the East African coast as the Japanese desperately rally their forces in the Pacific, where they are busy defending themselves against ever-growing Allied forces. Like his Axis compatriot in Berlin, Hirohito would benefit by recognizing he has bitten off more than he can chew."

"But, while Hitler, Hirohito, and Mussolini dare to fight on, the Allies still have to meet those threats on every front," Michael said. "Isn't that so?"

"Absolutely," answered Sir Richard, "and perhaps as seriously as at any previous time. When madmen sense the possibility of defeat, insanity often rules. Those who have followed them, having sworn to defend the pipe dreams of madmen, find themselves in the most danger."

"So, things are beginning to crumble from within?" Michael asked.

"Yes, and Hitler's Field Marshal von Bock and several of his highest-ranking Generals have already been dismissed because they dared to challenge demands from which Hitler would not yield. His second front offensive against the Soviets remains the most obvious error," said Sir Richard.

"Those closest to him must find themselves at their wits' end," Michael agreed.

"Sometimes a rational force from within will find the strength to withstand the apparent lunacy, while hoping others will join. To date, there have been several attempts on Hitler's life by those who still retain a rational mind. Mussolini, another madman, is also on the brink of defeat. Hitler will soon abandon him, because Hitler will not share Europe with anyone. In the Pacific, Hirohito maintains the Japanese mindset of nobility that ends only with sacrifice. Sadly, he will likely defend his cause until defeat is imminent and dangerously final for him and his people," said Sir Richard.

"So," Michael asked, "what do you see for the immediate future?"

"I believe the United States, in concert with all the aid we can offer, will fight on to victory in the Pacific. Together, we will take back every acre the Japanese have conquered. The war in the Mediterranean and North Africa will soon prove a distraction compared with what will be required on the European continent. Nothing short of an Allied invasion from the south in Italy or from the coast of France that marches straight to Berlin will defeat what is left of the Nazi forces. Assuredly, any invasion will be a costly one, but we will be victorious. Germany will lose heart as the Allied forces surround Berlin. Right will triumph, but the war will not yet be over," Sir Richard said solemnly, as he stood, walked to an east window, and stared into the distance.

Michael waited in silence. Sir Richard looked suddenly weighted, like a man who has just taken on a burden heavier than he can bear. Michael could only conclude that the contents of intelligence reports meant for his eyes only also brought sadness to his eyes and a weight to his brow. After a long moment, Sir Richard spoke again.

"Our final battle of this war will be fought by whole generations who will be left with only memories of innocent men, women, and children who suffered the horrors that a madman and all those who followed him inflicted on humanity. Those wounds may never heal. Those who stood by or turned their backs on the evil they ignored will live with those wounds forever."

Sir Richard stood silently for another moment before concluding.

"Decades will pass before Europe will have reason to hope there can be sufficient healing to promote a real measure of peace. We have years and years of work to do, Michael. My generation will pray that yours has the strength to continue the work that we won't have time to accomplish,"

Michael nodded and looked solemnly into Sir Richard's eyes before he spoke.

"There will not be another generation like unto yours, sir, not in the Commonwealth nor among our allies who have fought beside us throughout this war. When hostilities have ceased, and the victory has been won, it will be left, not only to your generation but also to mine to take on the challenge of reclaiming the truth and decency that can flourish only in the freedom of democracy," Michael said. "I pray we will find the strength and determination that you and all our forebears owned so that we can reclaim those treasured principles for which so many have given their lives."

Chapter 14

"You know that my Ernst is very fond of you, don't you?" Elke asked with a twinkle in her eye.

Brenda, not knowing how to respond, said simply, "Well, I've hoped so," as her blush rose to her cheeks.

"Forgive me," Elke said, shaking her head. "I shouldn't have been so forward with you. Perhaps I've simply enjoyed seeing him happy after so many years of unhappiness."

"Thank you, Mrs. Hoffman," Brenda said as Elke interrupted.

"Please, Brenda. Please, let me be Elke," she asked.

"If you like, of course, Elke," Brenda said a bit uncomfortably. "Forgive me, but I simply don't know how to deal with becoming a couple, especially with a man like Ernst. I've never been close to anyone other than my family before."

"I think I understand," Elke said, "although it has been many, many years since I found myself in your position. It was certainly different in those days. We lived in a smaller world. My beau was a neighbor. You and Ernst have come from different continents, and you never knew each other until you met when he was nearly twenty-five, and you were. . ."

"Seventeen," Brenda said, "and I was alone and without a family, suddenly on my own in a city far from home."

"That's what Ernst told me," Elke said. "There you were, all alone on a train platform, yes?" Elke asked.

"Yes," Brenda answered. "I had never traveled, let alone by railway. I was in a new city, and I didn't know what to do or where to go. I had nothing."

"You must have been so afraid," Elke said.

"Yes," Brenda replied, "I was, and suspicious, too, especially when Ernst approached me. I had no reason to trust any man I might meet, but Ernst was different."

"Different?" Elke asked.

"Yes. I could tell he was sincere and didn't have any agenda. I suppose you could say he was simply honest. I could tell that he wasn't looking for anything from me," Brenda said. "Instead, I somehow knew he wanted to help me, and with no thought of recompense. I don't know why I went with him that night, but somehow, I knew I would be safe. Your Ernst rescued me."

"I'm sure he'd been in your position before, Brenda. He knew what it was to be alone. Tell me, now, has he said anything about his father?" Elke asked.

"Yes," Brenda replied, "but I'm sure he hasn't told me everything. He's always been short-spoken and reserved when he mentioned his father. It's as if he doesn't want to speak ill of anyone, but I could see the hurt in him was bone deep."

"Then you've seen correctly, Brenda. In his most difficult moments, he remains an injured boy. At other times he seems unscathed by his injuries. Did he tell you about his last meeting with his father, far from here in the United States?" Elke asked.

"He told me he had tried several times over several years to find his father. He also told me he tracked him to Michigan and that his father died the very day he found him," Brenda said.

"That's correct," Elke began, "but Ernst was already a trained soldier then, and part of him wanted nothing more than to kill his father, a man who many would say deserved killing. But when his father ran from him, and Ernst caught up to him, his father was already dying. He died sobbing in his son's arms. Ernst was still looking for a way to please his father, to hear his father say just once, 'Well done.' Ernst made the scene of his father's death look suspicious, but only so that no one would consider that a family member could have been involved. He always wanted two things. First, he wanted to protect me. Second, he wanted to find peace with his father before he died. He was there to see the end of the final sad chapter of his father's life."

"I see," Brenda said quietly.

"So, now," Elke asked, "how do you see the next chapter of Ernst's life?"

"I don't know," Brenda said. "I know his work is very dangerous and could cost him his life, but I know he is devoted to it. I promised him I would be here, waiting for him when he came home, and I will keep that promise. I hope we can spend the rest of our lives together."

"I see," Elke answered.

"I hope that doesn't put us at odds somehow," Brenda said anxiously.

"Oh no, Brenda, it doesn't," Elke said, "not at all. Instead, it comforts me. Ernst and I have no family and no home waiting in Munich. My home is here now. His home will be with you. He needs to have a reason to come back to you, well and whole. You are that reason, my dear one, *meine kleine taube*," she smiled. "Ernst's Brenda. Nothing could please me more."

As Brenda leaned to meet Elke's embrace, Elke recognized the small six-pointed silver star around her neck.

"I see Ernst has entrusted our family secret to you," she said. "It brings me joy to see you wear it. Nothing could make me happier, Brenda," she said as she squeezed her hug even tighter.

"When he gave it to me, I promised him I would wear it until he returned," Brenda said as she reached to hold the star between her thumb and forefinger. "I haven't taken it off since then."

"That star, once worn by my grandmother, my mother, and then by me—after Conrad left—is now yours to wear," Elke said. "You are keeping our family's memories alive. I believe nothing could make our Ernst more content or give him more reason to come home to you."

Brenda was quiet for a moment before she said, "I need to give him the freedom to return to Germany if he wishes. He may need to find some healing there, helping those who have suffered from evils so horrible he dares not describe them. Every day he risks so much to preserve the best of his memories of his homeland—before the politics and the war changed everything, of course. He knows I am resolved to follow him wherever he feels he needs to be."

"He is a most fortunate man to find one like you, Brenda," Elke said quietly. "When he was a boy, I prayed with him through the years of his father's rages. When he was older, I prayed he would find his way safely through *Hitlerjugend,* and later I prayed for him during his years at university. Then I prayed when the Wehrmacht and the Abwehr sent him away. Only later did I learn he was in America. Now Ernst and I have found one another here, and he has found you, a faithful young woman with whom I hope he will share his life. Once more, though, he is away, and I have but one prayer remaining. Please, Lord, bring him home to us, well and whole."

Chapter 15

Lois Boucher had just finished setting the table for supper when she heard Luc's truck drive into the driveway and park beside the house. As he turned off the headlights, she looked out the kitchen window to see him get out and reach back into the truck's cab to retrieve something. The kitchen lights shone through the window into the yard just far enough to reveal a package with blue wrapping paper and a white bow. With the package under one arm and his lunch box under the other, he disappeared as he walked toward the back entry. As the back door opened, she heard his voice.

"The kitchen lights are on," he called, "so I know you're home. Is there no wife about who is ready to greet the man of the house on a cold February afternoon?"

As he placed the package on the kitchen table, Lois appeared from the dining room, smiling and wiping her hands on her apron.

"I'm right here, 'Mr. Man of the House,'" she laughed. "The 'Lady of the House' has been busy preparing your supper."

As she fell into his arms and they shared their first kiss since lunch, he said, "I hope you've prepared something special for the occasion."

"Occasion?" she laughed. "To what occasion are you referring, Mr. Boucher?"

"Alas," he said as he feigned an injury to his heart, both hands grasping at his chest, "you've not forgotten so soon, have you? My heart is cut to the quick!"

"Oh, stop it, you fop!" she chided. "Now tell me what occasion," she begged as the twinkle in his eyes grew ever more evident.

Turning toward the package on the table, he said, "Our anniversary, of course, my darling. How could you forget?"

"Anniversary?" she asked. "Our anniversary is, let me see," she said as she counted first backward to their wedding day, then forward in her mind, "not for another eight months!"

"Exactly!" he smiled. "Spot on! That makes today our four-month anniversary," he smiled as he pointed to her package, "and to mark the date, I bought you a gift."

"Oh, Luc!" she said as he placed the package in her hands, trying not to laugh. "So, this is like the one, two, and three-month anniversaries we've celebrated so far?"

"And why not?" he asked. "There's no other man on the island who gets to come home to a beautiful wife with that exciting British accent every night. Why shouldn't I celebrate? Now, my darling, open your package."

Beyond the ribbons, wrapping paper, and tissue paper in the box, Lois found a beautiful, full-length, light-blue silk nightgown with white lace trim at the neckline.

"Oh, Luc! It's lovely," she said as she reached to hug him, her head lying on his shoulder.

"I'm glad you like it," he said softly through her hair, "because I hope you'll wear it tonight."

"But," she said, "I feel so badly. You've bought me this beautiful gift, and I have nothing for you."

"Oh, not to worry, my sweet," he smiled. "I've thought of everything."

"You've thought of everything?" she said as he pushed the hair away from her neck and planted kiss after kiss beneath her ear."

"Of course," he said. "You see, tonight you get to put your new nightgown on."

"Yes. . ." she said, a question waiting in her voice.

"And then," he smiled, adding another kiss to her neck, "I get to take it. . ."

"Oh, you!" she laughed, "You never tire of that."

But before she could add another word, he said, "No, my darling, never."

"Well," she said, "tonight you'll have to wait until I return from my Red Cross meeting at Highfield. We're wrapping bandages and. . ."

Luc interrupted to groan, "And talking, talking, talking."

"Oh, fear not," she said, escaping his arms, putting her new nightgown back in its box, and straightening her apron. "You know that most of the women are older, and some have to travel home at some distance once we're finished. On a cold night in late February, we won't be very late.

"Well, I hope not, for your sake," he said, hiding his smile.

"Meaning?" she asked.

"Just that turnabout is fair play," he said.

"Meaning?" she asked again, matching the twinkle in his eye.

"Meaning," he said as he scooped up the box, "if you're late, it will be left to *me* to put this nightgown on so *you* can take it. . ."

Shaking her head and suppressing her laugh, she threw her arms around his neck and met his kiss with hers. In another moment, the ringing of the timer on the stove pulled both of them toward the stove.

A half hour later, when they had finished Lois's boiled dinner of corned beef, cabbage, potatoes, and carrots, Luc drove her to Highfield for her Red Cross meeting. He had arranged to work with Michael and Jacques to finish a couple of details on the *Lady M.* while the ladies wrapped bandages. With Lois safely delivered to Highfield's front door, Luc parked at the boatshed where the lights were already burning inside.

As he passed through the boatshed door, he could smell the fresh varnish on the newly refinished mahogany. Jacques was pleased to show him the results of the work that he and Michael had finished the previous week.

"It's a long, slow, tedious job," Jacques began, "and all the way through I've had to remind myself that admiring the finished project will make it all worthwhile."

"And now that you see it?" Luc asked.

"Well, what do you think?" Michael asked. "You were on the *Lady M* at the end of the season. You remember what shape she was in, don't you?"

"Well," Luc said as he took another look, "She looks brand new to me, now. You two have no reason not to be proud of this job. But, now that it's finished, what are we doing tonight?"

"Tonight is an easy one. We're installing new zinc anodes," Michael answered.

"You've got me there," Luc laughed, "never heard of them."

"You'll know all there is to know in a few minutes," Jacques laughed. "Follow me to the bench."

While Michael removed the old anodes from the keel, the shaft, and the propeller, Jacques explained.

"There's a thing called 'galvanic action' in salt water," he said. "Two different kinds of metal parts can cause one of them to corrode. Steel, even galvanized steel, will corrode if there are brass or bronze members in the water. To prevent corrosion, we attach a piece of sacrificial metal like zinc to various parts of the boat—the rudder, the drive shaft, and the propeller. That will be the metal that corrodes. What are called the more 'noble' metals, like copper and brass, will be preserved."

Luc looked at the shiny, clean zinc anodes on the bench and the gray, misshapen, corroded ones Michael had removed from the boat.

"Wow, there's a big difference in the old ones and the new ones. And they just bolt on?" Luc asked. "If you've already taken the old ones off, we should be done shortly."

"That's the idea," Michael said. "Early to bed, and early to rise. . ."

They were almost finished when Jacques asked, "Have you heard anything from Lois's mother lately? A while back, you told me her sister and brother were doing better at the sanatorium."

"That's right," Luc answered. "Both Biddy and Wilfred have made remarkable recoveries since being away from the city. The doctors say it's all because of a new drug treatment for lung diseases."

When Michael heard Luc's words, "a new drug treatment for lung diseases," he thought immediately of Bill Stewart. When the men were finished installing the last zinc anodes, Michael asked Luc to stay behind for a few minutes.

"I'd like to hear more about that new drug treatment you mentioned. What can you tell me?" he asked.

"Everything I know is in a letter on our desk at Spring Hill," Luc said. "I'm sure Lois will let me bring it over tomorrow so you can see for yourself."

"I'd like that, Luc. Thank you," Michael said. "Thank you very much."

Chapter 16

When the *HMS Revenge* sailed north from Durban on a course for Kilindini Harbor in Mombasa, Lt Boyd Moncrieff was among the happiest men aboard. The *Revenge* had sailed for Durban two months earlier, and only days after its arrival there, Cheryl Beatty, Kathleen's best friend, had sent the news of Kathleen's battle with malaria. Her fight with the disease had not been an easy one, but three weeks ago, she had been released from quarantine. Finally able to leave the malaria ward and the hospital, she was eager to return to her regular duties. However, her doctor's orders required her to limit her physical activity and to add several hours of bed rest each day. Ordinarily, Kathleen might have been piqued by those orders, but her one-block walk to the front door of the *Lotus Hotel* and the climb upstairs to her recovery quarters on the third floor were enough to convince her that a nap was a good thing.

Ordinarily, her canvas shoulder bag would have been large enough to carry the few personal necessities allowed at the hospital, but today it was overloaded and bulging at the seams. She smiled as she unbuckled the bag's cover flap and began taking out bundle after bundle of Boyd's letters and cards. Just as she finished, she heard a quick knock outside and watched as an envelope appeared under the door. She had no sooner picked up the envelope when there was a second knock at the door. She opened it to find Cheryl bearing a tall vase filled with flowers.

"He found me on the street," she laughed, "and that puppy dog of yours followed me home. These are for you."

"I wonder where he found them," Kathleen said as she admired the flowers and placed the vase on top of her dresser.

"I don't know," Cheryl said as she turned toward the door. "I only know I've got at least two more trips up and down the stairs. There's a basket of fruit, a box of candy, and heaven knows what else waiting down there."

"Oh, I wish I could see him," Kathleen said, "but my orders are to stay in my room for twenty-four hours before resuming normal activities."

"I'll give him that information, if you'd like, but instead, why don't I tell him which window is yours? I'm sure he'll appreciate a smile and a wave," Cheryl suggested.

"A capital idea, Cheryl," Kathleen beamed. "I'll be waiting right there," she said, pointing to the open window where the curtains fluttered in the breeze. After taking a moment to find her hand mirror and comb her hair, she hurried to the window.

Parting the curtains and raising the sash a little higher, she scanned the street below. She recognized no one until she saw Cheryl and Boyd crossing the street and turning to look back at the hotel. Then, Cheryl looked up and pointed to Kathleen's open window. As Boyd saw her waving, she blew kisses to him, he blew them back and then raised his hand to his ear as if he was holding a telephone receiver. She understood immediately that he wanted her to call him. He waved once more before running back to the Officers' Club to wait beside the telephone.

Twenty minutes later, she dialed the number she had lodged in her memory for months. As it rang and rang with no answer, her spirits began to fall until she finally heard Boyd's breathless voice.

"Communications, Lt Moncrieff speaking," he said, breathing heavily.

"Relax, Boyd," she laughed, "it's me."

"You have no idea how good it is to hear your voice," he said.

"Of course, I do, Boyd. I'm hearing yours, am I not? It's been so long!" she said.

"Too long," he agreed, "but how much longer are you restricted to your barracks?"

"Only until tomorrow, when I am allowed two hours outdoors in the afternoon," she answered.

"What time in the afternoon?" he asked. "I need to meet you outside your door and kidnap you for those two hours."

"Kidnap me?" she laughed.

"Yes," he answered, "and make you my prisoner. I need to look into your eyes, hear your voice, smell your perfume, and kiss you again and again."

"Oh dear," Kathleen said. "I'm afraid I can offer to help you with only three of those needs," she said.

"Three?" he asked.

"Yes," she said. "I have to wear my surgical mask when I leave the Infirmary for the next three days. They tell me my weakened condition may still cause risks for both of us. I'm sorry, Boyd," she said, sadly. "It's just protocol."

After a brief moment of silence, Boyd said, "Kathleen, it's been sixty-three days since I've looked into your eyes. I'll feed my eyes there for three days while I'm waiting for your kisses. But tell me," he added, "holding hands is allowed, right?"

"Yes," she laughed.

"And hugging? Not so tight you can't breathe, of course. Just a semi-polite embrace now and then?" he asked.

"Yes, again, Boyd," she laughed. "I'm sure we'll both find ways to express how much we've missed each other. I know I can't wait to have your arms around me."

"So," he asked, "how long do I have to wait?"

"Only until one o'clock tomorrow afternoon," she said. "I'll be waiting inside the door at the bottom of the stairs. I'll be the one in the mask."

"You know," he said, "I may find one for myself. Then we'll make a perfect couple."

"You make me laugh, and I've missed laughing for a long time," she said. "But now, I need to settle into this new room and enjoy my beautiful flowers, my fruit basket, and my candy. Can I trust you to take care of yourself until tomorrow?"

"Oh, yes, my love," he said. "I won't let anything keep me away from you."

After their goodbyes, Boyd set course for *The Nelson*, where he met two of his fellow officers. While his friends kept up their usual officers' quest among the women present, Boyd remained at their table nursing his Navy Grog. At the same time, Kathleen lay on her bed, waiting for the night air to cool enough for her to sleep comfortably. After a visit from the staff nurse who administered the last dose of quinacrine for the day, she slipped between the sheets, ready to enjoy the rest she needed to continue her recovery.

Her thoughts went to the next afternoon, when she and Boyd would enjoy a reunion of sorts after being apart for so long. She smiled and shook her head when she thought of being hidden from each other behind their gauze masks.

"I wonder how long we can make that last," she smiled. She always knew that men were the ones whose appetites needed checking, but now she was feeling some of the same energy Boyd never seemed to lack. She knew she'd never felt this way about any other man.

"He's the one, all right, Kathleen," she whispered. "But where will this war take us? Where will we be assigned next? How long will we be apart next time?"

Her thoughts were too much for her to bear alone. Thankfully, within a few minutes, the third-floor breeze prompted her to pull the top sheet over her shoulders. With the "Amen" of her evening prayers still on her lips, she gave in to the sleep her weary eyes craved.

In his bunk aboard the *HMS Revenge* that night, Boyd lay on his back with his hands folded behind his head, staring at the ceiling above. As the ship's senior Communications Officer, Boyd, among several other officers, had received a copy of the *Revenge*'s new orders from Captain Morgan. The single sealed folder was waiting for him at his desk when he returned from *The Nelson* an hour ago.

After mulling over the *Revenge's* new orders a second and third time, Boyd rose from his bunk and went to his desk. Taking his seat, he reached for the two volumes waiting on his desktop. One was entitled *King's Regulations* and the other *Admiralty Fleet Orders*. He leafed through one volume and then the other, finding the same well-marked pages he had surveyed night after night for the past several weeks. Satisfied he had confirmed the protocols he had already memorized, he returned to his bunk once again and lay on his back with his head resting in his hands.

A moment later, he promised himself, "I'll make an appointment to speak with Captain Morgan after tomorrow morning's briefing."

Chapter 17

A week after his last conversation with Bill Stewart, Michael was keeping an appointment with Dr. MacMillan at 9:30 on a Monday morning, right after Morning Prayer at St. Peter's. In his attaché, Michael carried a copy of the information Luc had gathered from the letter her mother had posted to Lois. Upon his arrival at Dr. MacMillan's office, he was happy to see Nurse Emily in her nurse's uniform standing with Andrew outside his office door.

"Michael," she called as she hurried in his direction, her arms extended, waiting for his embrace. "It's so good to see you. Andrew told me you had called, and I wanted to be sure to see you when you arrived."

As Andrew approached, Michael said, "It's hard to think we haven't been together since you were with us for our open house at Hillside, but that's what children will do, isn't it? We, parents of young ones, find little time to leave home, even to see our old friends."

As Andrew joined them, he said, "Exactly, Michael. Our Heloise has kept her mother at home for more than a year, but now we've found a way to bring our little one to work for part of each day. And Emily gets to teach and oversee the nurses' training program, her other love and joy."

"But not for too much longer," Emily said, looking left and right as if she were about to spill a secret. "You see," she said, turning to offer Michael a profile of her figure, "we have another on the way!"

The way she and Andrew beamed was infectious, and Michael joined them, with hugs all around.

"May I tell Susan?" Michael asked. "Your news is too good to keep secret," he laughed.

"By all means," Emily said, "and I'll make a point to call her so we can have a gab. But please excuse me just now. I need to get back upstairs."

With one more hug, Emily was on her way, and Andrew led Michael to his office.

"So, how can I help you?" the doctor asked. "You look healthy, and I hope your family is still well."

"Oh, yes," Michael said, "all the Morelands are well. I'm here on behalf of an old friend who needs some medical help."

Michael went on to tell Andrew about Bill Stewart, his wartime exposure to the gassings in Belgium, and his current recurring bouts of pneumonia.

"Did he tell you what kind of gas the Germans were using when he was exposed?" Andrew asked.

"It was early in the war when they were using chlorine gas," Michael said. "He said the Germans stopped using chlorine later and changed to mustard gas, but by then, he was no longer deployed. He heard about mustard gas from other soldiers in the hospital."

"And after the war? Did he get medical help then?" Andrew asked.

"He said he never got much medical help after the war, and he has no faith in medicine all these years later. But," Michael said, "I have a thought that might help him choose to get some treatment for his pneumonia."

"Tell me what you're thinking," Andrew said.

"Luc Boucher's wife, Lois, has a brother and a sister at Stannington, a sanatorium for children in England. They've had an almost miraculous healing from tuberculosis symptoms since their doctors have prescribed some new drugs. I was hoping you might know about these," Michael said as he handed Andrew the papers from his attaché.

Andrew took a moment to read before saying, "Yes, Michael. What I see here are sulfonamides or sulfa drugs, as they are known. They are now the most commonly used antibiotics for treating infectious lung diseases. We've had regular success using them with pneumonia cases, but," he said, sitting erect in his chair, "what a coincidence."

"Coincidence?" Michael asked.

"Yes," Andrew said. "You see, we've been fortunate here on PEI. We haven't been overrun with tuberculosis cases where sulfa drugs are regularly prescribed. However, Joseph Boucher has been interning at Montreal General Hospital on a ward where patients suffering from pneumonia and other infectious lung diseases are being treated. I'd like to speak with him about his experience with sulfa drugs and follow up with a conversation with the Chief of Staff there."

"That sounds wonderful," Michael said. "Bill gave up on doctors a long time ago."

"I understand," Andrew said. "Sulfa drugs weren't in regular use until the 1930's. If he had stopped seeing his doctors before that, he would never have known that an effective new drug for the treatment of infectious pneumonia had been discovered. If he's willing to give the medical world a second chance, he may enjoy some freedom from his chronic infections."

"When will you be in contact with Joseph?" Michael asked.

"We speak regularly on Tuesday afternoons," Andrew said.

"That's tomorrow," Michael said. "That couldn't be better."

"Yes, but we need to give him a day or so to collect some data and to compile a report, and I'll need time to consult with the Chief of Staff there," Andrew said. Looking at his desk calendar, he asked, "Can you wait until Thursday afternoon? I think we could give you something that might impress your friend, Bill, by then."

"Of course," Michael said, "Thursday will be great."

Michael stood and shook Andrew's hand before turning to leave the office. When he reached for the doorknob, he stopped, thought for a moment, and turned around.

"Bill owes me a favor," Michael said, "and I'd like to collect on that debt on Friday afternoon. Would you mind if I brought him here at about three o'clock then?" Michael asked.

Seeing the twinkle in Michael's eye, Dr. MacMillan smiled and yielded.

"It's not standard practice to advise a man about his physical condition when he's not a patient," he said, "so I'll just report everything I learn to you while Bill happens to be present to overhear the conversation. What do you think, Michael?"

"I think that's just what the doctor ordered, Andrew," Michael smiled.

Chapter 18

"Six letters?" Sqn Ldr Nigel Moncrieff asked as Able Seaman Walsh turned in the corridor below decks to continue his deliveries to the Officers' Quarters.

"Yes, sir," Walsh replied. "Six, sir. Four, sir, from a singular source, scented, sir, as the Squadron Leader will notice, sir," Walsh replied as he dared to smile.

Nigel raised his eyes and caught Walsh's smile, then half-closed one eye as Walsh raised his hand to salute.

"Will there be anything further?" Walsh asked, his smile still etched on his face.

"Not at the moment," Nigel said, returning Walsh's salute. "Just a word of encouragement. Continued deliveries of this character may earn you an early advancement in rank." Nigel's wink sent Seaman Walsh whistling as he hurried to the next officer's quarters.

It had been three weeks since Nigel received a letter from Cheryl. Besides her four letters in his left hand, there was also one from Boyd and another from his mother. While his brother's letter moved to the bottom of the stack, Nigel arranged the four from Cheryl by postmark—earliest to most recent.

Seaman Walsh had not misled him. As Nigel reclined on his bunk to read her first letter, Cheryl's scent transported him to the dance floor at *The Nelson*, where he held her in his arms, while her head rested on his shoulder. As he continued reading, he savored each line, even though her letter was the newsy kind, full of the ordinary day-to-day events in Mombasa.

It was her second letter that concerned him. Cheryl wrote about Kathleen's bout with malaria and her immediate hospitalization. Although he had no personal experience with the disease, the Royal Navy required strict adherence to prevention protocols and strict quarantine if the disease was diagnosed.

Cheryl's third letter was more reassuring, with news of Kathleen's continued recovery and further news of Boyd's imminent return from Durban. Her fourth letter was the most positive, with the good news that Kathleen's recovery was complete and that she had been released from the hospital.

Nigel's fifth letter was from Sir Richard and Lady Moncrieff. As usual, they spoke of their day-to-day routines with Susan's children. They assured him they were enjoying good health and enduring only the normal aging symptoms that others their age expect. As always, they were happy to report that all was well at Highfield, from which they sent their love, concern, and prayers for his safety.

His brother's letter was of an entirely different nature. Boyd had written while the *Revenge* was sailing north from its refit in Durban, a week from arrival at Mombasa. As Nigel continued reading, he realized he had never received a more heartfelt letter from his brother. What surprised him most was what Boyd wrote about himself and his feelings for Kathleen. There was no doubt that Boyd was deeply and helplessly in love.

"Those are the same feelings that have been echoing in my heart over these last few weeks," he said to himself. As Nigel read on, he began to ponder whether he, too, had been bitten by the same bug.

For Nigel, life as a Royal Navy officer had always had its protocols. Some were written codes of conduct, while others were unwritten, but clearly understood. Those protocols offered clear, logical, and safe boundaries. His father and his forebears had lived by those protocols and handed them down to succeeding generations. During wartime, those conventions were even more essential. There were things a Royal Navy officer could consider during wartime, and things he couldn't. For Nigel, marriage during wartime had never been a consideration. It was simply out of the question. For Boyd, however, it appeared that marriage had become a very real possibility, and one for which the Royal Navy had made provisions. What Nigel found in Boyd's letter was his younger brother's freedom to consider what his older brother would never have deemed possible. Boyd had suddenly provided Nigel with a menu full of food for thought.

Nigel re-read Boyd's letter to review his conclusions. First, Boyd was ready to marry, having found in Kathleen all he could desire for a life-long mate. Second, although Boyd had written while Kathleen was still in the hospital, he seemed assured she would enjoy a complete recovery. Third, he could hardly wait to propose to her. Finally, in the firm hope that her answer would be, "Yes," Boyd was preparing to ask her father for her hand. Lacking his permission, of course, Boyd and Kathleen would remain single.

Nigel discovered himself in a fraternal quandary. Actually, he was piqued. As the elder brother, he was supposed to lead and set standards of social behavior for his younger brother to follow. However, here was Boyd preceding him, daring to leap forward, to challenge familial protocols, and to dare to lead to places where his elder brother had not dared to go.

He smiled, shook his head, pushed the chair back from his desk, and stepped in front of the mirror on his locker.

"Good Lord, Moncrieff," he said aloud. "You've played everything so safe all your life that your younger brother has had to teach you to leave a few of your rules behind and live. He found a woman who has changed his life. So have you. It's time to do something about it."

Nigel knew his feelings for Cheryl had already led him down the same fearsome path Boyd had followed. That path was fraught with dangers of rejection and the threat of wounded pride that might never heal. Somehow, though, Boyd had been willing to take the chance. Nigel had to admit it; he admired Boyd. He was ready to accept a new and frightening challenge. Just then, there came a knock at Nigel's door.

When he opened the door, Able Seaman Walsh apologized, "Begging your pardon, sir, but another letter has been discovered at the bottom of the postbag. Here it is, sir."

The letter was a fifth from Cheryl, but this letter made no mention of Kathleen or Boyd. She was writing to tell him she was about to be reassigned and would soon be leaving her current post to travel to a new one. Of course, she could not divulge any further information concerning the WRNS travel schedule or her ultimate destination. Taking a suggestion from Kathleen, however, she offered enough information for him to know where she was being assigned.

She wrote, "You may remember a couple we met at *The Nelson* some time ago, Alex and Maria? Well, Maria has grown tired of her three-syllable name. She's going by Ria these days."

"Alex and Ria?" Nigel laughed. "The *HMS Formidable* has been patrolling the Mediterranean for months. We're due to make a stop in Alexandria soon. If Cheryl is posted there, I *will* find her."

Chapter 19

Boyd's conversation with Captain Morgan was a brief one. When Boyd asked if the captain would grant permission for him to marry, the captain asked only two questions.

"Lt Moncrieff, your family has a long and prestigious history with the Royal Navy. I am proud to captain a ship on which your father served in World War I. As your commanding officer, it is my responsibility to guide the men under my command in decisions that may affect their future ability to serve His Majesty's Navy, especially during wartime. Therefore, I must ask you several questions that are of a personal nature."

"Understood, Captain Morgan," Boyd replied.

Captain Morgan continued, "The young woman in question, where was she born?"

"In Windermere, sir," Boyd replied," two years after I was born in Suffolk."

"So, she is a British citizen?" Captain Morgan asked.

"Yes, sir. Her family name is one you may recognize. Balfour," Boyd said.

"Balfour?" the captain asked, "of the lineage of the former Prime Minister?"

"His grand-niece, sir," Boyd replied. "Kathleen is in service here in Mombasa with the WRNS."

"And her parents?" the captain asked, "Have you approached them for their permission to marry their daughter?"

"Not yet, sir," Boyd replied. "I have made it my goal to secure yours first, sir."

"Then go with my blessing, Lt Moncrieff," Captain Morgan said as he stood and extended his hand. "Given your father's years of distinguished service to King and country, I hope that Miss Balfour's parents will grant their permission without hesitation."

"Thank you, Captain Morgan," Boyd smiled as he shook the captain's hand. "I will inform you immediately of their response upon receipt."

Boyd wore his smile all the way to the *Lotus Hotel*, making only one stop between Captain Morgan's office and the hotel's front entrance. As he was donning his gauze mask, Kathleen stepped out the door. Their embrace was immediate.

"I dare not hold you too tightly," Boyd said, "I know you need room to breathe."

"Not that much room," Kathleen smiled as she tightened her grip.

Though neither could see a smile through their masks, their eyes told them everything. Kathleen took Boyd's arm as they began the fresh air stroll that all the medical personnel had prescribed.

At an outdoor cafe two blocks away, they sat at a table in the shade of an awning. Boyd ordered a pot of tea and *a mahamri,* small doughnuts made according to a local recipe. Both had to giggle as they dared to remove their masks for each bite and sip. The small talk they had enjoyed over the last two blocks became serious as Boyd reached across the table to take her hands in his.

"I need to tell you about a conversation I had with Captain Morgan this morning. Please bear with me, because I've had to dispense with my customary habit of doing all things in order," he said.

With a puzzled look on her face, Kathleen placed her cup in its saucer and said, "All right, tell me."

Without hesitation, Boyd straightened in his chair, gripped her hands a bit more firmly, and said, "I asked him to grant me permission to marry you."

"You asked him for permission to. . .?" she said, hesitating and wrinkling her brow. "But we haven't talked about. . ."

"I know, Darling," Boyd interrupted, "but everything has to happen in a hurry, and his permission was the first step. If he said, 'No,' I wouldn't be able to ask you," he said as he released his right hand and reached toward his front pocket.

"What do you mean, 'Everything has to happen in a hurry?'" she asked.

Leaning in to speak in a whisper, he said, "The *Revenge* has new orders. We'll be shipping out soon, and I can't bear to think of leaving you unless you are my wife. Please," he said, as he stood, stepped back from the table, bent to one knee, and held out an open black velvet ring box, "please, Miss Kathleen Balfour, will you marry me?"

Kathleen was in shock, but the happiest shock she had ever known. Looking into Boyd's eyes as tears came to hers, she said, "Yes, Lt Boyd Moncrieff, I will marry you."

Only then did she look into the ring box in Boyd's hand. There she saw a yellow gold ring with a large, emerald-cut diamond flanked by two slightly smaller emerald-cut blue sapphires.

"Oh, my," she gasped, as Boyd placed the ring on her finger. "Wherever did you find something this lovely in Mombasa?"

"I didn't find it here," he said. "I found it in Durban, two months ago."

"In Durban? Two months ago? But that was when I was in the hospital," she said with a puzzled look on her face.

"That's right," he said.

"But, two months ago, they didn't know if I would live or die," she said.

"Yes, that's what Cheryl wrote me," he nodded.

"But, knowing that, you bought this beautiful ring?" she asked.

"Yes," he answered. "It didn't matter to me. We were called to be married. I was ready to marry you, whether you made a full recovery or not," he answered.

Looking into his eyes, she was unable to stop her tears, and, reaching for the gauze mask still hanging around his neck, she tore it away.

"Damn the rules," she laughed, as she stood, leaned across the table, and kissed him, long, hard, and deep. When their kiss ended, they sat again, leaning forward, giggling and rubbing noses between playful kisses, until Boyd looked out into the passing traffic and noticed a passing rickshaw.

"Did you see that?" he asked.

"See what?" Kathleen asked, her eyes captured by the glistening stones in her ring.

"I just noticed that rickshaw drivers have no rearview mirrors," he said.

Puzzled, Kathleen looked up and said, "So?"

"So, the driver can't see what's happening in the passenger seat behind him. We need to discuss a telegram conversation I'll be having with your father when I ask his permission to marry you," Boyd said. As he began to smile, he added, "And I could use some encouragement on our way back to the Lotus Hotel."

"Oh," Kathleen said, nodding, "then I think we *definitely* need to find a rickshaw."

Boyd was on the curb, hailing one before Kathleen could stop laughing. As they waited on the sidewalk, she licked her lips, checked her compact mirror, and said, "Ouch. . .too much time behind those dry gauze masks." As she extracted the lip balm from her bag and prepared to apply it, Boyd had another idea.

"There's a better way to put that on, you know," he said.

Puzzled, she asked, "A better way? What better way?"

"For guaranteed fuller coverage," he said, pointing to his pursed lips, "just put it here. I'll take care of the rest."

Chapter 20

E.D. and Jan spent four days hiding and five nights traveling from safe house to safe house from Hoek van Holland to the outskirts of The Hague. Near the center of the city on the following night, in the darkness of a windowless basement room lit by a single kerosene lamp, five members of the Dutch underground huddled together as E.D. and Jan revealed the outline of their plan for rescuing four downed Allied pilots.

"Call me E.D.," he said. "This is Jan."

One of the men, a barrel-chested man of about fifty, looked at the remaining four and asked them, "French, this time?" Receiving nods from all, he turned back to E.D. and said, "Call me *Un*." Pointing to the others, one by one, he said, "This is *Deux*, *Trois*, *Quatre*, and *Cinq*." Turning back to E.D. and Jan, he said, "Our apologies, friends, but if you know our names, you become a danger to us, and we to you."

"Understood," E.D. said, as Jan nodded.

E.D. began, "We have four downed pilots who are in hiding here in The Hague. We need to collect them and transport them to England. Our best intelligence tells us we will be able to drive to each of the locations where they are in hiding, pick them up, and return here in the same evening," Opening a well-marked map and placing it on top of a steamer trunk sitting in the center of the basement floor, he said, "Note these addresses. We hope to make a coordinated escape for all four in a single night while arranging a rendezvous with a boat to receive them at sea."

As their new friends nodded, E.D. continued. "We will need a smart-looking automobile large enough for a driver and five passengers, businessmen's clothing for five men, an SS officer's uniform, papers for all, a Luger, and four bottles of schnaps. Can all these be available?" E.D. asked.

Polling the group with his eyes as the other men agreed and nodded, *Un* replied, "All but the papers can be had by noon tomorrow. Papers take a little longer, but no later than tomorrow at day's end.

"Excellent," E.D. said. "Meanwhile, to protect those who are housing each man, we must confirm a pick-up location a short distance away from each of these addresses," E.D. said as he pointed to the map.

"Understood," *Un* replied.

E.D.'s plan was a simple one. In a city known for Dutch collaboration with the Nazi occupation forces, four members of the underground, posing as Dutch collaborators and accompanied by E.D. in an SS officer's uniform, would leave the city to attend an out-of-town party. In their car with the SS officer as their driver, the group would make themselves known to those on duty at the city-limits checkpoint. After driving to their four target locations and exchanging one of the car's passengers for an Allied pilot at each stop, they would return to the city limits checkpoint several hours later. There, the SS officer would pose as the only party member sober enough to drive. Buried beneath their fedoras, scarves, and overcoats, his drunken passengers would remain unrecognizable. After leaving a gift of several bottles of schnaps at the checkpoint, E.D. and his passengers would pick up the fifth underground agent in the city. That man would drive them to the coast, where Jan would be waiting with a boat ready to begin the first leg of their sea voyage across the Channel to England.

Fortunately, the pilots' neighborhood locations were familiar to the Dutch underground. After looking at the target addresses, each of the men spoke up.

Quatre, a younger man with short, sandy colored hair, volunteered, "I am familiar with Nootdorp."

The man identified as *Cinq*, a grey-haired man with a full beard, said, "And I know Delft." Then, turning to *Trois*, he added, "and this man once lived in Den Hoorn. Right?"

"For ten years," *Trois* confirmed.

'That leaves only Wateringen," E.D. said.

Deux, a man of about 40 with a bald head and sad eyes, said, "My mother-in-law lives there. Hopefully, she'll be in bed and snoring at that hour."

"Then you'd better be up early in the morning before she wakes," *Un* laughed.

The remaining men's laughter was brief but hearty.

After another look at E.D.'s map, *Un* polled the others and marked the map at four locations.

Pointing, he said, "Here are the best places to pick up each man away from the address where he has been sheltering."

"Excellent," E.D. said, "There's only one other detail. When each of you exits the vehicle, your hat, scarf, and overcoat must stay behind. The airmen we rescue will need to dress in them to disguise themselves for their return to The Hague. Finally, our street exchanges need to take mere seconds. We can't risk discovery."

"Understood," *Un* said, as each of his men nodded.

"You will be on your own for your return to The Hague. We will pray that you remain undetected and return safely," E.D. said. "We will rendezvous here at the same time tomorrow evening to set the date and review any final details."

To prevent discovery, the men left at broken intervals over the next hour. Once they were gone, E.D. and Jan retrieved two folding cots and some bedding from the steamer trunk that had served as their map table a few minutes earlier. Although both men were exhausted, physically, mentally, and emotionally, only Jan found sleep in the first hour after their meeting ended.

E.D. lay on his back, looking into the darkness overhead. His thoughts flew back to his last days and hours on Prince Edward Island.

"It's hard to believe that a place whose people I once considered enemies is now the only place I crave," he mouthed in the dark. "It has become Brenda's home and my mother's home. Perhaps that island, so far from here, from this war, and from the horrors that so many innocent people are suffering at this moment, can become *my* home. God, if you are willing, that is my prayer," he whispered.

Meanwhile, a young woman more than 3,000 miles away was holding a six-pointed sterling silver star between her thumb and forefinger. She counted all six points again and again. At each point, she offered the same prayer.

"Guard him, keep him, hold him, love him. Please, good Lord, bring him home to me again."

Chapter 21

Michael stopped to pick up Bill Stewart at Freeman Ford at noon on a cold Tuesday morning in February 1943. When Bill climbed in, he was surprised to find that Michael's flatbed truck was so warm inside.

"How do you get it this warm in here?" Bill asked, "And why, after you've been waiting for me these last few minutes in the parking lot, is your windshield not frosted over?"

"Well," Michael answered, "heaters weren't available on these older Ford trucks, so I installed one of the new hot water options available on the newer models. It takes the heated water used to cool the engine and sends it through a miniature radiator mounted on the firewall. An electric fan drives the warm air surrounding that miniature radiator into the cab."

"OK," Bill said, "I get it, but what about the windshield?"

"That was easy," Michael said. "Like the first time I came in to ask you for some sheet metal, I bent up a piece of ductwork to capture some of that extra hot air. Now I just direct it to the windshield through another couple of sheet metal ducts."

"Well, it works for me," Bill said, "cozy in here."

After another mile or two, Bill asked, "So why am I going to see your doctor at the hospital today? After all, you know I don't take much stock in doctors, right?"

"Oh, you've made that clear, Bill," Michael answered, "but I'm not convinced you've gotten the best information in the past."

After a quiet moment as they drove toward the hospital, Michael asked, "You were at Ypres during the war, right?"

"That's right," Bill answered. "In Belgium, the third week of April 1915."

"And that's when the Germans used chlorine gas for the first time?" Michael asked.

"That's right," Bill answered. "It was the French and Canadians on the front lines. The yellow clouds came out of nowhere with an overwhelming, noxious smell that filled our lungs and left us choking, gasping, throwing up, and collapsing on the field. By some miracle, our troops held the line."

"And you were there that day?" Michael asked.

"I was," Bill paused, "but it was the second day when it got me," he said quietly. "It was near dawn. It had been quiet all night, too quiet. Then it began."

Michael drove on in silence. A long moment passed before Bill continued.

"The wind rose and came in our direction. Within minutes, it brought the yellow clouds and the unmistakable stench of the chlorine," he said. "Suddenly, none of us could breathe. We'd been told to cover our noses and mouths with a handkerchief soaked in water or our own urine. Some of the harder hit men were spitting blood, others were running, directionless, rolling on the ground, trying to catch a clean breath."

Bill paused again while Michael drove on.

"You know, you can dive into a trench to escape machine gun fire, and you can raise your rifle to shoot at an enemy machine gun nest," Bill began, "but you can't escape the gas that follows you to the bottom of the trench where you're gasping for air with your face in the mud."

After a quiet moment, Bill spoke again.

"I was lucky," he said. "Some men passed out and died that morning when the second and third clouds came. Somehow, I made it through. In the end, they say we had over 6,000 casualties over those two days. The Germans had only a few hundred."

"And after the battle?" Michael asked. "How did the medics treat your injuries?"

"There was nothing to be done for us. It was all new to the medics and the doctors. They didn't know how to treat the kind of injuries we had," Bill said. "And once we were home, there was still nothing they could do for us."

"It's been a lot of years since then, Bill," Michael said.

"Yes, it has," Bill nodded.

"Let me ask you a question. Do you remember hearing about Joseph Boucher, Jacques Boucher's adopted son?" Michael asked.

"The young fellow from England who got hurt in that sawmill accident?" asked Bill.

"That's him," Michael said. "Well, he's studying to be a doctor now, at hospitals in both Quebec and Montreal."

"Uh-huh," Bill said.

"He's learned about a new medicine for the treatment of recurring pneumonia," Michael said. "Isn't that what you suffer from?"

"That's what they tell me," Bill answered.

"Well, that's what Dr. MacMillan will try to explain today. He got the latest research documentation from Joseph in Montreal a couple of days ago. I'd like you to hear what he's got to say. Are you willing to hear him out?"

"Only for one reason," Bill said.

"What's that?" Michael asked.

"Because you think it's a good idea. You've thought out a few other good ideas, so I'm going to trust you on this one. Just so you know, though, I think you're playing out of your league," Bill said.

"Out of my league?" Michael asked.

"Yeah," Bill answered. "You're good at solving problems, Michael, I'll give you that, but remember, this one isn't made of sheet metal."

With that, Bill had to smile. Michael did, too. Fifteen minutes later, they were parked at the hospital in Charlottetown.

When Michael and Bill stepped through the doors and into the hospital lobby, Dr. MacMillan was just coming out of the elevator, dressed in his white lab coat with his stethoscope around his neck, as usual. He saw Michael and Bill at once and strode in their direction.

"Michael," he called, "and you must be Mr. Stewart," he said as he offered his hand.

"Just 'Bill', if you please," he said, shaking the doctor's hand.

"Then, Bill it is," the doctor said, turning to Michael.

"I have a conference room waiting this way," he said, pointing down the corridor to their right. "Follow me."

Once seated at the table in the brightly lit conference room, Dr. MacMillan began.

"Bill, Michael has told me everything he knows about your condition and how he thinks we might be able to help you. However, I'd like to ask you some questions and follow with a brief exam to check your vital signs, you know, your heart rate, blood pressure, and so forth. Finally, I'd like to take an X-ray of your lungs. All the tests will be finished in about thirty minutes or so. Then we'll meet right here again to tell you what we've found. How does that sound?"

"Let's get on with it," Bill said. "I don't want to keep Michael any longer than we have to."

"Don't worry," Michael smiled, as he patted the attaché he carried over his shoulder. "I brought plenty to do, and this will be a good room to do it in."

Dr. MacMillan led Bill to an examination room down the first-floor hallway, and, true to his word, brought him back half an hour later.

"I'm going to collect the last test results," he said, leaving Bill with Michael, "and I'll be right back."

As Dr. MacMillan closed the door behind him, Michael asked, "So, how did it go?"

"All right, I guess," Bill said. "At least there weren't any needles."

"And the X-ray machine?" Michael asked.

"I've never had an X-ray before, but it was painless, too. I imagine it's going to be expensive, though."

"I don't think so," Michael said, "but the doctor can tell you about that."

When Dr. MacMillan returned, he sat across from Bill and opened the file folder he carried under his arm.

"Bill, lacking any previous medical history of your case means we have to start at the beginning. Because we can't measure the progression of your illness, we have to rely solely on what we can measure now. I can tell you that your heart rate, blood pressure, and resting respiration rate give us no reason for concern. The history of the bouts of pneumonia you've suffered suggests you've endured a series of infections. In the past, we had no effective way to treat those infections. However, a discovery of new drugs, sulfonamides, commonly known as 'sulfa drugs', have proved remarkably effective in treating and preventing infections such as the ones you appear to have suffered."

"Do you mean I can just take some pills and never have those two-week-long bouts of coughing when I can't catch my breath?" Bill asked.

"We'll know as soon as we get your X-rays developed," Dr. MacMillan said. "That will take a couple of days. Let's make an appointment to meet again on Friday, same time, if that works for you?"

Looking at Michael, who was already nodding, Bill said, "Fine. I'm guessing those X-rays and those pills are going to be pretty expensive, so we'll have to stop at the bank on our way here," he said, looking at Michael once again.

"Oh," Dr. MacMillan began, "you won't have to pay for anything, Bill. All your expenses will be taken care of by the DSCR, that's the Department of Soldiers' Civil Re-establishment. After Michael spoke with me about your case, I took the liberty of contacting them. It took several calls before I reached the right people, but your care, your medications, and any future needs for your rehabilitation will cost you nothing. Your country will be paying a long-overdue debt."

Bill sat speechless as Dr. MacMillan added, "Bill, it's because of men like you that we still live in this free country. Michael's father and mine fought in the same war for the same worthy cause. We owe you and men like them debts we will never be able to pay. Medical bills for men who risked everything for our freedom?" he asked. "I promise you'll never see them, Bill, not on our watch."

Bill could no longer hold back his tears. He could only stand, look Dr. MacMillan in the eye, and mouth his "Thank you," as Michael stood to walk him down the hall and out the hospital doors.

Once in Michael's truck and about a mile away from the hospital, Bill had collected his thoughts.

"I guess I'd convinced myself after all these years that nobody cared then and nobody would care now," he said quietly. "I was wrong. Thank you, Michael."

"Dr. MacMillan spoke the truth about the debt we owe to you and all the men and women who risked their lives for the sake of this country. In case you ever forget that, though, I'll be here to remind you, OK?" Michael asked.

"OK," Bill said, "but tell me something, why are you heading downtown when Freeman Ford is in the other direction?"

"I'm giving you your first reminder, Bill. I'd like to stop by the Soldiers' Memorial at Queen Square. I've stopped there before to thank my father for his service in the Great War."

"Where did he serve?" Bill asked.

"He served in the Royal Horse Artillery in Flanders in 1915," Michael said.

"Then he faced the gas there, too," Bill said.

"Yes, he did, Bill, and the long-term effects brought him to an early grave."

"I didn't know," Bill said. "I'm sorry, Michael. It must have been hard to lose him that way."

Michael stopped the truck in front of the memorial and the life-size bronze statue of three World War I Canadian soldiers. Both men got out to take a closer look. Bill read part of the inscription.

"In memory of those from Prince Edward Island who gloriously laid their lives in the Great War," he said.

"And here on the other side," Michael said, "it says. 'Lest we forget.'"

"We can't afford to forget," Bill said softly.

Putting his arm around Bill's shoulder, Michael said, "And we won't, Bill. We won't."

With his eyes locked on the three bronze soldiers, Bill whispered, "Thank you, Michael, thank you."

Chapter 22

"Case and Reed are off to the henhouse with Miss Kimble, Michael," Sir Richard said as he motioned toward the leather chair in front of his desk, "and Susan is stopping over with Christine in a few minutes. We've just enough time for you to tell me how things went at the hospital with your friend, Bill."

"Bill didn't have the most positive attitude toward doctors before he arrived at the hospital, but by the time Andrew's examination was complete and the chest X-ray was behind him, he learned some things that left him very hopeful," Michael said.

"Then his malady is treatable?" asked Sir Richard.

"It appears so," Michael began. "Andrew believes the recurring bouts of pneumonia can be treated with what he called 'sulfonamides', drugs that fight the related infections that have caused Bill so much distress for so many years."

"Then there's hope his illness will respond to treatment in the same way that Lois' brother and sister have? Lois was here just this morning with another letter with good news from her mother," Sir Richard added.

"Hopefully," Michael said. Pausing for a moment before continuing, he began, "Before I left, Andrew mentioned attending a conference in Toronto with representatives from a number of hospitals, especially some with medical schools and research facilities. He said he noted nothing out of the ordinary except the addition of some military personnel and some discussion of potential British and American collaboration on the production of a new drug. I believe he called it *penicillin*."

As he rose to close the study door, Sir Richard said, "Let me tell you a little more."

Returning to his desk and retrieving a folder from his top drawer, he continued, "This report is only a week old, but it brings the kind of good news that will last for years."

"How so?" Michael asked.

"Because this drug, penicillin, was discovered in 1928," Sir Richard began, "but it has only recently been produced in quantity. Its ability to fight off infections far surpasses anything man has ever known, even the sulfonamides that are already saving lives. On the battlefield, more men die of infections from their wounds than from the wounds themselves. If the Allies can produce and distribute an adequate supply of penicillin, thousands and thousands of lives can be saved."

"So, that's why Britain, Canada, and the United States are all accelerating research and production of this drug?" Michael asked.

"Exactly," Sir Richard answered, "and that tells me something more."

Answering the quizzical look on Michael's face, he continued, "The Allies see a crucial need for a life-saving drug, and they are working to produce thousands of doses in at least three countries on two continents."

"All right," Michael nodded, tentatively.

"I have to believe they are trying to accelerate its production for a very specific reason, something they anticipate will be forthcoming. . ." he said.

"Do you mean an Allied attack on the Western Front? The one you've mentioned before?" Michael asked.

"Exactly," Sir Richard answered. "An effort this concentrated with unprecedented collaboration across the Atlantic means something big. An invasion like the one we've discussed may be as much as a year away, but unlike the Wehrmacht, which is driven by one man's lunacy to massive defeats costing hundreds of thousands of lives, the Allies are already planning far enough ahead to win their battles while *saving* lives."

At that moment, the men heard a knock at the door as Lady Moncrieff, Susan, and Christine appeared.

"Your playtime, Richard, and a tour of the henhouse were enough to wear the boys out," Lady Moncrieff said. "They're asleep in the library."

"And Christine is just nodding off here in my arms," Susan said.

Michael, standing while the ladies found their seats, said, "Richard and I have been trying to solve the problems of the world, but so far, to no avail."

"How sad," Lady Moncrieff said as she gave her husband a knowing nod. "However, Richard and I have some news that arrived by telegram this morning from British East Africa. We wanted you to hear it in person."

Retrieving a telegram from under the blotter on his desk, Sir Richard was preparing to read it when Lady Moncrieff interrupted him.

"Oh, I can't wait for the long version," she said, taking the telegram from his hand. "It's just this. Boyd is to be married to Miss Kathleen Balfour the day after tomorrow!"

Wide-eyed and taken aback, Susan asked, "Then she's recovered from her bout with malaria? And Boyd has his Captain's permission? He's spoken with her father and received his blessing?"

"All of the above," Sir Richard nodded.

Passing Boyd's telegram to Susan, Lady Moncrieff added, "Richard also heard from her father by telegram."

"I hope his message was cordial," Susan said as she lifted her eyes momentarily from the telegram in her hands.

"More than cordial," Sir Richard said as he perused the first page. "He wrote, 'You may not recall our introduction shortly after the end of the Great War. I was honored to be present when King George recognized and commended your bravery and acts of valor aboard the *HMS Revenge*. When our Kathleen wrote to us about her warming relationship with your son, we could not foresee that they would consider marriage so soon, particularly during wartime. Nonetheless, we hope you are as pleased as Lady Balfour and I remain.'"

"My, but that is more than cordial," Susan said as her mother nodded.

"It seems that Boyd has found the one for whom he's been waiting. I hope they will remain posted together in Mombasa for some time," Michael added.

"Unfortunately, that is not to be," Sir Richard said.

"No?" Susan asked.

"I'm afraid not," Sir Richard began. "The *Revenge*, accompanied by the *HMS Resolution*, will be escorting a convoy carrying the 9th Australian Division to Australia. The 9th, a division praised by both Montgomery and also by his enemy Rommel, will sail from Egypt in two weeks."

"Then their honeymoon will be cut very short," Susan said.

"Yes, so it will," Lady Moncrieff agreed.

"Perhaps the *Revenge* will escort another convoy back to Mombasa so the newlyweds can be together again," Michael offered. "After all, she's been escorting convoys from the Suez to Mombasa for months now."

"We can only hope," Lady Moncrieff said, "we can only hope."

Chapter 23

"It's called *Before the Storm*," Lois said as she emptied the puzzle box onto the dining room table at Hillside. "There are over five hundred pieces, so we may not finish it tonight."

"Oh, look at all that stormy blue and gray in the sky where it meets the sea," Patrice said. "I think you're right. It won't be easy."

"Well, the lighthouse with its red and white stripes won't be too hard, but all that beach sand will take some time," Hugh agreed.

"If the three of you will turn the pieces face up and find the edges, I'll put another log on the fire and make the popcorn," Luc laughed. "Just leave a few pieces for me."

Before he left for the kitchen, Luc turned on the radio and tuned in to the *Jack Benny Show*.

"Just a little background comedy while we concentrate on the puzzle," he said.

"Please, don't be too long in the kitchen," Lois called. "We need your help on this one."

Gatherings for these four at Hillside had become a once or twice a week habit in the winter of 1943. The ten-room house begged for more company than Luc and Lois could provide, and Patrice and Hugh were always happy to see one another. The days in mid-February were short, but there was always work at Highfield. Livestock, an icehouse to fill, firewood to replenish, and a special project here and there filled the daylight hours. Evenings were made for the kind of quiet entertainment the two couples were enjoying tonight.

"I had a letter from Mother in the post today," Hugh said when Luc returned with a warm bowl of popcorn."

"It's been some time since you heard from her, hasn't it?" Luc asked.

"Yes, that's true," Hugh said. "She tends to delay writing until she has something important to share."

"What was it?" Lois asked.

"She'd had a letter from Father," Hugh said, "a rather rare occurrence, you see."

"When was his last letter?" Patrice asked.

"I believe it's been some four months or more now. The Germans read and censor the letters before they are posted, you know. They're afraid of secret codes and such," Hugh answered.

"Did your mother tell you what your father had to say?" Lois asked.

"Oh, yes," Hugh said. "He wanted to let Mother know he was well and not suffering particularly, although he said he misses the roast of beef he enjoyed so much with her on Sundays at home. It appears the rest of his officers are well, though they also miss home terribly."

"And did he ask after you?" Patrice questioned.

"Not that she mentioned," Hugh said as he searched among the puzzle pieces. "Ah, here it is!" he said, "the last of the edge pieces. I'd like to have a go at the lighthouse if no one minds," he said as he began separating all the red and white pieces.

Catching Luc's eye, Lois said, "Let's get a second batch of popcorn going. I'll go with you. I need to get a pitcher of cider and some glasses, too."

After Hugh and Patrice had worked alone for a few minutes, Patrice could wait no longer to speak.

"Aren't you hurt with your father, Hugh? Not asking your mother anything about you after so long? You told me you've sent several letters to him with no response," Patrice asked, "isn't that true?"

"Yes, I've sent some letters, but perhaps he never received them. I understand the Nazis cull and sift everything, looking for coded correspondence. Besides, he has himself and his men to attend to," Hugh answered, still concentrating on the puzzle.

"But if he never received your letters, he would have all the more reason to ask your mother about you, wouldn't you think?" she reasoned.

"Perhaps," he said, "but you folks don't really know what it means to be a son in a family like the Buchanans."

"What it means to be the son of a Buchanan?" Patrice asked. "Is that something different from being a son in a family here?"

"Oh, my, yes. My father expects me to meet the same standards that were placed on him and on generations of Buchanans before him. Already, he has reason to be disappointed in me. Good Lord, I work with my hands as a common laborer. Do you see these nails? Some broken, and others, even worse, stained with every manner of dirt, stain, or varnish? Have you ever shopped in Charlottetown for a decent nail brush? I spent most of Saturday searching for one. Few of the merchants here have any idea what a nail brush is! And trying to find a decent pocket handkerchief, one with even a hint of linen in it, is not to be done. Every handkerchief here is a different color of plaid—red, green, blue, even brown. What happened to white? If they met me on the street today, few of my family would claim me."

Patrice looked down at her nails. She knew they weren't dirty, but two were broken from opening canning jars in the kitchen at home.

"I suppose these," she said, holding up her hands so he could see, "are something I should be ashamed of, too?"

"No," he said, rolling his eyes, "you folks here don't live as we do in Scotland."

"I see," she said, "because you live to a different standard, a higher one, right?"

"Exactly," he replied. "In our family, everything for us is prescribed. When I was your age, like all my family, I went away to boarding school. I was one among a hundred others, all in uniform, and all striving to be better than the rest. The teachers always dressed in mortarboard caps and gowns. My younger sister is at a boarding school like that even now, in wartime."

"And we 'folks' here attend school in a one-room wooden schoolhouse a short walk from home," Patrice said, "but we go home every afternoon."

"Right," he said, "and with all ages in one room."

"With a faculty of one," she continued.

"One?" he said, surprised.

"My sister, Ingrid," Patrice explained. "She just received her degree and certification."

"Trust me," he said, "she wouldn't be teaching in Scotland without years of further study. Faculty members in our schools climb a long and difficult academic ladder for most of their teaching years, clambering over one another to prove they are masters of their disciplines," he said as he turned his attention to the puzzle again.

"No, I suppose Ingrid wouldn't be teaching in Scotland, because we 'folks' here have simply not been able to meet your superior standards,

Mr. Buchanan. But fear not. Let me save you the embarrassment of condescending to socialize with us in the future," she said softly.

With all of his attention on the puzzle, Hugh didn't notice her rise silently from the table and hurry to the kitchen. There she found Lois, who agreed to drive her home.

"What happened?" Lois asked as Patrice hurried to the car.

"I'll tell you on the way," Patrice said, "I just need to be away from him."

As she started the car, Lois said, "I must apologize in advance, Patrice. If I seem a bit nervous, it's because I've been driving for only a month, and I'm not very good at shifting. With Luc so busy every day, Mrs. Moreland volunteered to be my teacher. She told me Mr. Moreland taught her to drive in England and again over here, where the cars are larger, and the roads are wider."

"Not to worry," Patrice said as she stifled her sob. "We have only a short drive to my house."

"So, tell me," Lois said as she backed out of the driveway. "What is it? What happened?"

"He is so, so superior," Patrice sobbed. "He despises every detail of who we are and how we live."

"Are you sure he wasn't having a hard time over his father's letter?" Lois asked.

"Maybe," Patrice agreed, "but he has an opinion on everything from plaid handkerchiefs to higher education. He knew which was better on every count, and, to him, we are obviously examples of a standard inferior to anyone bearing the name, Buchanan."

"Oh my!" Lois said quietly.

"He'll remain no more than a casual acquaintance as far as I'm concerned. I can consider nothing more familiar than that," Patrice said solemnly.

Lois waited a long moment before saying, "Before you close a door and lock it, perhaps you should speak to Mr. or Mrs. Moreland. They know what it means to navigate the problems that class and status pose. They may have some wisdom for you."

"Perhaps," Patrice said, under her breath, and then aloud, "Perhaps, Lois, but I don't think I'll be ready to bother them with a problem like this anytime soon."

Chapter 24

It had been two years since Sqn Ldr Nigel Moncrieff had been in Alexandria. When serving in the Mediterranean in May of 1941, the *HMS Formidable* had been hit with two 2,200-pound bombs dropped by Luftwaffe Junker 87's. Damage to her flight deck and hull kept her in port in Alexandria for the next two months before she sailed for permanent repairs at the Norfolk Navy Yard in the United States. She didn't return to regular service until February of 1942.

Since then, the Formidable has been stationed in the Mediterranean and was not scheduled to be in port in Alexandria. Fortunately for Nigel, however, RAF *Aboukir* lay only seven miles from Alexandria. With a variety of aircraft aboard the *Formidable* requiring maintenance that was best carried out in hangars there, Nigel hoped to find time to locate Leading Wren Cheryl Beatty whenever the Corsairs, Martlets, and Seafires aboard the *Formidable* could be ferried to the airfield.

As Squadron Leader, Nigel led every flight group both ashore and for their return to the *Formidable.* While the aircraft were in the hands of the air crews in the hangars at Aboukir, Nigel would not be denied a foray to the Ras El Tin quarter of the city, where Egypt's King Farouk quartered the British Forces, some in his palace, and others, like the Wrens, elsewhere on the palace grounds.

With no way to contact Cheryl, Nigel applied at security gate after security gate, requesting directions as he went. He wasn't the first RAF pilot to appear unannounced, but he might have been the luckiest, because when he applied at the office outside the Wren's barracks, he learned that the regular eight-hour shift change would bring most of the Wrens back to the barracks within half an hour. Still, Nigel wasn't sure that Cheryl was assigned to an office on the palace grounds. She might have been reassigned to any of several locations outside the city. Though not yet desperate, he was still an anxious officer in search of the one he loved.

So much had happened since he and Cheryl parted in Mombasa. The *Formidable* had sailed around the Cape of Storms and followed a northern course to Rosyth in Scotland for a refit that lasted a month. After they loaded new aircraft at Scapa Flow, they charted a course for the Mediterranean, where their orders kept them in the Western Mediterranean for months. Finally, new orders took them far enough east of the Algerian coast to make a day or two in Alexandria possible.

Nigel was sitting on the stoop at the Wren barracks, waiting where he had been directed, when he felt a tap on his shoulder.

"Sqn Ldr Moncrieff," a voice said. Leaving his daydreams and memories behind, Nigel rose to say, "Yes."

As he turned toward the voice, he discovered a woman of nearly forty years who looked him in the eye with her own eyes of steel. There was no hint of a smile anywhere on her face.

"It is my understanding that you are interested in securing a meeting with Leading Wren Cheryl Beatty. Is that correct?"

"Yes, Chief Wren. . .Wright," Nigel responded, as he squinted to read her name tag in the sun. "Leading Wren Beatty and I met when she was posted in Mombasa, some months ago. I was hoping to spend a few minutes with her when she is not on duty."

After Chief Wren Wright circled him and assessed him from every angle, she said, "You seem to have arrived at an opportune moment, Squadron Leader. Leading Wren Beatty has just finished her shift and is not due back on duty for another two hours and thirty-four minutes," she said as she looked at her watch.

"Thank you, Chief Wren Wright," Nigel said. "Please, tell me, how will I find her?"

"Fear not, Sqn Ldr," Wright said. "Be assured, she will find *you*."

Chief Wren Wright had no sooner turned her back when Nigel heard his name, coming from behind him. As he turned, Cheryl ran down the steps and fell into his arms.

"I can't believe it," she said. "You're here. We're together. Oh, I really can hardly believe it."

Nigel, never having been greeted like this before, was happily overwhelmed, as his arms held her more securely than ever before. He didn't notice the many other Wrens craning their necks and peeking past the blinds to watch them as they walked away, arm in arm.

"How could I stay away?" he asked. "I've waited and dreamed for months about the next time I would see you."

Cheryl led him into the shade of the tall hedge at the end of the walk where they couldn't be seen. Their kiss was immediate, lasting a long moment until their breath was spent.

"Well," Cheryl said, giggling with her cheek buried into his shoulder, "that just about says it all, I think."

As she looked up into his eyes, he said, "I was so afraid I would lose you, that I'd never see you again, that another would take the place I so hoped would be mine."

"And I have charted the *Formidable* every day since you arrived in the Mediterranean," she smiled. "It's part of my job, of course, but, oh, how I've loved seeing you sailing east, ever closer after all this time."

The part of Nigel that still wondered if Cheryl's feelings for him matched his feelings for her, faded in their next kiss, warmer and deeper than their first.

When their lips parted, they found themselves giggling again. Voices behind them drew their eyes toward the barracks, where the windows were still filled with faces, laughing, waving, and cheering. Waving back, the couple turned as Cheryl guided Nigel to a walking path toward the palace grounds.

"I'm busy ferrying aircraft back and forth to RAF Aboukir for the next few days. I need your help to find time to see you," he said, "as often and for as long as you can manage."

"You've arrived at the perfect time," she said, "for tomorrow evening, my shift ends at 8:00 PM, and curfew is at 11:00 PM."

"And how much time have we today?" he asked.

"We have another hour and eighteen minutes," she answered, "so let's go to the beach."

"The beach?" he asked.

"Right this way," she said as she led him down a path toward the palace and the sun that was waning in the west.

The breeze disappeared when they took off their shoes and their feet hit the sand. With his arm around her waist, he was content to follow her lead. Together, they celebrated all they had heard about Kathleen and Boyd's wedding, laughing as they admitted that neither was surprised and both were delighted that the newlyweds had at least a few days to be together after they had taken their vows.

When Cheryl checked her watch, she said hurriedly, "We need to go soon, or I'll be late."

"Then allow me just one more moment," Nigel asked. "I promise, I won't be long."

Cheryl nodded as Nigel stood opposite her with the sun behind him.

"Miss Cheryl Beatty," he began, "I have waited a lifetime to find you. Now that I have, I don't intend to lose you to another. I can only hope and pray that you have feelings for me that match mine for you. If so, then I ask you," he said, as he retrieved a small square box from his pocket, opened it, and took one knee, "to make me the happiest man I can imagine, and consent to be my wife."

The blue velvet box in his hand held a yellow-gold ring with a brilliant-cut center diamond, flanked by a pair of sparkling emeralds, which the afternoon sun set ablaze.

"Oh, my lord," she exclaimed, looking at the ring. "Where did you? How did you? Oh, never mind," she whispered as tears clouded her eyes, "Yes, yes, Nigel, a thousand times, yes."

This kiss, ruled by the tears they shed together, was brief, but just as warm as any before. They had to rush now to meet Cheryl's schedule, but with the ring on her hand, nothing interfered with their chatter on the way.

"But tell me," she laughed as they ran together, "how did you find a ring like this today?"

"Today?" he asked. "It wasn't today."

"Then, when?" she asked.

"I took a lesson from my brother," he said.

"From Boyd? What do you mean?" she asked.

"He bought Kathleen's ring months before he proposed. Two weeks after I left you in Mombasa, months and months ago," he said, "I knew I was in love with you and wanted to spend the rest of my life with you. When the *Formidable* shipped out, eventually taking me back to Rosyth while she was refit, I had a month to find a ring to match the sparkle and color of your eyes."

Cheryl, looking at the ring on her hand, then back at Nigel, said, "You knew in Mombasa?"

"Come now, Miss Beatty," Nigel laughed, "with your eyes, your smile, your wit, and the life you exude with every breath? I was smitten from the day we met, helpless but to wait for an opportunity to beg you for your hand. I knew if I rushed you, you might run away from me. But ever since I had to ship out, I've been afraid I might lose you. So, damning all the rules that would prevent us from becoming one, today was my first opportunity, and I dared not wait for another."

"Oh, you," she said, draping her arms around his neck, "you melt me, you do."

And after one more kiss, lasting longer than all the others, they rounded the corner and turned onto the path that led to Cheryl's barracks, where several dozen eager Wrens waited in the afternoon shade of the front porch.

Chapter 25

"Thank you for taking the time to see me, Sir Richard," Brenda said. "I know you have a very busy schedule."

Sitting at his desk in the study, Sir Richard answered, "Not at all, Brenda. I'm glad to be able to talk with you. Tell me, please, what's on your mind?"

After taking a deep breath, Brenda began.

"I came to apologize," she said. "When I arrived here, Michael and Susan were the first to receive me. I had invaded your property to use your radio to contact your enemies, but Michael and Susan, at your behest, befriended me. Since then, all of Highfield has treated me like family. You've welcomed my father, my mother, and my brothers and provided not only a home, but also work and wages that make our lives happy once again. After that, you sponsored Ernst's mother, making their reunion possible. In all that time, though, I've never asked to speak with you and apologize. So, I want to say I'm sorry for the things I did after I left home, things that hurt many people, but especially you and Lady Moncrieff.

"Of course, I forgive you, Brenda, but I hope you know I've really held nothing against you from the beginning," he said.

"That is very generous of you," she said, "but the anger I held against those who hurt me and my family ended up here, and that wasn't fair."

"I can see that happening in a case like yours," he said. "Sometimes our injuries cause us to lash out in an effort to try to make something fair. We have a sensitivity within us that demands justice. After you and your family were so vilely wronged, seeking retribution was a natural reaction."

"But I was striking out against people I'd never met," she said, "and at least one person was terribly injured."

"But all that is over now, Brenda. Now you and Ernst are helping people who want to end this senseless war. Ernst has just found a way to rescue four Allied airmen in Holland, and though you don't know this yet, you rescued us from a German spy on Canadian soil," Sir Richard smiled.

"I did?" she asked. "How could I have done that?"

"Do you remember a German spy who was supposed to arrive by U-boat to infiltrate Quebec City?" he asked. "You were to meet him and help him to melt into the local community, work with him on his language skills, and inform him on local customs."

"Yes," Brenda said, "but I never met him in Quebec. I was still trying to make contact with him when Michael and Susan discovered me in the fire tower."

"Exactly," Sir Richard agreed, "but you gave up trying to help him, then, didn't you?"

"Yes," Brenda said, "but are you saying that by doing nothing, I rescued Canada from a spy I never met?"

"It's like this," Sir Richard said. "If you had been intent on helping him, he could have endangered many lives. By not meeting him, not helping him with his language skills, not teaching him the local customs, and not finding a place for him to live, he might still be here, infiltrating banks and other organizations crucial to the war effort."

"I understand," she said, "but still, I did nothing."

"And that, for us, was the best thing you could have done," he said as he leaned forward, his elbows on the desk. "Would you like to know the end of the story?"

"Yes, please," she answered.

"His name was Werner von Janowski. He came ashore smelling of diesel fuel from weeks of sailing on a U-boat. He was wearing clothes that were decidedly not Canadian. Had you met him upon his arrival, you would have provided him with clothing that wouldn't have drawn attention. Although he was German, he tried speaking with a Parisian accent, something your help would also have prevented. He also tried to spend outdated Canadian currency. The local people he encountered knew immediately that something was wrong, and he was in the custody of the Royal Canadian Mounted Police a day after his arrival. He is now in Canadian custody, where he will probably remain until the war ends."

"So, you're saying that not helping him was helping you and all of Canada?" Brenda asked.

"Exactly," he agreed. "You made a choice in the tower, but don't forget, you made another choice overnight."

Puzzled, Brenda asked, "What was that?"

"Your cottage wasn't locked," he said. "You were free to go at any time. But you didn't run. You didn't give in to your angry side, the side that wanted to get even."

"No, I didn't," she said quietly.

"But you did consider it overnight, didn't you?" he asked.

"Yes, I did," she said, looking at the floor.

"Any of us would have as well, Brenda, but you *didn't* run. You stayed, and that's when you abandoned our enemy and chose something better," Sir Richard said.

"Yes, I did," she said, looking back at him.

"Now, considering everything that could have happened, how would you say things have turned out?" he asked.

Brenda could only shake her head and laugh. Lifting her face and looking back at him, she said, "It's been a miracle. My family has been rescued from those horrible camps and reunited here. Our new home and our life here are better than any we have ever known. Father's wounds have healed, and his illness has passed. Mother smiles and sings again, and my brothers have filled out and learned how to laugh once more. Ernst and his mother have been reunited here in safety, and Ernst and I found each other at last. When he returns, we're hoping to make a new life together."

Sir Richard left his desk and walked to the leather armchair beside Brenda's. After turning the chair to face her, he sat down and smiled. When he offered both hands to her, she smiled and placed her hands in his.

"Fr. Hunt had something to say about all this in his homily last Sunday," Sir Richard smiled.

"What was that?" Brenda asked.

"It was something about our God being the God of second chances," he said, "something I hope all of us will appreciate at some time or another in our lives."

"Well, then," Brenda smiled as she squeezed his hands, "I thank God for second chances."

Chapter 26

Lois couldn't help feeling defensive with Hugh Buchanan when he arrived at Spring Hill with Luc at the end of a workday at Highfield. Two days earlier, following a conversation with Hugh, Patrice had come to Lois more hurt and upset than Lois had ever seen her before. Lois knew that Patrice was a sensitive young woman, especially sensitive to condescension. She came from simple, hard-working stock and when she was very young, she had learned her place during the brief moments when she encountered a number of wealthy visitors who summered on Prince Edward Island. Later in life, despite her training in manners and deportment at Highfield and her remarkable success in her studies under the tutelage of Susan Moreland, she still feared that her birth among the salt-of-the-earth folks on Prince Edward Island would always invite scorn from those higher born. Patrice's last conversation with Hugh had incited those fears and left her in pieces. Sadly, Hugh seemed to have no idea why Patrice suddenly abandoned him in the midst of their last conversation, and why she had avoided him since. When Hugh came to Lois to see if she knew what was wrong, he was surprised to learn what Patrice had told her.

"Oh, my Lord! Is that what she thought I meant?" Hugh exclaimed as he stood at the kitchen table at Spring Hill, hat in hand.

"She felt you were comparing what it means to be born a Buchanan with what it means to be a person like her from Prince Edward Island," Lois said. "Evidently, the comparison you made left her feeling very small, perhaps even insignificant."

"Oh, Lord," Hugh said, his head down, as he wandered in a circle.

Luc, sitting at the kitchen table, sat silently for a moment before he spoke. "Do you remember anything you said that night that could have made her feel that way?"

Turning to Luc, Hugh began, "I remember she asked if I was hurt that Father never mentioned me in his letter to Mother. Of course, I was hurt, but I didn't feel I could tell Patrice that."

"Why not?" Lois asked.

Looking toward Luc for help, Hugh said, "Because a man can't tell a woman that he has hurt feelings, can he?"

"And why can't he?" Luc asked quietly.

"Because it's just not what a man does," Hugh said authoritatively, as if he were explaining the law of gravity. "We simply don't."

"Ah," Luc smiled. "I think I understand part of the problem, then. Patrice said something about what it meant, 'to be the son of a Buchanan'. So, is that part of it, Hugh? Is hiding hurt feelings from a woman part of what it means to be a Buchanan?"

Hugh was silent for a moment before saying, "Yes, it's part of being a Buchanan, but I think it's also part of being from Scotland, too."

"Well," Lois asked, "what about the things Patrice mentioned about having to work with your hands, your inability to find a decent nailbrush or a white linen handkerchief in town?"

Shaking his head, Hugh heaved a sigh and said, "Those are all Father's standards I learned as a boy. Our birth to the Buchanan name has required us to separate ourselves from those who were 'not born into a family with a history like unto ours,'" Hugh quoted. "Our Coat of Arms requires that we always live to a standard better than most." Suddenly, ashamed by the words that still hung in the air, he sat at the table with tears filling his eyes.

Lois and Luc waited quietly for a long moment before Hugh spoke again.

"When I came here to Highfield," he began, "it took some time before I could relax enough to take a place like any other man working for my uncle. Although I had no experience in carpentry, had never worked with my hands in any trade, and even lacked the vocabulary to speak intelligently on a building site, several men I had just met helped me relax and learn without shame. I always felt I had to appear to know more than I knew, but, in very caring ways, they tried to relieve me of that burden."

Lois and Luc nodded as Hugh continued.

"Then I met more and more of the Highfield family, and you," he said, looking at Luc. "You received me at face value, with no explicit or hidden expectations, and you endured my ignorance. You took the time to teach me skills that made me proud of our work at the end of the day. I earned honest callouses on my hands and found pride in my work. But," he paused.

"But, what? Luc asked.

"But at the end of the week, when I collected my wages, I was ever reminded that Father, were we together, would be shaking his head, ashamed of me for being no more than a common laborer," he said, looking toward the floor.

"So," Lois began, "how does Patrice fit into all this?"

"Oh, my," Hugh said, shaking his head and looking up. "Patrice brought bright moments that lit up every day we met. I couldn't tell her how nervous I felt when she came to the worksite, but I never had to wonder what *she* was thinking. I could be damning myself for a blunder when measuring or cutting at one moment and forget it all a moment later when we were together. She never made me feel judged or ashamed. I suppose for the first time, I felt it was entirely permissible for me to be, well, just me," he said.

"She also mentioned that there was something you said about your schooling that hurt her feelings," Lois said. "Do you recall?"

Taking a moment to think, Hugh exclaimed, "Oh, what an ass, am I! I thought I was complaining about being shipped off to boarding school and all the formalities that accompanied my education in Scotland. There's really no comparison with a student's life here at Highfield. In Scotland, friendships were secondary to achievement, and making parents proud was primary. The headmaster was distant, and the faculty lived in constant competition. What I found here at Highfield was entirely different. I heard about the personal attention each student receives here and discovered that the caliber of your curricula is more than a match for everything I endured as a student. However, students here learn without the constant and unrelenting pressure of competition for their family's sake. Patrice's classical repertoire, covering everything from Homer to Chaucer and on to Dickens, rivals anything I gained in my years away, and all under the tutelage of so very few."

Hugh paused a moment before saying to Lois, "Could I ask a boon of you? Would you be kind enough to explain to Patrice that she was correct? I was injured when forgotten in Father's correspondence with Mother. I've always felt I've been a disappointment to him. I believe those feelings, old and unresolved as they are, unfairly hurt Patrice. If she were willing,

I would welcome an opportunity to apologize. Our relationship means a great deal to me."

Hugh looked from Lois to Luc and back to Lois before she stood and stepped toward him with open arms. As he rose to receive her embrace, Luc stood ready to offer his hand.

"I'll be speaking with Patrice before the night is over," Lois said, "but a personal apology would likely be more readily received than any I could relate, wouldn't you agree? Perhaps a conversation with Patrice tomorrow evening would prove a convenient preamble to a second go at that puzzle we need to finish. A red and white lighthouse awaits completion."

Hugh's smile told Luc and Lois all they needed to know.

Chapter 27

The gentleman who stopped at the farm stand at the end of Highfield's driveway wasn't the typical visitor Elke Hoffman had seen in the past. His car was newer and larger than most, and he was dressed in a business suit, wearing a topcoat, and sporting a fedora.

Elke had just filled the shelves with three dozen eggs and several canning jars of green beans when he stepped out of his car.

Looking at the sign, he said, "Highfield. Is that the name of this estate?"

"Yes," Elke said, "the home of Sir Richard Moncrieff and his family."

"I see," he said as he looked up the driveway. "Tell me, if you will, is Sir Richard at home today?" he asked.

"I'm afraid I don't know," Elke said, "but I'll be returning to the house shortly. Would you like to leave a message for him?"

"That would be very helpful," the man said as he reached into his breast pocket and retrieved a business card. After writing a short note on the back of the card, he handed it to Elke.

"Thank you," he said. "You've been most helpful."

A moment later, he was back in his car and driving toward Charlottetown.

With her work done at the farm stand, Elke stopped at Highfield's kitchen door to give the card to Doris.

"A man I've not seen before, well-dressed and driving a very nice car, left this for Sir Richard," she said. "If you don't mind, I'll be on my way to lunch with Greta and Gerhardt next door. Please call if there is anything more I can do to help you this afternoon."

Sir Richard was in his study with Michael when Doris delivered the business card. As he read it, front and back, Sir Richard wore a quizzical look, then handed the card to Michael.

"Stephen Lytle?" Michael asked. "How curious. It's been more than five years. I never expected we would hear from him again."

"Neither did I," Sir Richard said. "After all, I've never met the man. He was simply a man whose name was on all the necessary purchase agreements and the deed to Highfield when we bought the house all those years ago. This note on the back of his card inviting me to lunch at the Charlottetown Hotel is quite a surprise."

"Does your schedule have room for you to meet him this week?" Michael asked.

"I'm sure I can find the time," he said, "especially since my curiosity is up."

Just then, Doris knocked at the door.

"I'm sorry to interrupt," she said, "but I just remembered one more thing Elke told me. The license plate on the gentleman's car was from the United States. She remembered seeing the words, 'District of' and a third word she couldn't read."

"Thank you, Doris," Sir Richard said, "that information is most helpful."

Once Doris was out of earshot, Sir Richard said, "That must have been 'District of Columbia', Washington, DC."

"Interesting," Michael said. "I can tell by the look on your face that lunch in Charlottetown just moved up a day on your calendar."

Sir Richard nodded, saying, "Yes, it has, Michael. How would you feel about joining us?"

"I wouldn't miss it," Michael said.

The luncheon appointment was made for one o'clock on Wednesday. Michael and Sir Richard left Highfield in Lady Moncrieff's sedan a little after 12:30 that afternoon.

"What did he sound like on the telephone?" Michael asked.

"Quite businesslike, actually, though personable enough. I still remain curious about what we might discuss over lunch," he said. "Perhaps he'll have something surprising for us."

"I suppose we'll know soon enough," Michael said, "since we'll arrive at the Charlottetown Hotel within a few minutes."

The maître d' surprised Sir Richard and Michael when he escorted them to a private dining room apart from the other patrons. There at the single central table, a tall man of about fifty years stood and extended his hand to Sir Richard.

"It is so good to meet you, Sir Richard. Finally, after too many years, I am able to make your acquaintance."

"Likewise," Sir Richard said as they shook hands, "and as I mentioned on the telephone, this is Michael Moreland, my son-in-law."

"So good to meet you, Mr. Moreland," Mr. Lytle said as they shook hands.

"Just 'Michael' is fine with me, Mr. Lytle."

"Then let it be 'Stephen' for me," Mr. Lytle said. "Please, gentlemen, make yourselves comfortable."

After a brief look at the menu, the sommelier arrived with a bottle of chardonnay and a bottle of cabernet sauvignon, and appetizers soon followed. With their lunch orders complete, Lytle addressed his guests.

"I will confess that I would not have made a return to Charlottetown, Sir Richard, had I not enjoyed the opportunity of hearing your remarks in Washington last year."

"So, you were in attendance for the Joint Resolution of the United Nations?" Sir Richard asked, as he tasted his wine.

"Yes," Lytle said, "I work for the Department of the Treasury, and I was present during the hearings between our OSS and your SIS concerning the horrors that continue wherever Jews are discovered under Nazi rule."

"Is that a new position for you?" asked Sir Richard. "I had understood that you were a banker who, like so many others who worked in finance circles, found the American stock market crash a tragedy for their businesses."

Holding up one hand and shaking his head, Lytle confessed, "I'm afraid I started the rumor that business reverses caused by the failure of the stock market forced me to sell the estate here on Prince Edward Island. In truth, gentlemen," he continued, "the stock market had nothing to do with my reasons for divesting myself of the property now known as 'Highfield.'"

"Then there was another pressing reason?" Michael asked.

"Yes," Lytle said, but he hesitated, seeming uncomfortable at answering Michael's question.

"Please forgive me," Sir Richard began. "I should inform you that Michael shares with me all the confidences you heard at the hearings in Washington. You enjoy my guarantee of security for anything we discuss in his presence. My confidence in him is without question."

"Thank you, gentlemen," Lytle said, relieved. "Forgive my reticence, for there is a great deal of history in my reasons for not disclosing a story that is becoming all too common these days. Allow me to continue."

With Sir Richard's nod, Lytle began again.

"My business with you is of a personal nature, much of which has been held in secret for many years," he began. "To begin with, I was not born 'Stephen Lytle'. I was born Simeon Levi in Munich, Germany, but I arrived in New York as Stephen Lytle."

"I gather from your surname that you are Jewish?" asked Sir Richard.

"Yes," he answered. "My parents were among the earliest Jews to suffer under the Nazi regime. By German standards, they were wealthy and very successful entrepreneurs who owned several manufacturing facilities, producing everything from coat hangers and curtain rods to aircraft engines. They became targets of Nazi hatred shortly after 1934, when Hitler declared himself Führer."

"That must have been terribly frightening," Michael said.

"It was horrible for me, because I had come to the United States as a young man, hoping to finish my studies and begin a career. Soon after I married, my work in finance was more successful than most of my peers could believe, but there was an underlying reason. My parents were forward thinkers and had begun to divest themselves of their assets in Germany before the Nazis could appropriate them. When those assets arrived in the United States, I managed their fortune until they found a safe exit from Munich." As Lytle stopped to pick up his water glass, Sir Richard spoke.

"May I hazard the guess that Highfield was intended as a home for your parents, then?"

"Correct," Lytle answered, "but they first spent two years in England. Then, concerned that Germany would invade Britain, they decided to sail for Canada. Sadly, when their ship arrived, they found they were not welcome in Halifax, and they had to continue south to the United States."

"We've seen others experience similar difficulties at Pier 21," Sir Richard said, shaking his head.

"Do you have siblings remaining in Germany?" Michael asked.

"No, he answered. "Thankfully, my brother and his wife fled to Switzerland, and they are safe there."

"I'm sorry to have taken advantage of your family tragedy," Sir Richard said.

"Oh, you took no advantage, Sir Richard, I can assure you. There were no buyers for an unfinished home of that size on this side of the ocean. Your purchase freed my parents to find a home in Washington Heights in New York City," Lytle said. "At about the same time, my wife, Elaine, began her battle with cancer and died three years ago this spring. Our daughter, Susan, twenty-two, is a student."

"You've had your share of suffering," Sir Richard said, "but I sense we are meeting at your invitation today for a reason not related to family history."

"You are correct," Lytle said. "It began in Washington last year, when you and the young man who accompanied you offered your testimony concerning Jewish persecution in Europe. I knew then that I had to contact you. I need your help."

"Then, is there a specific situation that prompts our meeting today?" asked Sir Richard.

"Yes," Lytle nodded. "It's my daughter, Susie. Well, Susie is what Elaine and I named her, but now she goes by *Sybil.* If you knew her, you'd understand. She's always had a mind of her own, you see. She's all I have left since Elaine died. But now I fear for her," he said.

"Is she in some danger?" Michael asked.

"Yes," Lytle said. "She had spent two years with my brother and his wife in Munich and wanted to continue her studies there. When my brother and my sister-in-law escaped to Switzerland, she refused to join them. She also refused to return to the United States. She had become very active in a student resistance movement called 'White Rose.'"

"We know of it," Sir Richard said. "They've published anti-Nazi leaflets and distributed them in several countries."

"Yes, and, as I remember, the young man who testified with you in Washington spoke of it," Lytle said.

"And you believe she is in grave danger?" Michael asked.

"Yes," Lytle nodded, looking back at Sir Richard. "I must find a way to get her out of Munich. I need your help."

"Then, I am afraid I have no good news for you," Sir Richard said, gravely.

"What do you mean?" Lytle asked.

"We've had some recent news from Munich. Three leaders of White Rose, a brother and sister, and another young man were captured by the Gestapo a little over a week ago. They were incarcerated in Munich."

"You're sure it was a brother and a sister?" Lytle asked desperately.

"Yes," Sir Richard said. "The surname was Scholl, as I recall."

"Then Sybil is still free," Lytle sighed.

"Hopefully," Sir Richard said, "hopefully."

Sensing Sir Richard had further information, Lytle looked at him intently and asked, "What are you not saying, sir? Please, I need to know."

Sir Richard paused for a moment before leaning forward to say, "I am sorry to tell you that the three captured by the Gestapo a week ago have already been tried and found guilty of treason." Sir Richard paused again before adding, "They were executed in Stadelheim Prison two days ago."

Chapter 28

With four downed airmen—two British, one Pole, and one American—along with Jan Ingwersen safely aboard the Dutch fishing vessel, *Lotte Noor,* sailing west for England, E.D. and two members of the Dutch underground made their way inland and back to The Hague before dawn.

Over the next three days, E.D. traveled the city on foot and on bicycle, meeting with one underground cell after another. By day and by night, he learned a great deal about life in the Netherlands under Nazi domination.

Collaboration with the Nazi occupation forces was rampant among the Dutch population, especially when it involved the capture and deportation of Jews to Germany. Dutch police and other government officials regularly identified Jewish citizens, sometimes placing bounties on them, encouraging the Dutch, who were dealing with hard economic times, to turn their neighbors in for profit. At the same time, active resistance had grown as German economic pressure on the Dutch economy increased, stripping the country of its wealth. As a result, members of the Dutch underground had learned to trust no one, making E.D.'s job all the harder.

On his third night at The Hague, E.D. rode a bicycle to a meeting in the basement of a three-story building a block from the Peace Palace. The building had been owned by a wealthy Jewish family whose import/export business dealing in fine gems was no more. The entire family had disappeared in a single night. Their home and business had been looted and remained empty.

Not surprisingly, the basement contained a small windowless room, but not one constructed for hiding. The room had been used as a safe beneath the store above. Its thick walls and steel door made it an excellent place for underground members to meet.

"Where did you find such a fine bicycle?" asked one of three men meeting E.D. by candlelight.

"On the street about a half mile from here," E.D. answered. "You could say I appropriated it for a good cause. I've found that a man dressed well and riding a fine bicycle is less apt to be stopped for questioning by the authorities, be they German or Dutch."

"So, you're a bicycle thief?" the man asked as the other men laughed.

"The best," E.D. confessed with a smile. "I highly recommend it to you when you haven't time to walk to your destination."

With a smile, the man said, "Call me Hans. My associates are Hans 2 and Hans 3," he said, pointing to the other men. "We have little time. We know you are seeking safe passage for airmen to reach the coast. We have successfully arranged for travel overland to Switzerland, Portugal, and Spain in the past."

"So, I understand," E.D. said. "Thank you. We just completed the delivery of four men to the Channel and across to England. We need your help to make future rescues by sea."

"Understood," Hans said, nodding. "We will need everything you can tell us about your contacts and the means by which your escape was made successful."

"Understood," E.D. agreed. "Is this a safe destination for a second meeting?"

"Only well into the evening, perhaps the day after tomorrow," Hans said. "We make it our practice not to meet in the same place on two successive nights."

"Of course," E.D. said, "but in the interests of time, can you provide another address for a meeting tomorrow?"

"It can be arranged, my friend the bicycle thief," Hans smiled, "but you haven't given us a name. What do we call you?"

"E.D.," he said.

"E.D.?" Hans asked as E.D. nodded. Hans looked to his two friends to note their reactions. When he turned back, E.D. found all eyes trained on him as the men sat forward. No one was breathing. Hans broke the silence with a question.

"Tell me, E.D., were you aboard an RAF bomber that was shot down near Strasbourg sometime a year or more ago?"

Cautious with his answer, E.D. said, "Perhaps."

"If so, then I must tell you that your reputation precedes you. To most, you are a ghost," Hans said, "but we are seeing you in the flesh. When we part tonight, however, none of us will attest to your presence here. A ghost you shall remain."

E.D. nodded his appreciation as Hans continued.

"This," he said as he retrieved a canvas backpack and handed it to E.D., "is for you. And this," he said after scribbling on the back of a business card, "is how we can be reached until tomorrow night."

Minutes later, E.D. was on the bicycle with the backpack over his shoulder. It weighed very little, leaving E.D. in some suspense concerning its contents during the short trip back to his lodgings for the night. Having left the bicycle a block away, E.D. forced himself to walk at an even pace until he was safely off the street and indoors. There, he opened the backpack and found among its contents a sealed envelope. The message within was encoded, but thankfully in an SIS code he recognized. He had it deciphered within minutes. His orders had changed.

His new orders took him not south and west back to England, but south and east to Munich to locate and extract a young woman, a student in the city he knew so well.

"But what could her strategic value be?" he wondered aloud. Missions with this kind of risk weren't made for personal reasons.

"She must know something or have something very valuable to the Allies," he said to himself, "but what could that be?"

At the same moment, some 500 miles away, a young Jewish woman was sleeping on a pew near the organ in the Asamkirche in Munich. Only votive candles lit the interior of the church where Sybil Lytle lay, dozing fitfully, using her bookbag as a pillow. On the floor, less than an arm's length away, stood a pair of knee-high brown leather boots with tall, stacked heels, but these were not ordinary heels. No naked eye would detect that the heels were hollow. Each contained two canisters of 35 mm film. Unlike the film canister in the camera Sybil carried in her backpack, the film in these canisters had not recorded photos of historic sites on Munich's city streets. No, the film in the heels of her boots documented horrors in places called Sobibor, Treblinka, Chelmno, Auschwitz, and Majdanek, places the free world needed to see. They were the last possessions entrusted to her before a dozen or more Gestapo agents descended on her three closest friends at Ludwig Maximilian University and took them into custody.

Sybil craved sleep as she lay on the pew, but she dared not sleep past dawn. Before the morning sun, she would need to search for another place to hide, somewhere her face was not known, somewhere out of the February cold and wind.

She dozed but found no rest. She woke at the slightest sound, fearing she had been discovered. The winter wind whistling through the tall carved doors at the front of the church offered no note of peace. When she closed her eyes, all she saw was Hans and Sophie and Christoph, captured, struggling, shouting, and manhandled by the Gestapo.

Eventually, toward dawn, she slept. When she awoke, light from the votive candles near the altar were still reflecting in the stained glass. She sat up slowly, revealing her profile above the back of the pew. Turning toward the front of the church again, she looked past the crucifix to the vision of heaven in the apse beyond the altar.

"Heaven," she whispered. She wasn't sure she believed her friends were in a better place now, but she closed her eyes and tried to imagine them there, laughing once more, happy, bright-eyed, and full of peace.

"Perhaps they've found their peace now," she whispered, but try as she might, her tears would not be denied.

Chapter 29

It seemed to Michelle that she and Logan hadn't been more than half a mile from home in a year. Since the air raid in New Mills seven months ago, Michelle had limited their walks to the streets only a few minutes from Fletcher Hall. Today, however, she thought Grayson would be proud to see her and Logan driving south toward Buxton with his mother and sister on a crisp winter day in Derbyshire.

"We'll be there shortly," Nancy said. "Furness Vale is only a few miles away."

"Yes," Mother Royce said. "Once we reach Buxton Road, we're all but there. But tell me again, where are we having lunch?"

"It's a pub called the *Soldier Dick*," Michelle said. "Several years ago, our friend Michael Moreland told me a charming story about it."

"Michael Moreland, yes," Mother Royce said, "he's the young man in the picture with his wife and children, the picture on your desk."

"That's him," Michelle agreed. "Funnily enough, were it not for Michael, I might not have met Grayson."

"Then, although I haven't yet met the man, he gets high marks with me," Mother Royce said, smiling and slapping the armrest as if she held a gavel.

Nancy's driving directions were correct, for after a few more turns down the winding road, the *Soldier Dick* appeared on their right. She parked the Rover at the curb near the front door.

"We may be a few minutes early for lunch," she said, "but I can see the lights are burning inside. I'm sure they'll accommodate us. Come along, Mother."

As Michelle climbed out of the rear seat with Logan, Nancy retrieved his diaper bag, and the foursome started toward the pub's front door. Before they arrived, however, Michelle had a favor to ask of Nancy.

"I have my camera in Logan's bag," she said. "Would you retrieve it and take a photo of Mother Royce and us here?" she asked, pointing to a spot under the sign.

"Of course," Nancy said. "I hope your camera is similar to mine, though. I'm no expert when it comes to photography."

"It's quite simple," Michelle said. "Fear not. After you've captured us at the door, perhaps Mother Royce will hold Logan while I take a photo of you three?" she asked.

"What fun," Mother Royce agreed.

With their photos finished, the party moved inside and found a table opposite the bar. The story Michael had told Michelle about his grandfather's visit to the pub at least fifty years earlier was a story Michelle couldn't wait to tell.

"Michael's grandparents on his mother's side lived right here in Furness Vale before the turn of the century," she began. "As the story goes, his grandfather was here at the pub one evening when a young American man arrived from London after a tour of Europe. The fellow was on his way to Manchester, where his ship to America was due to sail the next day. Sadly, the young man discovered he didn't have enough money to pay for his fare home."

"What a predicament," Nancy said. "So, what did he do?"

"Amongst his luggage, he had a guitar, and he became a minstrel for the evening, earning tips by playing and singing whatever would please the patrons," Michelle said.

"So, everything turned out for the best?" Mother Royce asked.

"Sadly, no," Michelle answered, "for at the end of the evening, he discovered he still hadn't made enough money to pay for his ticket home. There was only one thing left to do."

"And what was that?" Nancy asked.

"He offered up his guitar for sale. When none of the other patrons showed an interest, Michael's grandfather had pity on the young man and bought the guitar. He made it a birthday gift to his daughter, Michael's mother, a week later," Michelle laughed. "Eventually, the guitar came to Michael, who learned to play it when he was young. The instrument is with him on Prince Edward Island to this day."

Michelle had just finished her story when an older man who had been sitting at the bar stepped away from his barstool and approached the ladies at their table.

Holding his cap in his hand, he said, "Begging your pardon, ladies, but sometimes a bloke can't help but overhear things in a pub as close as it is here at the Soldier Dick. I couldn't help but hear you relating that story, Miss, about the young man and the guitar. Would you favor me by answering a question?"

"Of course," Michelle said, "if I can. The story isn't mine, you see. I can only repeat from memory what my friend told me."

"That's all good and well," the man said. "I won't hold you to nothing. Just one question," he said, his cap still in his hand. "Did your friend happen to mention his relative's name, the one who purchased the instrument?"

Michelle thought for a moment, trying to recall her conversation at Highfield that was several years old now. After a long moment, she said, "I'm sorry. I don't recall a family name, but I do remember that his mother's name was Amelia."

Michelle looked at the man as a tear appeared in his eye, and he prepared to speak again.

"Could it have been Amelia Rose?" he asked.

Surprised, Michelle exclaimed, "Yes! That's right, that's how Michael told me his father always addressed her. 'Amelia Rose'. Did you know her?"

Retrieving his handkerchief from his back pocket, he said, "Only as well as a fellow born when his elder sister was fourteen years old could know her. Amelia Rose Swindells was my sister's name. Married a man from Suffolk, as I remember. Died too young with the Spanish flu at the end of the war, God rest her soul."

"Then, that would make you Michael's uncle," Michelle marveled.

"Michael?" he asked.

"Yes, Michael Moreland," she said, "her son."

"Ah, yes," he said as he recollected, "that's right. Moreland was her name. Yes, I remember now. We had a letter saying that she'd borne a son. Named the lad for Father, as I recall now, yes, it would have to be Michael."

"Yes, Michael Moreland," Michelle confirmed.

"Once the war began," the man continued, "we lost touch, you know, and then, so soon after," he hesitated, "she was gone, she was." He hesitated another moment before saying, "Begging your pardon, Miss, I'm Jimmy, by the way. Well, James is my given name, James Swindells, but I'm known to all as Jimmy. Thank you for letting me interrupt your lunch."

As he turned toward the bar, Michelle stood and put a hand on his shoulder.

"Please," she said, "I know Michael would like to know more about his mother's family. His father died a number of years ago. Michael lives in Canada now."

"Ah," he said. "I could hear something of Canada in your voice, I could," he smiled.

"If you wouldn't mind, Mr. Swindells. . ." Michelle began.

"Just Jimmy is fine," he laughed.

"All right, Jimmy," she agreed, smiling back. "Would you let me take a photo of you for Michael? And if you would give me your address, I would be pleased to let him know about his uncle so that you could correspond, perhaps?"

Smiling, Jimmy said, "I would like that. Thank you, Miss."

After Michelle had taken the photos and had Jimmy's address in hand, the ladies enjoyed their fish and chips and were ready to begin the short ride home. Michelle, however, asked Nancy to make a detour.

"Jimmy said he still lives in the family home where Michael's mother was born," she said. Handing Nancy a slip of paper with Jimmy's address, Michelle said, "I need to take one more photo on our way home."

Chapter 30

The weather had been cold on Prince Edward Island in February of 1943, but the snow of the last two weeks had melted, and the sun was shining. Bill Stewart and his wife, Marge, were driving north up Suffolk Road on a Monday morning.

"We're not far away now," Bill said as he shifted into second gear. "I've heard about the farm stand at the end of the driveway. I'm sure we won't miss it."

"But we can't simply arrive there, uninvited, Bill," Marge said.

"Oh, I'm not intending to venture farther than the farm stand that's open to all. That's why I've brought the trunkful of parts from the shop. We're welcome to leave the inner tubes, spark plugs, radiator hoses, and such that folks can use, but just can't afford these days. Freeman Ford was glad to help."

Bill was still unloading the trunk when Michael's flatbed showed up at the end of Highfield's drive. Michael got out and left Simon sitting in the passenger seat. Simon was busy sniffing at a covered pie basket on the truck floor.

"Bill Stewart!" Michael called as he stepped their way. "And this must be Marge," he added.

"Yes, it is," Bill laughed, putting his arm around her shoulder. "At last, the two of you get to meet."

"It's good to put a face to the name," Michael smiled, as Marge offered her hand,

"And it's good to meet you, Mr. Moreland," she said, "and finally get to thank you for many, many blessings."

"Well," Michael said, "Bill set me on a path that made everything possible. He's the one I'll always be ready to thank."

"But I'm guessing you don't know the latest," Marge said. "Have you told him?" she asked, looking at Bill.

"Not yet, but give me a few minutes," Bill said as he closed the trunk on their car.

"Before you do," Michael began, "I'd like to offer an invitation. I have two warm pork pies in a basket in my truck. My watch tells me it's just about time for lunch. If you're not too busy, would you follow me across the road to our home for lunch? I'm sure my wife, Susan, will be glad to meet you both. Then you can tell us the latest while we eat. How would that be?"

Bill and Marge couldn't contain their smiles. As they looked at each other and nodded, Bill turned to say, "We'll be right behind you."

After Michael introduced Susan, he gave the Stewarts a quick tour of the house while Susan set the table. Along with the pork pies, she served green beans and pickled beets from the larder.

Once at the table, Michael said, "So, tell me, Bill, what's the latest news you mentioned? It's easy to see you're feeling well, with all that color in your cheeks."

"That's just it," Bill began. "With Dr. MacMillan leading the way, I've been back and forth to Montreal, where I've become part of a test group of folks with lung problems like mine. At first, they gave me some medicines you might remember Dr. MacMillan mentioning when you were with me at the hospital."

"Sulfa drugs?" Michael asked.

"That's right," Bill said, "and they were doing a good job at keeping the pneumonia infections down for a while, and then. . ."

Marge interrupted, "And then, thanks to that young intern, Joseph Boucher, Bill became part of another test group using the latest medicine."

"It's called *penicillin*," Bill interrupted. "It's the latest of what they call *antibiotics*, and look at me! You see the difference, don't you?"

"I certainly do," Michael said, as he looked toward Susan. "You wouldn't believe how much better Bill looks, Susan, and," he continued as he turned back to Bill, "you climbed up and down the stairs a few minutes ago with no problem at all."

"And he was shoveling snow at home the other day when we got that last six inches," Marge said, beaming. "He's a new man."

"And there's one more change that has nothing to do with my health," Bill smiled.

"What's that?" Michael asked. "Don't leave us in suspense!"

"It's about work," Bill said. "You notice I'm not there today, don't you?"

"That's right," Michael answered. "When I saw you at the farm stand, I wondered at first if you weren't well enough to report this morning, but clearly that's not it."

"No, it's not," Bill smiled. "You can say I'm what they call *semi-retired* these days."

"That means he only works half the hours and is training a new man to take over completely before spring," Marge smiled.

"And then we're going to take some time to travel to a few places we haven't seen in years," Bill said.

"To see our children and grandchildren in the States," Marge added.

"But none of this would be possible if you hadn't dragged me to the hospital, Michael," said Bill.

"And none of this," Michael said, smiling and indicating the dining room, the kitchen, and the rest of the house, "would have been possible without the push you gave me to file for a patent, either, Bill."

"It seems that we're all in this together," Susan added, "blessed beyond our expectations." As everyone agreed, Susan said, "Now, give us a moment to clear these dishes, and we'll be able to enjoy what's left from the peach cobbler Michael started on last night."

"I only ate half of it," Michael complained.

"That's right," Susan said with a smile, "and that's why I baked two."

Just then, Christine woke from her nap, and Brenda returned with Case and Reed from Highfield. While Michael served the cobbler, Bill and Marge enjoyed meeting the children. When dessert was finished, Bill and Marge said their goodbyes, and Michael retired to the kitchen and the dishes.

On the kitchen counter next to the sink, however, Michael found a sealed envelope.

"Brenda must have brought this over with Case and Reed," he said to himself. Turning it over, he recognized Sir Richard's hand in four letters: FYEO—*For Your Eyes Only*.

Chapter 31

Michael took Sir Richard's letter to his bedroom desk before opening it. When he sat and turned on his reading lamp, he read,

It appears that the Munich witness in question has gone to ground. She has not been seen since the others were taken into custody. Reliable sources indicate that she may be in possession of evidence that the Gestapo and SS would be eager to retrieve.

E.D., already in the Netherlands, has orders from our office to reach the city in question with all due haste to locate and secure the witness and any evidence she bears. We have left all travel details to him on the ground and notified all agencies to aid him in whatever way he may require.

The Prime Minister has followed White Rose for some time. He is highly interested in aiding our efforts to retrieve this witness. If and when we have any update on this intelligence, we will determine our ability to update our visitor from the States. Until then, we remain in silence.

We will speak of this case at our next opportunity.

R.M.

Michael sat back in his chair to peruse the letter once more before crumpling it and throwing it into the fire in the fireplace. With no other way to be of service in this case, Michael sat back in his chair to say, "God help this young woman to stay hidden until Ernst or another capable agent can find her. When they do, for I trust they will, grant them all safe passage to a friendly home. Amen."

While Michael prayed in his bedroom, E.D. had made his way back to the Dutch coast. Having determined the fastest route to Munich was via air from Britain to Spain and overland to Germany, he had contacted Jan to meet him at sea near Hoek van Holland. Though more dangerous than an overland route to Munich, E.D. knew that the sooner he was in the air, the more likely he would be able to find Sybil Lytle and the evidence in her possession.

Jan's Dutch underground compatriots were a hardy, highly skilled group of men. Hours after E.D. reached the coast, he heard Jan's voice come out of the dark as the water slapped the hulls of the two fishing boats that brought them together.

"No time to lose. Aboard and gone," Jan said in a hoarse whisper.

Wasting no farewells, E.D. was aboard Jan's craft and bound for the English coast in no more than a minute. As they sailed in the darkness, the two men kept a quiet conversation.

"Bound for?" Jan asked, adding, "if you can say."

"RAF Honington in Suffolk, then RAF Gibraltar, and overland to Munich in haste," E.D. said. "A life-or-death situation. A young woman."

"I see," Jan said, "and speaking of a young woman, I received this for you in London. The scent on the envelope is the basis for my conclusion regarding its sender," he smiled.

Jan handed E.D. a letter from Canada, postmarked in Charlottetown four weeks earlier, and posted in care of Jan at his Hyde Park address. E.D. could see little in the darkness with only the captain's single oil lamp in the boat's cabin. In the flicker of the tiny flame, he could make out Brenda's name on the return address label. That was enough to hold his attention until the morning sun provided sufficient light to read. Until then, exhausted, he slept. It would be two days before he would reach RAF Honington. After that, another long trek by air, boat, train, and foot stood between him and his arrival in Munich. He could only hope to locate his target before the Gestapo did.

It was four hours later when E.D. awoke. Midway across the channel, the sun was rising, but the temperatures remained bitterly cold. Remnants of bread, cheese, and milk, along with a cold pot of tea, sat on a small shelf in one corner of the cabin. E.D. settled for a slice of bread and some cheese before settling back on the bunk where he had spent the night. He opened Brenda's letter and, holding it up to the morning light, he read,

My Dear Ernst,

I am writing this letter on the first of February, knowing you may not receive it for some time. Please know that I miss you terribly and pray each day for your safety and your soon return, well and whole, on this side of the ocean.

I want you to know that your mother is well and thriving. She and my mother have become fast friends and spend much of each day together. Elke, as she insists I call her, also dedicates several hours each day to serving in the kitchen at Highfield and wherever else she might be needed. Friedrich and Carl attend the school just a short walk from our home, and they keep a daily afternoon schedule caring for the livestock at Highfield. Father and Sir Richard have become fast friends and enjoy breakfast together every Monday. The remainder of Father's days are spent working at Highfield or in our barn and sheds, preparing for what spring will bring in the fields.

I know you cannot risk writing, but any communication you can venture would be a treasure for me. Please take care of yourself, not just for yourself, but for me as well. I will be waiting for you, and I hope the wait won't be long.

With all my love and prayers,
Brenda

Ernst had never had more reason to ache for home, even though the place he considered his home had never really been his. However, the only two people he truly loved, his mother and Brenda, were waiting on Prince Edward Island, an ocean away. He had once called Munich his home, but now it was a place of danger where evil lurked in every doorway. Despite the danger and the darkness, everything in him felt an urgency for his mission, a need that called him to rescue and retrieve a young woman now alone and hunted by those who remained relentless in their pursuit.

His thoughts returned to Brenda. Closing his eyes, he could feel her in his arms once more, enjoy the scent her letter brought him, and feel the softness of her blonde hair on his cheek. Her kisses, warm and willing and matching his filled his memory as he nodded off again.

It was Jan's voice that woke him next. Their Dutch craft was about to raft up with an English boat for the last leg of their journey across the Channel. They would be boarding the boat from England in a few minutes.

"Gather your goods, my friend," Jan called into the cabin. "Our final stretch, about four hours in duration, awaits us. On deck now, step lively," Jan smiled.

Aboard the *Feathered Friend*, not a flat-bottomed Dutch boat but a proper British sloop that cut through the water, they made better time. Despite the fog that began to settle in, the English coastline came into view in a few hours' time.

"Our captain tells me there will be a car waiting to drive you to RAF Honington from Aldeburgh, where you'll be landing," Jan said, pointing toward the coastline. "The drive is less than fifty miles. With any luck, you'll be in the air after a good meal and a change of clothes," he said with a smile. Then, leaving his smile behind, he continued, "I know your mission is one of dire necessity and full of danger, or they wouldn't have sent for you. You're a brave and dedicated man, E.D., and it's been my honor to work with you."

"And it's been my pleasure working with you, Jan," E.D. said, "and with any luck, we'll never have to work together again."

Jan was quick to return E.D.'s smile. An hour later, E.D. climbed over the gunwale and dropped into a waiting skiff a few hundred yards off the coast of Aldeburgh.

Chapter 32

Hugh Buchanan spent most of the late afternoon alone in his cottage at Highfield preparing for an after-dinner conversation with Patrice. It felt like almost a week since he and Patrice and been together with Luc and Lois, one of the worst weeks that he could remember in his life. When they parted then, he didn't know why his conversation with Patrice had upset her so much. After he had an opportunity to speak with Luc and Lois, he discovered that his feelings about his father, his family, and his heritage ruled his life and could hurt others. Tonight, he was hoping to retrieve a relationship that, if not broken, was thoroughly bruised.

When he arrived at Spring Hill, he realized he was probably over-dressed. Luc wasn't wearing a tie or a tweed blazer. Neither were his shoes freshly polished. Before Lois arrived with Patrice, Hugh decided to dispense with his blazer and tie.

"I confess I'm a bit nervous," he said. "I've been such an ass. Of course, I didn't mean to be. Nonetheless, the result is the same. I've hurt Patrice."

"One misstep doesn't end a waltz," you know," Luc offered. "Most couples experience a number of these mishaps as they get to know one another."

"Thank you," Hugh said, "but mine has been a bit of a catastrophe. I've been an oaf, and I've offended her, making her think that I feel superior to her, when truly the opposite is the case."

"All parents set standards for their children," Luc began, "standards that were set for them by *their* parents. Fortunately, our small worlds have grown larger over the years, and sometimes we find that the standards we learned early in our lives need not limit us today. As we encounter people elsewhere, we'll find many whose hearts are honest and honorable, perhaps more honorable than our own. Although their outward training and experience may not mimic ours, their hearts will remain just as worthy."

"I understand that now," Hugh said, "but I only wish I had considered it then."

"Then, trust this," Luc said. "Generous people generally allow second chances. Would you say that Patrice is a generous person?"

"Yes, I would," Hugh answered with a smile, "and I hope that she will remain so tonight."

Just then, the two men saw the headlights from the Bouchers' car shine up the driveway. With one last hopeful look in Luc's direction, Hugh took his place next to his host with a gift box in his hand.

As the ladies arrived and entered the kitchen, Luc and Hugh stepped forward to take the ladies' coats. Although Hugh moved rather tentatively, Patrice remained gracious but cool. When he presented his gift of chocolates, she warmed.

"Thank you," she said, "but you shouldn't have."

"Oh," he said, "but I needed to. I hope you like caramels."

"They remain among my favorites," she answered.

Lois interrupted to say, "Why don't you two go to the parlor while Luc and I finish in the kitchen? The puzzle is still there, and while you get started, we'll get the popcorn ready."

"Thank you," Hugh responded, looking at Patrice. "That would be lovely," he said, looking for agreement in Patrice's eyes.

"Yes," Patrice agreed, "that would be lovely." Then, turning, she led Hugh toward the parlor.

Lois and Luc made sure that popping the corn took longer than usual, while occasionally lending their ears to the conversation in the dining room. When they eventually delivered the refreshments, Patrice and Hugh were laughing over the puzzle.

"Hugh had the lighthouse finished before I knew it," Patrice said.

"But the red and white stripes were half done when we arrived," said Hugh. "You've gotten all the rocks beneath the lighthouse sorted, so now we can start on the really difficult part, the sandy beach."

"Then let's have at it," Luc said as he placed the bowl of popcorn on the table.

"You two have gotten almost as much done as four of us did the last time we were together," Lois laughed.

"Well," Hugh smiled, "that's probably because I've not been the oaf that I was last week."

"An oaf last week?" Lois laughed. "No, I think not. Perhaps you were just a person, like the rest of us. After all, no one here was looking over your shoulder to make sure you were behaving."

"Behaving?" Luc interrupted. "Are we supposed to behave? Now, that's no fun."

"No, it isn't," Patrice agreed. "We simply need to be ourselves, not who we're supposed to be. None of us has ever found that to be fun."

After they had worked for a few minutes, Luc had an idea.

"You know, with most of this puzzle already finished," he said while looking at his wristwatch, "we still have time to get to the Capitol Theater in Charlottetown. They have a film called 'Casablanca' with Humphrey Bogart and Ingrid Bergman."

"Tonight?" Lois asked.

"Yes," Luc answered, "it's their Friday night special. It's here in the Charlottetown Patriot," he said, holding up the evening newspaper.

Looking over his shoulder, Lois said, "And they're offering a free bag of popcorn with every ticket, but," she said, reaching for Luc's wrist to check his wristwatch, "we'll need to leave right away to make it on time."

"There's no rush, Sweetheart," Luc laughed, "we'll only miss the same old newsreels. If everyone agrees, I'll start the car. In five minutes, it will be warm and cozy and ready to go."

"I'd be happy to go, if Patrice agrees," Hugh said.

Looking his way, Patrice couldn't help smiling as she said, "It sounds like a fine idea to me. I'll help Lois clean up while you men attend to the car."

With Luc's five-minute prediction correct, the four were in the car and on their way. In the back seat as they left the driveway, Hugh reached over for Patrice's hand and kept it secure and warm in his gentlemanly grip. In the darkness, he couldn't see the smile in her eyes. Neither could she see his.

Chapter 33

"Canaris?" Gerhardt Kimmel asked. "Yes, there was a fellow student by the name of Canaris when I studied at the German Imperial Naval Academy in Kiel. A brilliant young man, I believe he spoke five or six languages."

"Yes," Sir Richard said. "That would be the man who also commanded a U-boat in World War I."

"Correct," Gerhardt agreed, "near the end of the war, at about the same time that I was in command of a U-boat. Is he sailing with the Kriegsmarine presently?"

"No," Sir Richard answered. "He is serving in a completely different role now, directly assigned by Hitler."

The men were enjoying their Monday morning breakfast at Highfield when their conversation turned to the state of the war.

"As I said," Gerhardt began, "he was a brilliant young man. I'm not surprised that he has advanced to a high office, but can you tell me what the state of the war is now? I confess I have not followed the news recently."

"The Nazis have faced two major setbacks," Sir Richard began, "the first in their defeat by the Soviets in Stalingrad. Their North African campaign seems to be on shaky ground at present, so shaky that the Allied high command had enough confidence in their troops to schedule a meeting in Casablanca called the "Casablanca Conference" in January. Attended by President Roosevelt and Prime Minister Churchill, the conference ended with a call for the unconditional surrender of the Axis powers."

"So, Germany is trying to maintain a front in the east against the Soviets, a front in the west against Great Britain and the United States, and a third battlefront in North Africa?" Gerhardt asked.

"Correct," Sir Richard answered, "and Italian forces haven't proven a substantial help to the Axis cause."

"But there's no way to supply that many fronts with the required manpower, arms, air support, ground support, and the necessary supplies," Gerhardt said. "It's pure folly." "It becomes more obvious every day," Sir Richard said. "American attacks on the U-boat docks in Wilhelmshaven last month tell the tale. The US Air Force shot down twenty-two German aircraft and lost only three of their own. Fifty-three bombers, B-17 Flying Fortresses and B-24 Liberators, dropped over 130 tons of bombs, hitting oil refineries and factories. And that was just the beginning."

"The beginning?" Gerhardt asked.

"Yes," Sir Richard answered. "The RAF followed two weeks later, targeting the major Kriegsmarine facility at Wilhelmshaven. Arsenals holding mines, torpedoes, and ammunition were decimated. Using radar-guided bombing, the RAF obliterated facilities covering over a hundred acres, while losing only three Allied aircraft."

"It appears the Führer has lost his ability to defend his war machine," Gerhardt said.

"Yes," Sir Richard agreed, "and we continue to hope that he will sue for terms of peace soon."

"But from what we have heard, unconditional surrender would appear unlikely," Gerhardt said quietly.

"I would have to agree, my friend," Sir Richard said. "I, among many others, regret that so many lives, both among the Allies and our enemies, will be lost before this senseless war ends."

"But this Canaris you mentioned. What role does he play?" Gerhardt asked.

"He happens to be the director of the Abwehr, Hitler's military intelligence service," Sir Richard answered.

"I told you he was a brilliant man," Gerhardt smiled.

"Yes, but the Abwehr's history and performance since the war began would give us reason to believe that its leader has not been in complete agreement with his Führer," Sir Richard said.

"Ah," Gerhardt smiled, "another bit of history repeated."

"I agree," Sir Richard nodded. "It seems Canaris has a conscience, and after witnessing some of the Führer's most heinous acts, he is finding he can no longer keep his eyes closed to the evil, pretending he cannot see."

"And Brenda's friend, who is in Europe now, she tells me," Gerhardt began, "was helpful in revealing some of those evils when he accompanied you to Washington last year."

"Yes, he was," Sir Richard said. "Where he is now, we don't know, but he, and we, are in the business of saving lives."

"Mine being one," Gerhardt said quietly, "and my family's lives before that."

After the two men had finished their second cup of coffee, Gerhardt was on his way home. It was only a moment or two later that Sir Richard's radio came alive with a message relayed after it was decoded in London. Sir Richard donned his glasses to read it.

Arrived Gibraltar at 0:600 today. Anticipate two days to reach contact in Marseilles. Four more to Munich. No word yet from those tracking the package to be retrieved. More news as it becomes available.

Sir Richard sat back in his chair, shaking his head. He was remembering an earlier communique he had received that day. He opened the top drawer of his desk to find it again, but he stopped to say, "The French Revolution in 1789 was more than 150 years ago, and we might have thought that the guillotine would never have a place in history again."

Looking once more at the page in his hand, however, he read, "Sophie Scholl was the first to go under the blade, her brother, Hans, second. They died silently. As the blade was falling on Christoph Probst, he shouted, "*Long live freedom.*"

Sir Richard scanned the remainder of the document, shaking his head when he read that one of the charges against the three students was that they had "vulgarly defamed the Führer."

"A man who is responsible for killing hundreds of thousands, perhaps millions of innocent Jewish men, women, and children, now kills three students for distributing leaflets that quote the Bible and Aristotle. And the crime for which they were killed is that they 'defamed the name of the Führer,'" he said, shaking his head once again.

He placed the documents back in his top drawer, turned off his desk lamp, and left his study. As he hurried through the kitchen, he looked out the window and checked his watch. Reaching for his coat on the coat rack at the back door, he saw Michael getting into his truck. Hurrying out the door, Sir Richard waved Michael down.

"You're headed for Morning Prayer at St. Peter's, aren't you?" he asked.

"Yes, I am," Michael answered.

"Well, I've got a few things to pray for this morning," Sir Richard said. "May I tell you about them on the way?"

"Fr. Hunt is always happy to see another face at Morning Prayer, and I'll be all ears until we get there. Hop in."

Chapter 34

Professor Hans Gerber, his morning oblations and breakfast complete, left his flat and walked the four blocks that led him to his office at Ludwig Maximilian University. The streets in Munich were quieter than usual this week. A good number of the students one might ordinarily expect to see on their way to and from their classes had abandoned their studies following the recent capture and execution of three of their own. Professor Gerber was working actively to fight off his own feelings of depression, the quiet darkness that comes from grief and a sense of resignation. He could not help asking himself, "Who will be next?" and "Will it be another student, or will they make an example of a faculty member this time?" Habit took him to his office door as he walked head down, looking at the stairs to the second floor.

Again, by habit, he checked the small corkboard outside his office door, where he and his students left an occasional note for one another. He found one tattered piece of paper, carefully folded in three, with a thumbtack inserted at the outer fold. When he opened the note, he was surprised to read,

"Herr Professor Gerber, I have only one question. Are we meeting for our usual coffee and kuchen today or is it tomorrow? In either case, I will look for you there."

The note was unsigned, but the professor knew immediately who had left it.

In the days when Ernst Hoffman was studying at LMU, the professor regularly met students informally at *Cafe Luitpold*. Hoffman had become a regular patron because he often worked a late-afternoon shift at the café when classes ended. Taking the note into his office and depositing it in the fireplace, Professor Gerber determined to keep his coffee and kuchen habit that afternoon.

At precisely 3:45, E.D. arrived at *Cafe Luitpold*, found a table near the door that looked out on the street, and ordered coffee. When he saw Professor Gerber approaching on the sidewalk, he ordered a second coffee and kuchen for two. When the professor came through the door, E.D. stood and raised his hand in a congenial welcome. With a smile and a nod, Gerber joined E.D. at the table.

In low tones, E.D. said, "Maintaining your smile and the 'all is well' attitude must be rather tiresome for you, I would imagine."

"Yes, it is. I sense you know the history of the last few weeks here, then?" the professor asked.

"Yes," E.D. answered. "That's why I am here. I am searching for one in hiding."

"Female?" Gerber asked. "Foreign student?"

"Yes," E.D. answered.

"Let's finish our coffee and speak on the street," Gerber suggested. A few minutes later, they were walking through the *Odeonsplatz* as E.D. explained his mission.

"Her name is Sybil Lytle. She may be carrying some highly sensitive evidence of Nazi atrocities. No one has heard from her since the executions," E.D. explained.

"And no one will, if Kurt Huber has his way," Gerber explained. "He is a professor of psychology and music and a friend of White Rose. I understand he has the young lady in hiding. We need to contact him immediately, for I fear that his life may also be in imminent danger."

"How can we reach him?" E.D. asked.

"Leave that to me," the professor said quietly. "You need to stay away from LMU. Everyone is being observed. Fortunately, an old man who has served as a professor for many years is not of concern to the Gestapo at the moment."

"Understood," E.D. nodded. "Here tomorrow?" he asked. "Same time?"

"Not here," Gerber said. "Same time, but at the *Dallmayr*."

"Done," E.D. said as the two separated at the next corner, the professor bound for his office at LMU, and E.D., hiding in plain sight on the street, but bound for the basement of a safe house a mile or more away.

Since the executions, Sybil Lytle had not seen daylight. A slight young woman with golden brown hair and dark eyes, her nights had been spent in churches since the execution, a different one each night. Arriving in the dark before dawn, her days brought her to a different basement or warehouse, tenement or dormitory, as she varied her regular daily patterns for her safety and for the safety of those who risked hiding her. Professor Huber was her one hope. She knew that any opportunity to escape the city would come through him.

All those associated with White Rose had learned to memorize communications. No longer was anything written, so the message Sybil received from Professor Huber after his meeting with E.D., came to her from the lips of the church sexton who opened the door at Trinity Church, the Carmelite monastery church.

Careful to deliver the message as he had memorized it, the sexton began, "Tomorrow, at the Matins bell, this same door. Three knocks will come. You respond with two. Wait for three more, then unbolt the door. A man will hand you a pair of gloves. Put them on and follow him."

Sybil repeated the instructions word-for-word, as the sexton disappeared into the darkness. After she bolted the door, she found a paper sack containing bread, cheese, and a milk bottle filled with water. Since bottled milk had long since been rationed only to the Wehrmacht, the water brought no surprise. Behind the bottle was a ration packet of powdered milk. Sybil ate and drank gratefully, made her nest in a corner with her blanket, and used her backpack as a pillow. She slept fitfully, waking again and again, afraid she might miss the Matins bell which rang before dawn. Not surprisingly, though, she was well awake and waiting at the door when the bell sounded.

E.D. was waiting outside. He knocked three times and listened for her response. When he heard two knocks, he answered with three more and waited for the bolt to slide open. With only a moon for light, neither could make out the other's face. Handing her a pair of kid gloves, E.D. closed the door behind her. As she put them on, he said, "This way," and led her to the alley on the west side of the church.

Chapter 35

Sybil Lytle had no idea who was rushing her through the darkness in Munich. Neither did she have any idea where he was leading her. Fifteen minutes of racing from corner to corner, hiding in shadows whenever an automobile passed, changing directions, and doing all in silence made her frightened and insecure. At one corner, she stopped the man who towed her by her left arm.

"Who are you? Where are you taking me?" she said in a hoarse whisper. "I must know."

"You will know all you need to know in another fifteen minutes," the man said. "If you want to remain alive, simply do as I say. Otherwise, we may both perish."

Willing to wait for another fifteen minutes, Sybil yielded and followed his orders in silence. A short time later they arrived at the basement door of a bakery only a short walk from *Munchen Hauptbahnhof*, Munich's central rail station. Once in the dark basement, E.D. broke his silence.

"Your name is Elise Herschoff. You will address me as Oberleutnant Wagner. Here are your papers," E.D. said, handing her an envelope. As she opened the envelope to inspect its contents, E.D. said, "This is your story. Memorize it. Your father, Wilhelm, and your brother, Kurt, were both killed at Stalingrad. On behalf of the Führer, I am accompanying you to notify your mother, Helga, of their demise. She is living in refuge in Switzerland."

"But where are you taking me?" she asked.

"We are traveling by rail to Switzerland. There you will be released to your uncle and his wife. You must remember that you are in mourning. Your black gloves will be matched by the remainder of your wardrobe. You must play the part every moment, remaining always near tears. I will speak for you if we are stopped or interrogated. Do you understand?" E.D. asked.

Sybil nodded silently.

"I understand that you are carrying evidence in the heels of your boots," E.D. said.

Taken aback, she asked, "How do you know that?"

"You must begin to consider that I know everything about you. You can have no secrets from me. A secret could mean your life. I will be wearing an SS uniform until we reach the Swiss border. You will revere me with the same fear with which most of Germany's population reveres the SS. That is our best defense as we make our escape to Switzerland."

"So," Sybil asked, "you are escaping, too?"

"You can know no more than I have told you," E.D. said. "Now your name?"

Without hesitation, she answered, "Elise Hershoff."

"Your mother?" E.D. asked.

"Helga," she answered again.

"Your father and brother?" E.D. continued.

"Wilhelm and Kurt," she answered, "killed in Stalingrad."

E.D. continued, "Our experience in the Resistance is that hiding things in plain sight is the most successful option. You may keep your evidence in your boots until we leave the last train at Badischer Bahnhof near the Swiss border. Before we cross the border, you will give your evidence to me for transfer to our Allied friends. Do you understand?"

"Yes," she said quietly.

At that moment, a matronly woman appeared, carrying an armload of women's clothing. Amongst the clothes were a supply of mourning garments. E.D. left to confer with another member of the resistance in an adjacent basement room. When he returned in his SS uniform, Sybil Lytle, now Elise Herschoff, awaited him. With her face hidden by her black veil, she was unrecognizable.

"Admirable," E.D. said, congratulating Sybil's wardrobe matron and the work of her team of make-up artists. "Please prepare our bags, now. We depart for the rail station in half an hour."

Less than an hour later, the couple, now in the safety of their private compartment, were traveling toward Switzerland. Sybil could wait no longer to get the answers she craved.

"Pardon me," she whispered, "but I hope I do not sound ungrateful. I assure you that I am thankful for your work and for the risks you are taking while evacuating me from Munich. Still, however, since no one is listening, can you tell me anything further?"

"Such as?" E.D. asked.

"Why did you come to find me?"

"Your father asked for help," E.D. answered.

"My father?" she said, surprised. After a short pause, she asked, "But how did you find me when I was in hiding in Munich?"

"I was a student there some years ago," E.D. answered. "I made friends then who remain friends today."

"And when we arrive in Zurich," she began, "what happens to you?" she asked.

"I will disappear. You will forget we met. A ghost met you, led you to safety, and then disappeared, all in a dream. Now," he said seriously, "soon we will be arriving at *Badischer Bahnhof*, the last German checkpoint. You will find a pair of shoes in your travel bag. Your boots must remain with me."

Sybil removed her boots and handed them to E.D., who immediately removed the contents of their heels. With the four film canisters in his possession, he left their compartment and returned a few minutes later. No longer in an SS uniform, E.D. was wearing a railway steward's uniform. When they changed trains at the border, Sybil knew it would be several more hours before they arrived in Zurich, where her aunt and uncle awaited her. Once E.D. delivered her to her uncle's custody, she knew she would see him no more.

"Please," she said in a whisper, "you've risked your life to save mine. I know I would have been discovered within days in Munich, and save for you, I'd have died there. What could make you care for a stranger like that?"

It was a long moment before E.D. answered, saying, "I share a lineage with you. It has to do with our bloodlines. Too many of our forebears have lost their lives simply because of their bloodlines. If I can help to preserve even one, then I am the one who is rewarded."

He watched as Sybil's eyes filled with tears. "And," he continued, "you have a father who loves you and is desperate to have you return to him. If there is any debt you feel you owe me, please pay it by returning to him. Fathers who love as he does need their heartaches relieved."

An hour after E.D. left Sybil at the platform in Zurich, her four canisters of film were safely in the hands of Allen Dulles at the US Office of Strategic Services. Dulles provided SIS in London with full copies of the photos two weeks later. At the same time, microfiche copies filled the heels of E.D.'s boots for his travel back to Munich, where he arrived a week later. Shortly after his arrival, a knock at Herr Gerber's flat brought the professor to the door.

"Who is calling at this hour?" he asked.

"I have only one question," E.D. said, smiling in the darkness of the hallway.

The door opened immediately, and Gerber rushed E.D. in.

"Were you able to transport the subject and her package safely away?" Gerber asked.

"Safe to the hands of her family," E.D. answered, "and the package to those who could make the best use of its contents."

"A miracle," Gerber said, happily.

"And," E.D. said, "other copies went to international Allied locations, and one last copy is to remain in safekeeping here in Munich."

"Safekeeping?" the professor asked. "With whom?"

"With the most trusted man I know in the city," E.D. said. "A microfiche copy for your files," he whispered, handing the professor a small package. "Others will make their copies public when it profits the Allies. You may need a copy for your own reasons one day. Until then, I must offer this parcel and disappear at once."

The men embraced, an embrace more fitting, perhaps, to a father and a son than to a professor and his former student—even more fitting, perhaps, to quiet men-at-arms, partners in defending those who were unable to defend themselves. With one last wave and a look over his shoulder, E.D. disappeared into the Munich night.

"Auf Wiedersehen, my dear friend," Herr Gerber said quietly. "Mach's gut."

Once more, E.D. found his way to *Munchen Hauptbahnhof* in the darkness, there to board a train for Zurich where he had some unfinished business.

Chapter 36

"What have we here?" Michael asked as he sorted through Highfield's mail at the Charlottetown post office. He was holding a large, thick envelope posted from England. As he turned it over, he found a return address label from Fletcher Hall in New Mills.

"Ah, this will brighten Susan's day," he said to himself. "She always enjoys hearing from Michelle, and based on the size and thickness of this envelope," he said as he tapped the weighty envelope against his hand, "I'd wager there are photos enclosed."

Michael had two more stops to make on his way home, one at Verrier's Hardware and one at Freeman Ford. An overnight snowfall kept traffic light and made the streets quiet under the flatbed's tires, and Michael drove more slowly than usual, easing the truck to the curb in front of the hardware store. Armand was at the front door with a stiff broom. He looked up when he heard Michael's truck.

"It's cold enough that a broom will do a shovel's job," he said, "but later when the sun comes out, I'll have to scrape these steps down before they freeze overnight."

"Typical island weather," Michael agreed. "I wouldn't expect anything else."

Once the men were inside, Armand asked, "Need help finding what you're looking for?"

"Not this time," Michael said. "I'm just finishing a bird feeder for Susan and the boys. There's a perfect spot for one behind the main house between Susan's art ell and my shop. She and the boys like to watch from the kitchen window or from the breezeway. I just need a couple of eyebolts and some light-duty chain to suspend the feeder where the squirrels can't bother it."

"Well, you know where to find what you need, I'm sure," Armand said. "I'll see you at the counter when you're done. I'll be sweeping the back step in the meantime."

At the cash register a few minutes later, Michael said, "I just picked up a letter from New Mills. I'm guessing there are some photos inside. If so, I'll be stopping by to show you soon."

"That would be nice," Armand smiled. "We had a letter about two weeks ago. I know Anna would love to see some new photos."

When Michael stopped at Freeman Ford a few minutes later, his tire tracks told him he was one of the first to arrive that day. As usual, Michael found his way directly to the parts department. Bill Stewart was sitting behind the counter.

"Michael Moreland," he called. "Our first customer on a snowy morning."

"As I was first at the post office and at Verrier's Hardware just now," Michael laughed. "I might be the early bird, but I'm not digging through the snow to find any worms this morning," he smiled.

"Well, what can I help you with, then?" Bill asked.

"How about windshield wiper blades for all my cars and trucks. It seems none of them are wiping clean right now," he said.

"Coming right up. We've got them on a shelf out back. Give me just a minute or two to find the right lengths," Bill said.

Bill was no sooner on his way, when Steve Freeman arrived from the parking lot.

"Michael," Steve called as he came through the door in his overcoat with a newspaper under his arm. "I recognized your truck outside. Is Bill getting something for you?"

"Yes," Michael answered, "some wiper blades."

"Good," Steve said, "and I must say, since you got Bill to the right doctors, he's like a new man. We've never seen him look better."

"It's modern medicine," Michael said. "This new one they call 'penicillin' is a miracle drug."

"Well, it's doing miracles for Bill," Steve said as he walked toward his office.

A few minutes later, Michael was on his way home. After he parked his truck in the garage and left his hardware in his shop, he went to the kitchen with the mail. Case and Reed had just finished their breakfast, and Susan was feeding Christine in her highchair.

"Let me take care of that young lady, Mother," Michael said. "You've got mail to open."

As he handed her Michelle's envelope, Susan's quizzical look turned to joy when she recognized the return address. As she turned to the table while opening the envelope, Michael said with surprise, "No tip for the delivery boy?"

Susan turned back, rolling her eyes as always, and gave him a quick kiss. Of course, he swarmed her in his arms and refused to let her go without a second. When he left a mock bite on her neck, she couldn't suppress her laughter, and wriggled free while he took her place with Christine.

As he added sugar and cream to the last cup of coffee the pot had to offer, Michael watched his wife spill several photos on the table from the folds of a three-page letter. While stirring his coffee, he heard her ask, "I wonder whose house this is?"

Christine was ready for her last few bites of warm cereal, and Michael was glad to oblige. Meanwhile, Brenda had come for the boys and taken them upstairs while Susan finished reading. She sat pensively for a moment before turning to Michael.

"There are some photos you should see here, Michael," she said quietly.

After wiping Christine's face and placing her in her playpen, he joined Susan at the table.

"All right," he said, "show me what you have there."

Handing him a photo of an older man standing at a bar in a pub, she asked, "Do you recognize this man?"

Taking a quick look, Michael answered, "Can't say that I do. Should I?"

"No," Susan answered, still holding the letter in her hand, "but I hope you will have an opportunity to meet him someday. He's your Uncle Jimmy. James Swindells, your mother's older brother."

Sitting up and full of attention now, he took a second look. "And Michelle took this photo?" he asked. "Where could she have met him?"

"In a pub called 'The Soldier Dick' in a village called Furness Vale in Derbyshire, only a few miles from New Mills," Susan answered.

"But that's where my mother's father bought. . ." he began.

"Her guitar, right? The whole story is here," she said as she handed him the letter.

After he read the first page, he looked up at Susan. "I didn't know I was named for my grandfather," he said with tears in his eyes, "and I didn't know he died the same year my mother died. I didn't know I had an uncle, either."

Susan handed Michael two more photos. One showed a long, broad cobblestone driveway leading to a three-story stone house, two smaller houses, several barns, and two stone outbuildings. A second photo offered a view from atop a hill, showing a swift-flowing river several hundred feet from the house, where a stone mill with a water wheel stood.

Handing Michael another page of Michelle's letter, Susan said, "Read this page."

After reading the page, Michael was overcome. "This is the house where my mother was born. It's called 'Sunrise,' because it faces east, where the sun rises over the tall, pastured hill before it. It's where my mother, her parents, grandparents, and generations before them lived," he said.

"Yes," Susan agreed, still reading from the final page, "And Michelle writes here that the main house has twenty-seven rooms, including a chapel. There are two guest houses, several barns, garages, and a water-powered gristmill."

As he shook his head, Michael said, "My father always told me he felt he had stolen a rose from a rich man's garden when he married my mother, but I never gave it a second thought."

"There's still more to tell," Susan said as she continued reading.

"More?" he asked.

"Yes," she said. "Listen to this. 'Sunrise' covers three hundred and twelve acres. But there is also the Swindells Mill several miles away not far from the pub in Furness Vale."

"More than three hundred acres? The estate, and a mill in Furness Vale?" Michael murmured as he looked again at the photos.

"There's one last thing, Michael, something very important," she said quietly as she finished reading to the end of the final page.

"How can there be more?" he asked, looking up from the photos.

"Listen," she said as she sat down beside him, her hand on his arm. "This is what Michelle wrote."

"Michael's uncle lives alone at Sunrise. He has no brothers or sisters. He never married. He is the last surviving member of the Swindells family line in Derbyshire. It appears that Michael is his sole heir. At Jimmy's request, I gave him your address. I expect that you will be hearing from him sometime soon."

Chapter 37

"The war has become a bookkeeper's nightmare for the Axis powers," Sir Richard said, as he sat in Highfield's dining room, stirring his morning tea. "It has come down to numbers, numbers that require neither strategists nor analysts to decipher."

"Then could you enlighten us in layman's terms, Richard?" Lady Moncrieff begged, "Or, perhaps by example, for those of us who lack your military mind?"

"My apologies, then, Angela," he said. "I'll proceed to explain by example. You've heard me speak of the Battle of Guadalcanal in the Pacific?"

"Yes, the Japanese invaded the Solomon Islands sometime in the early summer of 1942, and the American forces took it back after some fierce fighting," she said. "Is that correct?"

"Spot on," Sir Richard answered, "but the cost in lives tells a bit more of the story. The US forces began their attack in August of last year. During the time it took to retake the island, they lost fewer than 1,700 men. Over the same time, the Japanese lost over 24,000."

"That is an incredible difference," Lady Moncrieff said. "Are there similar results on the European front?"

"There are," he answered, especially if we consider the Battle of Stalingrad as an example. Axis casualties numbered half a million, including 90,000 who were taken prisoner. Most of those men died for the sake of Hitler's pride. With his forces surrounded, he refused to listen to those in command on the ground. The Soviets also incurred tremendous losses of life, but they have a much deeper well from which to draw. More important for the Allies is that while Hitler was looking East, we in the West have been preparing for our own future offensive."

"And in Africa?" Lady Moncrieff asked.

"The British Eighth Army has pushed Germany's Rommel back to French Tunisia. He won't be back, I can assure you," Sir Richard smiled. The Allies suffered 250,000 casualties in Africa while Axis casualties numbered over 620,000. And if you consider the war at sea," he said, "the Axis forces endured severe losses at sea this year as well, including 30 U-boats and 13 surface vessels."

"And Allied naval losses?" Lady Moncrieff asked.

"Our losses were primarily limited to shipping vessels, 45 in number, and only one United States submarine," he said.

"In each case, it seems the Axis powers will not be able to continue with such losses of men and naval vessels of war," Lady Moncrieff concluded.

"Correct," he responded, "and we can't forget Axis losses in the air. Last month alone, Germany lost nearly 250 aircraft, while Allied air losses totaled fewer than 50."

"So, for the sake of our sons at sea," Lady Moncrieff began, "can we assume that Nigel in the Mediterranean and Boyd somewhere between Mombasa and Australia may be in less peril than they were at the beginning of the war?" she asked.

"Statistically speaking, my dear, I would agree, but I'm sure our prayers will remain constant," he said.

"Yes, they will," she agreed, "yes, Richard, they will."

Just then, Michael knocked at the door.

"Begging your pardon, Richard and Mother," he began, "but a communication from abroad has arrived. Armand believes it may require your immediate attention, Richard."

"Then I'll take this cup with me," he said as he retrieved his teacup and saucer. "I'll check in with you at lunch, my dear?" he asked.

"Of course," she answered, "of course."

On their way to Sir Richard's study, Michael said, "It's from Zurich, from E.D., perhaps. Armand is decoding it now."

After donning his headphones and listening intently for several minutes, Sir Richard made some notes and removed his headphones.

"Not from E.D., but *about* E.D.," Sir Richard noted. "He accomplished his mission. He delivered the package to her family in Zurich."

"Remarkable," Michael said. "It's been only a week since he began the mission. And his whereabouts at present?" Michael asked.

"Known to none, at the moment," Sir Richard answered. "As is often the case, he's probably gone to ground to avoid detection after delivering the goods."

"And is the package willing to travel back to the States, where her father is waiting?" Michael asked.

"It seems not. She's more interested in pursuing resistance efforts from Switzerland. It appears she is dedicated to honoring the work her friends began, the friends who died for their cause," he said.

"Not an entirely predictable decision, considering the dangers she faced before her rescue, but not entirely surprising either. Her father did warn us that she had a mind of her own. Will you be updating Mr. Lytle?" Michael asked.

"I'll arrange for someone in Washington to make that contact," Sir Richard said. "My primary interest is securing the remaining parcel now in E.D.'s possession, the evidence the Lytle girl was holding. Its discovery could mean a death sentence for anyone possessing it. The Gestapo will have it no other way, I'm sure," Sir Richard said. "His safest option remains in Switzerland."

"In Switzerland?" Michael asked.

"Yes," Sir Richard said. "The closest option would be to deliver the parcel to the US Office of Strategic Services in Zurich. Of course, he could also deliver it to the British embassy in Berne. Sir Clifford Norton is the envoy in charge there. That's a riskier option, though, because it requires travel. The Allies have many enemies in Switzerland. The Swiss government may be officially neutral, but few of its citizens are."

Just then, Sir Richard's private line rang. When he answered, Michael could hear only one side of the conversation.

"Hello. Yes, Armand, thank you. Right away. Will inform you as necessary. Yes. Of course. Until then," he said.

Sir Richard replaced the receiver and reached for his radio headphones. He waited for a moment while Armand relayed another message. He listened and made some notes. Taking off his headphones, he turned to Michael.

"E.D. left a copy of the package with Allen Dulles at the OSS office in Zurich. E.D. will be resuming his previous assignment in the Netherlands. We believe he is still in possession of the original. After a pause, Sir Richard said, "Returning to the Netherlands means several hundred miles of risky travel through Germany."

"But no one is better equipped than E.D.," Michael said. "He is an expert at hiding in plain sight."

"That he is," Sir Richard agreed, "and I pray that he remains so."

"Amen," Michael said. "Amen."

Chapter 38

"Joseph," Dr. MacMillan said as he rose from the chair behind his desk to offer his hand. Smiling, he continued, "It is so good to see you here in Charlottetown again. I want you to know that your work while you've been in training and, most recently, at Connaught Laboratories in Toronto, is already saving lives here on Prince Edward Island. Please, sit down so that we can talk for a moment."

As Joseph Boucher sat opposite Dr. MacMillan at Charlottetown Hospital, he felt a bit confused. He didn't know how his work and studies in Quebec, Montreal, and Toronto could directly impact the lives of the people on Prince Edward Island.

"Dr. MacMillan," he began, "I have been the fortunate recipient of many opportunities, some that I followed and others that I did not. If the choices I made have proven helpful to you here, I can take no credit. I pray, and I try to listen, and I try to follow. Most often, I find that I am the one who is blessed when those choices help people find healing and live longer, happier lives. But all the same, it is not I who has the power to make that happen."

"Well spoken, Joseph," Dr. MacMillan said, "well spoken. Nonetheless, because you began your training here and requested that our hospital be considered a partner in implementing your research program, lives are being changed for the better. At your recommendation, our hospital has access to new medications. Few Canadian hospitals of our size have been chosen to participate in these tests. We owe you our gratitude for this opportunity."

"I'm happy that Charlottetown Hospital can be part of the program," Joseph said.

"I would like you to meet one of our patients who came to us on Michael Moreland's recommendation," said Dr. MacMillan. "If you will accompany me on my rounds this morning, I hope you will be able to meet and examine several others, as well. I think you will be blessed when you hear their stories."

"By all means, Doctor," Joseph said. "It will be my pleasure."

"Splendid, Joseph," said Dr. MacMillan, handing him a stethoscope and a white lab coat that matched his own. Joseph was confused by the embroidered name tag on the coat that read, "Dr. Joseph Boucher."

"There must be some confusion," he said, pointing to the name tag, but Dr. MacMillan waved him off, saying, "Consider it a necessary formality for the sake of our patients." Walking toward his office door, he added, "I'll tell you more about it later. Now, let's be about it, Dr. Boucher, our patients are anxious to see us."

Dr. MacMillan led Joseph to the first examination room, where Bill Stewart was waiting. A nurse handed Joseph Bill's chart, on which she had just recorded his vital signs. As she left, Dr. MacMillan said, "Bill, I'd like you to meet Dr. Boucher. He's been working with the laboratory that is providing your medications.

"It's my pleasure to meet you, sir," Bill said as he rose and extended his hand. "Six months ago, my wife and I weren't sure I'd be here now. Those bouts of pneumonia wouldn't quit, and I was getting weaker and weaker. Now, though, most of those symptoms are gone. I haven't had a bad spell since we began treatment here."

Looking at Bill's chart, Joseph commented, "Yes, I see the original prescription treatments with sulfonamides had an immediate positive effect. However, the more recent treatment with penicillin has provided even greater relief of symptoms. Now that we can effectively treat the infections, the symptoms often disappear."

"I understand that you're the one who got me into the test program, right?" Bill asked.

"I can't claim that responsibility, although, as part of my training, I had an opportunity to intern in Toronto, where new medications were being tested," Joseph began. "When Michael Moreland and Dr. Macmillan contacted me, I promoted your case, complete with your military history, to those in charge."

"But, that made a difference, didn't it?" Bill asked.

"Yes, I believe it did," Joseph said. "A major factor in their decision was due to the war. There is an ever-present need for more effective medications for soldiers who are injured on the battlefield. Your case, Mr. Stewart, captured their interest. Because you suffered from untreated injuries in the last war, they felt they owed you an opportunity to participate in testing their new medication."

With eyes filled with tears, Bill said, "Thank you, Dr. Boucher. I'm proud to be one of those you have helped. I'm sure there will be many others."

"And we're going to visit several more on Dr. Boucher's list right now, Mr. Stewart," Dr. MacMillan said. "I'm sure you will meet with Dr. Boucher again soon." Then, after checking Bill's chart, he added, "Yes, here it is. Dr. Boucher will be seeing you next month for your regular check-up."

Dr. MacMillan's rounds brought him to three other patients that morning. Joseph accompanied him to each. One involved a potato farmer injured in a farm accident. A severe cut on his lower calf, left untreated, had become infected. Treatment with penicillin had helped Dr. MacMillan avoid amputation. The remaining two cases were similar. Both involved families who felt they could not afford treatment at the hospital. Both had wounds that were infected. Again, the difference between amputation and healing lay in the drug that could treat the infection, allowing the patient to heal.

With their morning rounds complete, both men retired to Dr. MacMillan's office where they resumed the seats they left in the morning.

"I have a confession to make," said Dr. MacMillan.

"A confession?" Joseph asked. "What kind of confession?"

"A professional one. I wasn't entirely forthright with you this morning concerning your lab coat," he said. "There is more to the story."

"Please, tell me, then," Joseph asked.

Dr. MacMillan took a breath before he began. "Joseph, your academic case before the medical review board defies description. Nothing about it could be described as 'regular' or 'customary.' You began your studies here in Charlottetown and continued them in Quebec. After securing your nursing credentials, you pursued pre-med training here and later in Quebec and Montreal. Your on-the-job training statistics dwarf those of any other men who finished a college degree before applying to medical school. Furthermore, you have continued your classroom and on-the-job hospital training more consistently than most pre-med students have done."

As Dr. MacMillan poured glasses of ice water for himself and Joseph, he took a sip and began again.

"When the medical review board added your experience in the Connaught Laboratories in Toronto, they found more reasons to abandon some of their usual requirements."

"Requirements for what?" Joseph asked.

Pausing a moment, Dr. MacMillan continued, "Requirements for licensure as a practicing physician."

Joseph sat in silence as Dr. MacMillan explained.

"The Commonwealth, at wartime, is in desperate need of physicians. The usual four-year training program had already been shortened to three years, but in your case, Joseph, you have far more hospital experience than any other man currently in training. Thankfully, your previous physical injuries preclude your service as an enlisted man on the battlefield. As a result, your medical expertise will be available to patients both in hospitals and in their homes during and after the war."

Joseph nodded, assuring Dr. MacMillan that he understood.

"Now, to my confession, Joseph," the doctor began. "Based on all the factors I have listed, including your hospital experience as a nurse, your training in Quebec and Montreal, and your research experience at Connaught Laboratories in Toronto, the medical licensing board has agreed to place you here in Charlottetown as an intern while I serve as your attending physician this year. The label on your lab coat, *Dr. Boucher*, was not an error nor a formality for the sake of our patients. It is, if you will accept it and remain in training here with us this year, your professional title, Dr. Boucher."

Joseph, the gentle soul that he was, succumbed to his tears. When he recovered a few minutes later, Dr. MacMillan ushered a smiling young physician to the hospital dining room, where Ingrid, his intended, and the rest of his family, Highfield included, waited to congratulate him. In the end, it was clear to all that although Joseph Boucher had entered the hospital that morning, it was Dr. Boucher who would be leaving this afternoon.

One further surprise awaited the assembled group that morning. After taking a private moment to talk together, Joseph and Ingrid were happy to announce their wedding plans and to invite all to attend their nuptials in two weeks' time.

Chapter 39

The war in North Africa that began on the Libyan-Egyptian border in the summer of 1940 eventually spread to include campaigns in Morocco, Algeria, and Tunisia. By the spring of 1943, with Allied codebreakers decoding many German communications, Allied forces had regularly interrupted critical German supply lines. By April that year, the Axis defeat was imminent. Lacking adequate troops, munitions, food, fuel, and other basic supplies, it was certain that the Axis forces would soon be forced to withdraw.

After the British Eighth Army advanced west into Tunisia in early March, the British First Army followed with an offensive from central Tunisia in mid-April. During that time, the *HMS Formidable* had been relieved of its assignment in the western Mediterranean off the Algerian coast and ordered to Alexandria to provide convoy defense. Their re-assignment took them through the perilous waters south of Malta.

In a crucial location between Italy and Libya, where Allied air and naval forces launched attacks on Axis convoys, the island of Malta had survived both German and Italian sieges aimed at interrupting essential Allied shipments of food, fuel, and armaments. Enduring more bomb attacks than any other Axis target, the population of the island was often forced to seek refuge by living underground. With several airfields and the only British harbor between Alexandria and Gibraltar, Malta was a strategically vital Allied asset, a location serving both the Royal Navy and the RAF.

As the *Formidable* sailed east, Sqn Ldr Nigel Moncrieff and the rest of the Fleet Air Arm airmen spent most of each day in the air, primarily doing reconnaissance as the *Formidable* proceeded through dangerous waters toward Alexandria. Meanwhile, the ground war in Tunisia continued. Upon arrival off the coast of Alexandria, the ship remained at sea in defense of convoys carrying both troops and vital supplies. After more than a month at sea in the Eastern Mediterranean, the captain offered a long-awaited report from British troops fighting in Tunisia. On May 13, 1943, the Axis forces under General Rommel and General Von Arnim had surrendered, and more than 270,000 German and Italian troops became prisoners of war. Following the surrender of the First Italian Army soon after, the remaining Italian colonies in Africa were finally under Allied control.

Over the next several weeks, aircraft from the *Formidable* were able to make required flights for refit and maintenance at RAF *Aboukir* in Alexandria. Not unlike his last visit to Alexandria, Nigel was intent on making his way from the airfield to King Farouk's palace grounds and the Wren's barracks. This time, however, he telephoned Chief Wren Wright before leaving the airfield.

When the operator connected them, Nigel began, "Chief Wren Wright, this is Sqn Ldr Nigel Moncrieff from the *HMS Formidable*. Thank you for taking my call."

"Yes. We met some months ago when you arrived unannounced to call on LWren Beatty, as I remember. Your reason for calling today, Sqn Ldr?" she asked. Her tone told Nigel that Chief Wren Wright was all business.

"I am calling today with Captain Talbot's knowledge and permission to request a second appointment with LWren Beatty," Nigel said.

"Noting your mention of your Captain's knowledge and permission, Sqn Ldr Moncrieff, would one be correct in assuming that your intentions include a proposed commitment of a serious nature?" she asked.

Taken aback by her directness, Nigel said, "Yes, that would be a correct assumption. I have a copy of the letter he issued me, which I will be happy to offer you, at your pleasure," he added.

"Following the scheduling limitations that accompanied your previous visit," Chief Wren Wright said, the slightest smile appearing in her voice, "I would recommend that you arrange to arrive at 12:00 hours today when LWren Beatty will have finished her overnight shift."

"I will make plans accordingly," Nigel said.

"Our security personnel will be apprised of your imminent arrival," she said, "and a pass will await you at the gate."

"Thank you, Chief Wren Wright," Nigel said, surprised at such a courtesy. "I will look forward to seeing you when I apply at your office."

Noting her reaction to his mention of Captain Talbot's permission for his visit, Nigel understood that Chief Wren Wright was no stranger to the Royal Navy's protocol for marriage during wartime. Clearly, Nigel could be sure he was not the first British naval officer to seek the hand of a Wren under her command. He thought back to his conversation with Captain Talbot.

"So, you are following your younger brother's example?" the captain smiled.

"So, it seems, sir," he answered, "especially since it was he who introduced me to LWren Beatty."

"And, assuming the young lady's response will be positive, you expect no surprise or objection from her parents?" he asked.

"No, Captain," Nigel answered. "They were quite supportive at the time of our engagement."

"So, the only question will be one of leave from your duties, then," Captain Talbot said.

"Yes, sir," Nigel agreed.

"Then, let us plan on one week, as our duty allows, and that week beginning on the schedule the Wren's require," the Captain smiled.

After leaving the Captain's office, Nigel rushed to check in with the motor pool to find a vehicle for his drive to the palace grounds. A Jeep was available, and with the dry weather and spring temperatures, an open Jeep was ideal. If he had the best part of six hours to spend with Cheryl on a day like this, the sun and the breeze in a Jeep would be icing on their cake.

When he arrived on the palace grounds, Nigel stopped at Chief Wren Wright's office to offer her an opportunity to review his letter from Captain Talbot. A few minutes later, he arrived at Cheryl's barracks, where the covered front porch was full of Wrens once again. Cheryl emerged from the crowd in uniform and met Nigel halfway up the front walk. Nigel might have limited his public greeting to a kiss on the hand she offered, but one of the Wrens shouted, "Kiss her, Flyboy!" joined by several more a second later. Laughing, Nigel and Cheryl obliged her fellow Wrens before the couple ran hand-in-hand to the Jeep.

"I'm sure you're hungry after your shift," he said, "so I'd love to find a quiet place where we can eat and talk. I'm a stranger here, so what can you recommend?" he asked, as he steered with one hand and held hers with his other.

"How about the *Casino Petrou*? she asked. "It's not far away, and the water view is lovely."

"Just point the way, then," he smiled, "because after lunch, I want an hour or so alone with you on the beach before dinner."

Only a few minutes later, they were seated in the open air at the restaurant. With a chilled bottle of white wine on the table and their lunch order made, Nigel couldn't wait to tell Cheryl about his conversation with Captain Talbot.

"If you agree," he said, as they held hands across the table, "I have Captain Talbot's permission and a week's leave. I don't want to wait any longer, Cheryl. Please," he said, his fingers gently caressing her ring finger and her engagement ring, "please, let me put a wedding band on your finger as soon as we can."

"You understand that I will need Chief Wren Wright's permission, too, don't you?" she asked.

"Yes," he said, nodding.

"And, that my decoding work has been vital with all of the radio traffic and the remaining Axis activity only a short distance from here?" she asked.

"Yes," he nodded again.

"Well, I spoke with Chief Wren Wright earlier today when she called to say she had received your call, and she said. . ." Cheryl paused.

"Yes?" Nigel asked as he leaned toward her.

"She said that based on the letter from your Captain, she would arrange for my leave to match yours," she laughed as she stood to kiss him across the table.

As they sat again, Nigel was still shaking his head. "You had me for a moment there, Miss Beatty, but don't forget, we still need to send a telegram to your parents. I must ask your father's permission."

"Then, fear not, Darling," she smiled. "Remember, please, that I work in a communications office. We can send a telegram from there after lunch."

Smiling his knowing smile, Nigel responded, "No, we can't."

Surprised, Cheryl asked, "Why not?"

"Because after we finish lunch, Darling, we need to spend an hour alone at some secluded spot at the beach. We will have just eaten, of course, but I know I'll still be hungry for something sweet."

"Well, there's no time like the present," she smiled, as she leaned across the table to reach him. Taking hold of his tie, Cheryl didn't have to pull very hard to bring Nigel's face toward hers until they were nose-to-nose and eye-to-eye.

"Let's not waste a minute, *Flyboy*," she said.

And Nigel didn't.

Chapter 40

"Of course, we were delighted when the house was finally finished, Lois," Ingrid said. "I remember the day you and I completed these stencils in the dining room. That was months ago."

"Yes, but *finishing* a house and *furnishing* a house are two entirely different tasks," Lois said.

"And that's why I need both your practical experience in the kitchen, the laundry, and the bathrooms, as well as your artistic gifts to help me get the remainder of the drapes and other decorating done before the wedding," Ingrid said. "We need to be able to move in right after the wedding."

"Fear not, my friend," Lois laughed. "I know it feels overwhelming, but with a bit of planning, some shopping, and some help from the men to hang the curtains and drapes, we'll finish on schedule, I'm sure. Let's get your notebook out so we can make a battle plan."

An hour later, Lois had a list of tasks to complete, a list of materials to purchase, and a schedule for the next five days that would turn the bare cottage into a home. From can openers and colanders to potholders and placemats, Lois had a plan.

"Now, we'll need more than the two of us to get all of this done," Lois advised. "You and I need to pick out curtains and linens in town, so we won't be available here to fill the kitchen cabinets. Have you spoken with Patrice?" she asked.

"Yes," Ingrid answered, "and she should be here in a few minutes. I also asked Brenda, and she said she'd be happy to help."

"Smashing," Lois said. "Then you and I need to get to town to choose not only the bathroom and kitchen curtains, but also drapes for the parlor and bedrooms, and shades for all the windows. If we had a man to install the curtain rods and other hardware, we could make a good start."

Just then, the telephone rang, and Ingrid went to the entry to answer it. Before she got there, though, the women heard a knock at the door as Patrice and Hugh arrived.

"Hello," Patrice called on the way in the door.

"In the parlor," Lois called back.

"Hugh is with me," Patrice said as she crossed the kitchen. "We brought some tools and some hardware from Hillside."

"Mr. Moreland had a whole bucket of extra curtain mounting hardware and some more for the shades, too," Hugh offered.

"Lovely," Lois said, "and I see your hammer on your belt, Hugh. Could you help to install the curtains and drapes?"

"Of course," he said, "but some of this work requires two hands and an eye from across the room to make sure things are straight."

Returning from the kitchen, Ingrid said, "That was Brenda calling. She'll be here in a few minutes."

"Then you and I can drive to Charlottetown with our shopping list while Patrice, Hugh, and Brenda work here," Lois said.

"If you could spare a moment," Hugh said to Lois, "I'd like to speak with you and Patrice. I'll only be a few minutes," he said, looking from face to face, a little nervously.

"Certainly," Lois said as Ingrid nodded and made her exit to the kitchen. "I'll check the shopping list one last time," she said over her shoulder.

As Lois and Patrice sat on the couch, Hugh sat forward in a chair opposite them.

"I wanted you to know," he began, "that I had a letter from my mother. My father wrote to her and included a page for me. Mother forwarded it to me," he said as he removed an envelope from his pocket.

"Had he written to you before he was captured?" Lois asked.

"No," he answered, "and not since. This is the first time he has written anything intended for me," Hugh said.

"Is it something you can share?" Patrice asked.

Hugh nodded, but hesitated for a moment before saying, "I'm not sure how I feel about what he has written. I believe that his time in captivity could affect whatever he might write. His lines in this letter encourage me at this moment, but I'm not sure he will feel the same way forever."

"Forever may be too much to ask in a time of war, Hugh," Lois said. "Sometimes today is all we can hope for."

Nodding again, Hugh said, "I think I understand. Please bear with me."

He took a small page out of the envelope and read,

Dear Hugh,

It has been many, many months since I last saw you. I hope you are faring well in Canada.

I confess that it was with some shame that I became a prisoner of war. I learned something that soldiers older than I have known for generations—on a battlefield, a bullet is no respecter of persons. I ordered my men to surrender solely to save lives. As a prisoner, however, I have come to see some things differently than I have seen them before, many of which concern us.

I fear that my disregard for the physical problem you endure has caused a breach in our relationship. Please understand that I believe that no failure of honor on your part has kept you from the battlefield. I know that you have always been eager to serve. Many senior men in command, I among them, have come to understand that men on the battlefield who ignore or disguise a physical disability place others in danger. A wise man honors others by respecting his limitations. Your asthma has never been your fault. A good God has kept you from the horrors from which many others will never heal because He has plans for you, plans yet to be realized.

I am writing to apologize. By ignoring your health and expecting you to meet an impossible standard—my impossible standard—I have challenged your honor. Please forgive me. I am not worthy to be any man's judge.

I look forward to our reunion when this conflict ends.

I remain your dedicated father.

Hugh looked up with tears in his eyes.

"I feel that I may have my father again," he said, "though we have been estranged even before he went to war. I will write to him and look forward to a second letter in return."

"That sounds very wise," Lois said. "Your relationship is a precious gift, Hugh. Value it highly."

Patrice said nothing but opened her arms to offer a hug. Hugh received it gratefully.

When they parted, Patrice offered a suggestion.

"Let me help you with the hardware on the windows," she said. "I don't know anything about installing it, but I can hold things while you're on the ladder."

"That would be a boon," Hugh said. "I'm sure we will make a good team."

Offering her customary over-the-shoulder smile to Lois, Patrice followed Hugh to the dining room.

The window shade hardware proved easy to install. Patrice kept Hugh supplied with the brackets and nails while he was on the stepladder at each window. With one bracket on the left and one on the right, each requiring only two small nails, they finished the dining room windows in minutes.

On the way to start on the parlor windows, Hugh asked Patrice a question.

"Tell me, it you will, Patrice, how was Luc injured on the battlefield? He has told me only that he was wounded and was discharged from the RCA."

"I'm not surprised he hasn't said anything, even after all the time you've spent together. Luc doesn't like to rehearse those days. Sometimes those memories keep him up at night," she said.

"Perhaps, I've asked amiss, then," Hugh allowed. "I think of my asthma and how a cough like mine on the battlefield could reveal my squad's location to the enemy, or a long bout of coughing could keep me from advancing on the battlefield or helping a wounded comrade find cover. Although my symptoms have proven less serious since I arrived here, I know I still don't qualify to serve."

"Then your cough is very much like Luc's glasses," Patrice offered. "He doesn't like to wear them, but just as you need your medicine from time to time, Luc's injuries have left him needing his glasses."

"So, his eyes were injured?" Hugh asked.

"That's right," Patrice answered.

Patrice explained that on his first day on the battlefield, Luc, serving as a sniper, saved lives by stopping two enemy snipers. As he did, however, one of their bullets found him.

"Have you noticed a pendant that Lois wears around her neck?" Patrice asked.

"Yes," Hugh answered. "I've never seen her without it."

"That pendant is part of the shrapnel from the enemy bullet that shattered the lenses in Luc's scope, wounding one of his eyes," she began. The bullet went on to lodge in his shoulder. When he returned from the battlefield, he gave it to Lois. She had it made into the piece of jewelry she has worn every moment since."

Hugh hesitated and worked quietly for a few minutes before saying, "Luc wears glasses that keep him away from the battlefield, and I have an epinephrine inhaler that keeps me away. He was fortunate to come home alive. How can I complain about my state in life?"

"And Luc has no need to apologize to anyone for being here at home," said Patrice, "and do you know what, Hugh? Neither do you."

Hugh looked down from his perch on the ladder and smiled.

"Would you do me a favor, Miss Boucher?" he asked.

"Certainly," she answered.

"Would you kindly hand me a bracket for the left side of this window as well as a couple of nails?" he smiled.

Chapter 41

Lady Moncrieff's regular letter from Millie, Clifton Manor's housekeeper and cook, arrived as usual by the tenth of the month. Millie's previous monthly reports customarily concerned routine business and news concerning the health and welfare of the personnel, the state of the grounds and gardens, and any further concerns she might have for property maintenance during the Moncrieffs' absence. With only three members of the staff employed at the manor, there was usually little to report. In March of 1943, however, Millie's letter brought unusual news and a wave of concern.

After reading the letter, Lady Moncrieff called Susan right away. Her voice on the telephone told Susan something was wrong.

"Hello, Susan?" Lady Moncrieff asked.

"Yes, Mother. You sound upset. Is something wrong?" she asked.

"Perhaps. Your father is not here, and I've just received a letter from Millie with some worrisome news. Could you stop by sometime soon?" she asked.

"As soon as the children wake from their naps, Mother, perhaps thirty minutes from now?" Susan replied.

"Of course," Lady Moncrieff said, "but, earlier, if possible, please."

"Yes, Mother," Susan said, "as soon as I can."

When Susan arrived and had the children settled with Brenda, she found her mother in the east sunroom. Lady Moncrieff was looking out the window with Millie's letter in her hand.

"Is there a problem, Mother? You've got me worried," Susan said. as she took a seat beside her mother on the settee.

"It's all in Millie's note on the fourth page," she said as she handed the letter to Susan.

When she had finished reading, Susan turned to say, "So, it appears that Millie met a visitor to Clifton Manor claiming to be Joseph's uncle, his father's brother."

"Yes," Lady Moncrieff agreed, "He first called at the orphanage in Ipswich, and they directed him to Clifton Manor. He is claiming to be his father's heir."

"But that could strip Joseph of his inheritance," Susan said quietly.

"Exactly," Lady Moncrieff said. "That gentle young man, about to be married, with a new career ahead of him at the hospital, would be penniless again."

"But the solicitor in London made a thorough search for any surviving relatives before he discovered Joseph was here years ago," Susan said. "I'm sure there must be some mistake."

"Perhaps," Lady Moncrieff said, "but we won't know anything more until you consult with the solicitor. You are still Joseph's legal guardian, are you not?"

"No," Susan answered. "He reached the age of majority on his twenty-first birthday. There were reams of documents delivered here, all bearing Joseph's name and replacing mine."

After thinking for a moment, Susan said, "I suppose I could seek the counsel of the London solicitor before we consider speaking with Joseph, to see if he has heard from. . .," she said, looking again at Millie's letter, "Mr. Arnold Fenton."

"Of course," Lady Moncrieff agreed. "Joseph and Ingrid don't need this kind of worry this close to their wedding. For all we know, the man could be an impostor. As I recall, the solicitor required written proof of Joseph's identity, in a document long hidden in a family prayer book. Isn't that correct?"

"Correct, Mother. That original certificate of Joseph's christening provided irrefutable evidence of Joseph's identity. This new Mr. Fenton would need some equally convincing evidence of birth and heritage, to make a credible claim, I believe," Susan said.

"Well, this is no time to worry those two who will soon be newlyweds," Lady Moncrieff said, "so I shan't say a word."

"And I'll join you there, Mother," Susan agreed. "I'll speak with Michael tonight to get his thoughts as well."

Two days later, Susan received a letter from Ipswich, this one from Mr. Arnold Fenton.

"I find it odd," Michael said, "that this man hasn't engaged a solicitor in Suffolk or approached the court. A personal letter offers no legal standing or authority. Let's see what he has to say."

While Susan changed Christine's diaper, Michael read the letter and sat back in his chair to ponder.

"What is his story?" Susan asked.

"He says he lost contact with his father and brother when he was away in the Great War. As a result of his war injuries, he says he was left with amnesia and has been living in a veteran's hospital since 1918. He only recently recovered memories of his father, Amos Fenton, and his brother, Bruce Fenton, and their home in Suffolk. After traveling there and making some inquiries, he discovered they were both deceased," Michael said.

"Then, as a veteran, he must have credentials on file with the Royal Army or the Royal Navy," Susan said.

"Or the Royal Air Force," Michael added. "Of course, the burden of proof remains with him."

"Then, it could be a long time before he could verify anything. I'm sure that none of our military services has time during the war to search for records that are almost thirty years old," Susan said.

Michael was silent for a moment before adding, "There's still a chance the man deserves an inheritance, you know."

"Agreed," she said, "but since there is nothing we can do on this side of the ocean, I think we should leave well enough alone. We could suggest that he discuss the case with a solicitor of his choosing."

"And, as far as Joseph is concerned?" Michael asked.

"Joseph is a new intern at the hospital and about to be married. He probably has enough on his mind at the moment, but I have another idea," she said.

"And what is that?" Michael asked.

"I'll wager Father has access to military records from the Great War and SIS personnel who could complete a search for us. He could find a name like Arnold Fenton from Suffolk, don't you think?" she asked.

"A capital idea, Darling, a capital idea," Michael said. "You could see your father in the morning to make your request. I'm sure he'd be delighted to settle this mystery for us."

"I'll telephone Mother to get us on his schedule," Susan said. "I think we'll have an answer very soon."

"And only then will we consider informing young Dr. Boucher of his presumed uncle," Michael said. "Until then, we'll not bother him with anything other than pleasing his bride."

"Agreed," Susan said, "agreed."

Chapter 42

Nigel and Cheryl wasted no time communicating with their parents, offering them the good news of their nuptials. Thankfully, the return telegrams from both families arrived within 48 hours, both entirely supportive of their children's union.

With their wedding planned one week away, and both their leaves from active duty limited to seven days, Nigel and Cheryl remained on regular duty. Without the immediate need for an aircraft maintenance flight from the *Formidable*, the bride and groom were not scheduled to see each other again until the day they made their vows. Thankfully, the Air Engineer Officer aboard the *Formidable* was one of Nigel's good friends who discovered problems with two aircraft that week, requiring the skills of the personnel at Aboukir airfield. By some coincidence, the aircraft required overnight stays in the maintenance hangar, followed by flight tests each following day. Nigel smiled, understanding fully that he owed his friend several favors in port sometime soon, a debt he would be happy to repay.

At Highfield, the Moncrieffs couldn't have been more elated. They decided to celebrate with a midweek luncheon, where Nigel and Cheryl's nuptials dominated the conversation at the table.

"I wasn't sure that our eldest would ever find a young woman who could turn his head," Lady Moncrieff laughed, "but this one seems to have met the challenge."

"I think he was simply waiting for the right one. He probably isn't yet aware, though, that in the end, we chase them until they catch us," Sir Richard smiled as he raised his glass of champagne to his wife.

"Sometimes we have to slow down a bit to let you catch up," Lady Moncrieff said with a wink toward Susan, "so that you think you're in charge."

"But, in the end," said Susan, with a nod to her husband, "we don't mind being caught."

Looking at the photos on the mantle, Michael added, "It appears the Moncrieff men have very good taste. Your grandsons will be handsome; your granddaughters, beauties."

"Like these three?" Sir Richard added, pointing to a photo of the Moreland children.

"Well," Michael said, looking from the photo and back to Susan, "if Christine keeps up with her mother, I'm not sure Boyd or Nigel's daughters would have a chance. It would be unfair to expect Kathleen or Cheryl to meet the beauty standard Susan has set."

With a roll of her eyes and a shake of her head, Susan said, "What will I do with you, Mr. Moreland?" before quickly adding, "And don't you dare answer!"

"In the meantime," Lady Moncrieff began, "we have a beautiful bride and her groom to celebrate in town tomorrow."

"We seem to have no problem finding husbands and wives among our several families," Sir Richard laughed. "It's as if Highfield is the place to live and work if one is looking for a mate."

"But they are amazing matches, you must agree," Michael said. "Some local, most international, and more on the way, I'm sure."

"I'm keeping my eye on the Buchanan lad and our Patrice," Sir Richard said. "She's still a bit young in my estimation."

"And I agree, but fear not, Father," Susan smiled. "Our Patrice can hold her own. If Hugh decides to chase her, he'll end up either very tired or caught."

"Probably both," Michael added under his breath, earning one more roll of Susan's eyes.

Rising, Sir Richard said, "It's time we men retired to the study, ladies. We have some work to do, if you don't mind."

"Of course not," Lady Moncrieff said. "Susan and I will catch up on the last of the local wedding details."

On the way to the study, Sir Richard said, "We've heard from our friend abroad. I have an update for you."

With the study door closed, Sir Richard began. "As you know, E.D. and his package arrived safely in Zurich, and copies of the evidence in the young lady's boots have been safely transmitted to both the British and the US embassies. E.D. is currently in Zurich and will be traveling via Berne to debrief Miss Lytle on his way back to The Hague, where he has business to complete."

"That's quite a distance through some very dangerous territory," Michael said.

"Yes, it is," Sir Richard agreed. "Thankfully, he is remarkably skilled linguistically and has the support of resistance cells for at least part of the way. He is concerned about the level of capitulation of the population in the Netherlands and how many have joined the Nazis against their own people. He is also following some horrible leads from Latvia."

"Those poor people have endured multiple invasions by both the Soviets and the Nazis," Michael said. "They remain virtually defenseless."

"Correct. Both the Soviets and the Nazis have been brutal in their treatment of all three Baltic countries," Sir Richard agreed.

"For his sake, I hope when E.D. reaches the Netherlands again, he can finish his mission and find his way home," Michael said.

The two were silent for a moment, both realizing that E.D. had nowhere he called home.

"I was thinking this would be his home," Michael said. "Of course, Germany could also be his home, but probably not until the war ends."

"I had the same thought," said Sir Richard. "He is, to some degree, a man without a country."

"Or a man with several countries," Michael added.

"And it's likely that Brenda will be part of that decision," Sir Richard said.

"It certainly seemed that way when they were here together for those few days in the fall," Michael agreed.

"For the moment, however," said Sir Richard, "he plans to spend his last day in Switzerland in Berne, de-briefing the young lady he rescued in Munich."

"And Steven Lytle?" Michael asked. "Have you heard from him since we last spoke with him in Charlottetown?"

"Yes, once by telephone and once by the post," Sir Richard said. "Because the telephone is not secure, I suggested he write. He was most grateful for his daughter's extraction from Munich and happy that she had been reunited with her aunt and uncle in Zurich. Sadly though, his deepest desire, to have her at home with him in the safety of the United States, remains unsatisfied."

"Perhaps E.D. will have some influence on her decision when he meets with her in Berne," Michael said.

"Perhaps," Sir Richard agreed. "No one could know more than he about the potential dangers she will face as part of the Resistance, even in Switzerland. If she doesn't heed the advice he offers concerning her safety, I would wager that she will soon face new dangers for which she will find herself completely unprepared."

Chapter 43

It was early in the afternoon under cloud covered skies in Berne when E.D. located the flat where Sybil Lytle was staying. Surprised to see him again, she invited him in and offered him coffee at her kitchen table. When he suggested she might be safer with her aunt and uncle in Zurich, he found himself ill-prepared for her emotional response.

"No, no, no!" she cried as she rose from the table. "Sophie, Hans, and Christoph did not give their lives for nothing! Their deaths cannot be the end of our work! We cannot let the Gestapo's threats be the deciding factor in our battle for the truth. Were we to run away from everything White Rose has begun, we would be traitors to the memories of three martyrs. No, if no one joins me, if I must fight on alone, I *will* fight on alone."

E.D. hadn't seen this side of Sybil Lytle before. During their midnight escape from Munich, they had hardly spoken, but she had cooperated with his every directive. She had trusted his experience and yielded to his authority, and, with her cooperation, he had been able to guide her safely away from Munich and deliver her to her aunt and uncle. With the dedication she felt toward her cause, however, he knew now that returning to Zurich was not an option she would consider. Clearly, she had other plans that she hoped would honor the sacrifice her three friends had made.

"So, you will continue your work from Berne?" he asked.

Shaking her head, she said, "No, I can't work from here. There are no secrets among the Swiss. There are ears and eyes everywhere."

"I understand," E.D. said, "but how can you be safe outside of Switzerland?"

"Our work has earned us friends far from Munich. With their help, I will know when and where travel is safe and when I must disappear for a day. I need to go where the work is. I'm sure you understand," she said, nodding her head to urge his reply.

"Yes," he said, "I understand the dangers the Gestapo, the SS, and too many other Nazis offer, and experience has been my faithful teacher. That is why I would be derelict if I did not try to convince you to remain in Switzerland."

"Perhaps you don't understand," she began. "We have networks of people in cities like Stuttgart, Strasbourg, Cologne, Frankfurt, Düsseldorf, and even as far away as Hamburg. Our travel between those cities, though not without danger of discovery, is supported by scores of those who share our vision. I will face the possibility of discovery wherever I travel, just as you do, but it's a risk I am willing to take."

E.D. had been thinking as she spoke. His trek toward his destination in the Netherlands would take him through Stuttgart and Strasbourg and northeast through Cologne and Düsseldorf. He had few contacts in this part of Germany and planned to search out local resistance cells, a task that presented its own risks. Before he could say anything, though, Sybil had a question.

"You're quiet, and you're thinking," she began. "Thank you. My uncle would have interrupted me before now, using his logic to try to dissuade me from my goals. He has yet to understand that common sense doesn't work in a world gone mad."

E.D. nodded, but before he could speak, Sybil had a question.

"I saw your mind ticking through the cities I listed a minute ago. You were thinking about something, weren't you?" she asked.

"Yes," E.D. answered. "I was, but before I tell you, I need a few answers about your travel over the last six months or so."

"Ask away," she answered.

In the next few minutes, E.D. learned that Sybil had recently been in contact with her White Rose supporters in Stuttgart, Strasbourg, and Cologne. Following the brutal executions in Munich, she felt she needed to meet with as many White Rose supporters as possible to tell them the truth that no news source would dare to report. She also felt it was vital to remove herself as far as she could from Munich where the Gestapo would be searching for her. Her plan was to leave Berne for the short trip to Basel and then make her way to Stuttgart. From there, her itinerary would take her to Cologne by way of Frankfurt.

"So," E.D. began, "you have a reliable network of supporters who can offer you travel assistance and places to stay as you travel to Cologne?"

"Yes," she answered. "I've trusted them for several years now. We all have. The dangers we've faced have always been while traveling. The streets and railways are full of eyes. Backroads are slower, but safer. We try not to travel alone. Two pairs of eyes are so much better than one."

"But you're willing to travel alone and take that risk?" he asked.

"Yes," she said, "but only because there is no other option. Our people need to hear the truth."

"And if there were another option?" he said.

Puzzled, she asked, "How could there be another?"

"My orders take me to The Hague," he said. "Thankfully, I have several reliable associates in Frankfurt and Düsseldorf, but none in Cologne. Since you do. . ."

Interrupting him, Sybil said, "Are you suggesting we travel together?"

"The Gestapo are searching for a lone young woman, correct?" he asked. "Would you not be safer in the company of a man?"

"And we would have two pairs of eyes," she nodded.

"How soon would you be able to leave?" he asked.

"The train for Basel departs at 3:15 tomorrow afternoon," she answered.

"Then we'll purchase our tickets and be on the platform at 3:10," E.D. said. "Tonight, however we have much to settle."

"What do you mean?" she asked.

"First," E.D. began, "you can't travel with papers that bear your name. The Gestapo knows it all too well. You will need to use these," he said, as he reached into his bag, "the papers you carried when we left Munich."

As he handed them to her, he asked, "Do you still have your camera?"

With a quizzical look, she said, "Yes," but why would. . .

"And some film?" he asked.

"Yes, but. . ." she said as he interrupted.

"Because," he said, "we need to appear as a couple, perhaps traveling on holiday. We'll take some photos together this afternoon as if we've been touring. We can have them processed in the morning in Basel. They may be useful in keeping you from being recognized."

"All right," she said.

"Next," he asked, "are you familiar with firearms?"

Sybil answered hesitantly. "My father and I shot at targets with a rifle at home, once," she said, "but that was a long time ago."

"So, you've never handled a pistol?" he asked.

"No," she answered. "Why?"

E.D. reached down toward his left ankle to pull up his trouser leg, revealing an ankle holster holding an Astra 300 semi-automatic pistol. Removing the holster from his leg, he said, "You'll need to carry this, but first, you will need to strap it on above your knee, your *left* knee," he emphasized. "It will be invisible there, but it will be easy for you to locate under your skirt, should it become necessary."

Wide-eyed now, Sybil said, "But I don't know how to fire a pistol."

"Don't worry," E.D. said. "It's not there for you. It's there for *me*. If I need it, I'll know where to get it."

E.D. kept the pistol while Sybil, wide-eyed, took the holster to the next room to strap it on. While she was gone, E.D. removed his Walther PPK and shoulder holster from his bag. He donned the weapon and was just putting his jacket on when Sybil returned.

Surprised, she asked, "So, you have one, too?"

"That's right," he said, as he prepared to hand her the Astra 300. "Now, there isn't a cartridge in the chamber, so there's no danger that it will fire by itself. Just return the pistol to the holster and snap the strap over the grip to keep it there."

"That's all?" she asked.

Turning back to her he said, "Just one more thing."

"Yes?" she asked.

"Stay away from the trigger," he said.

"Don't worry," she answered as she started for the next room again.

When she returned with the pistol safely in its holster, E.D. was waiting in his overcoat and had his bag over his shoulder.

"Please," he said, "gather your camera, your coat and your travel bag. We need to go for a stroll, so you can become comfortable wearing the pistol. We'll find someone to take some photos, and we'll practice being close friends. There won't be time to rehearse tomorrow."

Though still reeling from all the details, Sybil was ready to leave within a few minutes. Thankfully, the day was overcast, but the remaining afternoon light was perfect for taking the photos they needed. They walked the streets of Berne as a couple for half an hour, returning with just enough time to debrief before dinner. Sybil was happy to surrender the pistol, its holster, and a canister of exposed 35mm film, which E.D. placed safely in his bag.

"I'll return at 2:30 tomorrow afternoon," E.D. said, "so that you can get comfortable with the pistol again before we walk to the depot. Meanwhile, rest well. Tomorrow will be a busy day."

With that, E.D. was gone, leaving Sybil Lytle's head spinning.

With some time to relax, she heaved a relieved sigh and said, "We have a consummate professional with a gun and me carrying another, strapped on my thigh. No one could have made me believe this kind of surprise would be waiting for me today."

She took a deep breath before her next thought arrived.

"I wonder what kind of surprises await me *tomorrow*."

Chapter 44

"Oh, my," Susan sighed, "that is a relief!"

"Yes, it is," Michael said, "and thankfully, Joseph never knew a worry."

Sitting at his desk and holding a folder that Sir Richard had handed to him after breakfast, Michael sat back in his chair to offer Susan the details.

"There were several families named Fenton who lived in and around Ipswich during and after the war. It can be hard to keep them all straight. It appears that Mr. Arnold Fenton served in the Royal Garrison Artillery in France. His Royal Army records list his father's name as Amos Fenton, and his mother as Maude Fenton, both deceased shortly after the war ended. He also had one brother, Bryce Fenton, who left one heir, named Joseph."

"Our Joseph?" Susan asked as she leaned forward in her chair.

"No," Michael said. "*Their* Joseph's grandfather's name was Amos. Thankfully, our Joseph's grandfather's name was Andrew. *Their* Joseph's father was named Bryce," he continued, "while our Joseph's father was named Bruce."

"So," Susan asked, "Mr. Arnold Fenton was simply barking up the wrong tree, as they say?"

"Yes," Michael nodded, "but only by a single branch."

"A single branch?" What do you mean?" she asked.

"Andrew Fenton and Amos Fenton were brothers," Michael said. That makes Joseph's father, Bruce, and Arnold Fenton, cousins."

"So, Mr. Arnold Fenton is Joseph's cousin, once removed, correct? Susan asked.

"Correct," Michael said, "but not his cousin Bruce's heir. Joseph is his father's only son."

"And only heir," Susan smiled.

"That's right," Michael said, "and it doesn't appear that any guile was attached to Arnold Fenton's inquiry. He simply needed someone who could do some proper research in a public records office."

"That is good news to get on a Friday, on the eve of Ingrid and Joseph's wedding," Susan said, "but I think we should wait to tell Joseph the long story until the happy couple returns from their honeymoon,"

"Agreed" Michael said, pausing before he added, "but regarding this wedding, I must confess, I feel a bit disconnected. Tell me again. Do we really need to do nothing except arrive as guests at St. Peter's for the vows and at Spring Hill for the reception afterwards?"

"That's correct," Susan smiled. "Luc and Lois, with help from Patrice and Hugh, have taken care of everything. Elke and Greta volunteered to watch Christine and the boys during the service and the reception. We'll be on our own for the first time in months," she smiled.

"I feel guilty to be looking forward to an afternoon without Christine and the boys, but my smile feels no need to recede," he laughed.

"You know," Susan began, "with these young men and women who've grown up with and around us during these last years, we've become family, like aunts and uncles of sorts."

"I don't know if I'm ready for that, though," Michael said, "I always think of aunts and uncles as old people."

Folding her last diaper, Susan walked to Michael's chair and looked over his shoulder at the letter in his hands. Then, draping her arms over his shoulders, she rested her chin against his neck and ear.

"Old people often have trouble hearing, I'm told," she smiled, "so I'm speaking directly into your ear so that you can hear me."

"Got it," he said as he placed his hand on her arm. "Now, if you'll just add a little nibble to that earlobe, maybe we'll find out just how old I really am, OK?"

Before she could answer, they heard a door close downstairs, and a voice calling, "Susan? It's Brenda. I've got the boys back from their romp with your father."

"I'll be right down, Brenda," Susan called back.

"Foiled again," Michael smiled as he let her go. "No nibble this time, so I'll let you go with a kiss."

"There's nothing old about you, Mister," she laughed, and with their kiss and a peck to follow, she was on her way downstairs.

After a few minutes of small talk, Susan noted something lacking in Brenda's usual energy. She wasn't wearing her customary smile, her shoulders were drooping, and she seemed distracted and distant. Susan had to ask why.

"You seem a bit out of sorts today, Brenda," she began. "Is anything wrong?"

"Oh," Brenda said, glancing toward the floor. "I was hoping it wouldn't show."

"What wouldn't show?" Susan asked.

"I'm sure it's just jealousy, you know. About the wedding," she said, still looking at the floor.

"Ah," Susan said, "I think I understand now."

"It's not that I'm not happy for Ingrid and Joseph, it's just that I'm sad for me. That sounds so childish, doesn't it," she said, hoping Susan would understand and change the subject.

"Let's sit down for a minute," Susan suggested as she pulled two chairs away from the kitchen table.

As they sat, Susan asked, "When was the last time you heard from Ernst?"

"I had one letter from London, but he doesn't dare write from any occupied country. He's afraid I could become a target simply by association, and he's especially concerned about Highfield and all of you," she said.

"So, you don't know where he is or how much danger he might be facing, right?" Susan asked.

"Yes," she answered quietly.

"And meanwhile, a couple younger than you and Ernst, a couple with a new home waiting just down the hill are getting married and going on their honeymoon tomorrow," Susan said.

"Yes," Brenda agreed.

"Then I'd say you'd have every reason not to be your usual perky self. How could you? Your beau is far away, potentially somewhere dangerous, and you haven't heard from him in months. What reason would anyone have to be happy?" Susan asked.

"None, I suppose. The loneliness is almost as hard as when I was in a cell in Halifax," she said, "only I didn't know he loved me then."

"I have an idea," said Susan, "but I can't be sure it will work just yet."

Brightening a little, Brenda asked, "What kind of idea?"

"While you unload the boys' gear, I'm going to make a telephone call. I'll be back in just a few minutes."

While Susan went upstairs to use Michael's telephone, Brenda loaded the boys' play clothes into the washing machine. By the time she had finished, Susan had returned.

"All right," Susan said with a smile, "here's what we can do."

With Susan's smile, Brenda's darkness began to lighten, and the two sat at the table again.

"Father has just given me some information that will not compromise security for Ernst or those with whom he is working. Here it is: Ernst is in a safe place at the moment. He will be traveling soon, as he usually does, but not alone this time. He has the support of several others who can help him as needed," she said. "I know that's not much, but it's what we have right now."

Brenda's eyes were alive again as she leaned forward to say, "Thank God. Ernst is safe."

"Yes," Susan nodded. "Presently, he is, and he is not alone. That's not a lot of news, but. . ."

"But it means a lot to me, just knowing he is in contact with someone here who knows him," she said.

"And that's the best part," Susan said.

"The best part?" Brenda asked.

"Yes, because Father has promised to provide whatever bit of information he can, whenever you ask," Susan smiled.

"I can ask him?" Brenda marveled, wide-eyed.

"Yes," Susan said, "but no more often that once every few days, all right?"

"Oh, my, yes," Brenda smiled. "I promise, I won't pester him. He's always been very generous with me. If the time is right and I can catch his eye, I'm sure he'll tell me what he can."

"There," Susan said. "Now you'll be able to go to the wedding without bringing the dark sky and clouds you've been under."

Brenda had to laugh, and both women agreed that a hot cup of tea and something sweet were in order on a damp spring afternoon. Case and Reed, worn out after their hour with Sir Richard, were content to enjoy their nap.

Chapter 45

E.D. arrived at Sybil Lytle's flat promptly at 2:30 PM as promised. Dressed as tourists in traveling clothes, no one would suspect that they were both carrying firearms. While maintaining their roles as carefree tourists, Sybil kept her camera handy, always ready to take one more photo. With their tickets in hand by 2:45 PM, they were ready to board the train before 3:00 PM. The train left the platform on schedule.

The rail trip to Basel offered no specific dangers, but crossing into Germany from Switzerland could only be accomplished with help from local Allied sympathizers. In every city and town on the German border there were Swiss merchants and businessmen who regularly found ways across the border to Germany. Some were well-known to German border patrols, merchants who supplied goods to both the Germans and the Swiss. Others aided clients like E.D. and Sybil, helping them to cross the border under cover of darkness, away from regular checkpoints. E.D. contacted a man known to him only as 'Karl' who met them at a beer garden not far from the train depot. While E.D. and Sybil enjoyed refreshments posing as carefree afternoon travelers, Karl took a seat at a table adjacent to theirs. While E.D. and Sybil appeared to be talking and whispering together, Karl was listening intently behind his newspaper. Every so often, E.D. spoke, and Karl responded by interjecting a word or two, as if reading aloud behind his paper. After a quarter of an hour their plans were laid, and E.D. and Sybil adjourned to the streets to return to their hotel. At dusk they appeared again, this time wearing long overcoats that disguised their overland travel garb beneath. Karl fell into step with them and led them away from the center of town.

"Many acres along our borders have become agricultural factories to help meet our country's needs," Karl explained, "and the Germans have fortified the border heavily with barbed wire in those locations. The same borders are guarded by other roving patrols whose schedules vary. With little cover of vegetation in this season, our crossing will be one of opportunity, but we will have to wait patiently for that opportune moment."

Their wait lasted almost three days. Arriving after 10:30 on the third night, the three hid among the last few evergreen shrubs at the edge of a field that had already been prepared for spring cultivation. It was a cool, damp night, and they could hear the laughter of German soldiers sitting around a fire a few hundred yards away. Suddenly, the laughter turned angry and was filled with shouts and challenges. What caused the ruckus didn't matter to the three hiding in the undergrowth. While the soldiers were occupied with each other, Karl led E.D. and Sybil through the darkness and over a series of barbed wire coils. Helping each other only in whispers, they managed to cross the border, but their trek through fields and underbrush wasn't over. At dawn, in the early morning light, Karl finally led them down a steep ravine to a pasture and the sounds of bleating sheep. In an aging barn with an unlocked rear door, three bicycles awaited them. Nearby was a farmhouse where smoke rose from a center chimney and a single kerosene lantern burned within.

"I am always happy to see that lantern," Karl said. "Had it not been lit or had there been two lanterns, we would not be stopping. Now, follow me."

Once in the house, the three warmed themselves at a woodstove and ate a breakfast of bread, cheese, and strong coffee. As the sun rose higher, E.D. and Sybil mounted their bicycles and rode with Karl toward Lörrach, a small town a few miles away. There, Karl left them with a handshake and a wink as he turned back toward Basel, ready to return with his next client.

E.D. and Sybil made their way to Strasbourg over the next four days and to Frankfurt a week later. Each noted a subtle, but welcome change in the attitudes of the people they met. Though once universally devoted to the war and their Führer, many wore a sense of weariness and resignation. With most of their days spent on the road, E.D. and Sybil found time to talk about the changes they were noticing.

"I think the breaking point for many was Stalingrad," E.D. said as they walked the last few miles toward Frankfurt. "There were so many casualties, so many sons and fathers who didn't come home."

"True," Sybil agreed, "but I noticed a decline in Hitler's popularity long before that."

"When?" E.D. asked.

"Early in the war, when the Luftwaffe couldn't send enough bombs to England to make a land invasion possible. Many began to lose faith long before Stalingrad."

"But there's been another factor coming to light more often every day," E.D. said.

"Which is?" she asked.

"The captures of the Jews, their deportations, and the atrocities everywhere—Germany, Poland, Belgium, the Netherlands, Austria. . ." he began.

"Yes," she agreed, "and Latvia, Yugoslavia, France, Luxembourg, and even Greece. The list goes on, with more horrors reported every day. And sometimes," she said with a voice full of grief, "sometimes it follows you home to places like Munich." E.D. watched as a tear began to roll down her cheek.

After a quiet moment, E.D. offered, "Let me give you a reason to be proud and to hope for a revival of White Rose's voice."

"Anything, please," she said as she dried her eyes. "I'll take anything."

"I was in contact with people in London while we were in Strasbourg," he began.

"That night when you were out until almost dawn?" she asked.

"Yes," he said. "They know what happened in Munich, all of it—the capture, the mock trial and the executions. They asked me to bring something back to England."

"What would that be?" Sybil asked.

"A copy of your sixth leaflet," he said.

"But why would they be interested in a document written for the eyes of Germans in Nazi Germany?" she asked.

"I am not at liberty to provide you with that information," he said, "but I can tell you that they rarely ask for anything for which they don't already have a well-laid plan."

Sybil thought for a moment before she brightened and asked, "Why can't I deliver it to them myself?"

Incredulous, E.D. turned to her to say, "Why? Because it's a long way to London and the travel is more dangerous the closer you get. Besides, I thought you had work to do in Cologne."

"Yes, I do," she interrupted, "but you're going back to England after your work is done in the Netherlands, right?" she asked.

"Yes, but those orders could change in a moment," he answered.

"But, if they don't change," she said, "I could get there with you and deliver the goods myself, couldn't I?"

E.D. thought for a moment before saying, "They already have the evidence on four 35mm rolls of film you provided. That's one hundred forty-four exposures that the world still needs to see. Then again," he said as he reconsidered, "I suppose they would be interested in interviewing the woman who supplied the goods."

Though she was elated, Sybil decided to hide her excitement, saying only, "Of course, we have a long way to travel and lot of work to do first. But we could make a destination in England a potential long-term goal. What do you think?"

Shaking his head in mock defeat, E.D. began, "You have a way of making your goals, *our* goals, Miss Lytle. Let's take this one day at a time. We can't let every new goal you imagine jeopardize those that remain first and foremost."

Nodding her head, Sybil agreed. "Understood. One day at a time." When she finished with a mock salute, E.D. couldn't hide his weary smile.

Chapter 46

Cheryl and Nigel were married on a Saturday morning at the chapel on the Royal Navy base in Alexandria. The base chaplain presided at the service and doubled as Nigel's best man. Chief Wren Wright gave Cheryl away and doubled as her Maid of Honor. The service was over in less than fifteen minutes, and when the chaplain pronounced Nigel and Cheryl "man and wife," the small, corrugated steel building shook with the cheers of the congregation—three dozen beaming Wrens.

Nigel and Cheryl ran to their waiting Jeep under a shower of rice and rose petals and drove directly to the Cecil Hotel on the Alexandria Corniche, not far from the Saad Zaghloul Square. Their leaves from duty were set to expire in five days when Nigel would return once again to the *HMS Formidable*, flying reconnaissance in the air over the Mediterranean, and Mrs. Nigel Moncrieff would return to breaking coded Axis communications in a basement office with five other Wrens. Neither could predict when they would see each other after their leaves expired.

Meanwhile, half a world away, Dr. Joseph Boucher and his bride, Ingrid, were spending their first wedded night at home at their Tudor cottage on Suffolk Road on Prince Edward Island. The honeymoon suite at the Château Frontenac in Quebec awaited them the following night. Their stay in Quebec would end the following morning, for their itinerary took them next to Montreal and the Mount Royal Hotel. Dr. Boucher and his bride were intent on spending an hour at a particular ice cream shop not far from Royal Victoria Hospital, the same shop where they had practiced their first kisses two years previously.

Two nights following the Boucher wedding, the Moncrieffs and the Morelands were at Highfield, enjoying dessert after dinner.

"It's so interesting watching these young people suddenly become adults, begin careers, and marry," said Lady Moncrieff. "Where did the time go? When I first arrived on this island, they were in knee pants and jumpers, and the girls wore their hair in braids."

"Wide-eyed Patrice," Michael laughed, "entertained us regularly by always saying exactly what she was thinking. The funniest part was that most times we were thinking the same thing, but we weren't bold enough to say so."

"And now, despite the world being at war," Sir Richard added, "both of our sons have found brides, women we've met only through the post, by telegram, and in these photos," he said, pointing to the mantle in the library. "Our whole family history appears in these photos, and now our sons and their brides have taken their rightful place. I raise my glass to them!" he smiled, as Lady Moncrieff, Susan, and Michael joined his toast.

"Of the original Highfield family, only Patrice remains unwed," Susan said.

"But we can hardly call her a spinster, now, can we?" Michael laughed. "Do you remember where we were at her age?" he said to Susan.

"I think you were teaching me to drive after my brothers gave up," she laughed, "back when we shared our first kiss."

Suddenly sitting erect, Lady Moncrieff said, "What was that about your first kiss?"

Susan and Michael looked at each other and began laughing. Michael gently waved his palm toward his mother-in-law, yielding the floor to Susan.

"It's not what you think, Mother," Susan laughed. "Michael had been so patient with me during my driving lesson that day. He coached me for mile after mile, and, for the first time, I drove without a hint of a mishap. When we returned home, he parked Bessie in the garage for me, and I was so elated with my lesson that I took off my bonnet to kiss his cheek. He happened to turn toward me at the same moment, and my lips landed on his," she laughed, "leaving both of us wide-eyed."

Lady Moncrieff looked over at Michael as he nodded. "Just as she said," he smiled.

"And the next one," Susan added, "was here at the top of the fire tower, years and years later."

"So, Angela and Susan," Sir Richard began, "concerning Patrice and young Master Buchanan, I would advise postponing your worries for several years."

"Oh, Richard," Lady Moncrieff chided, "we're not intent on rushing anything. Of course," she added, "if something develops. . ."

"To our wives," Sir Richard interrupted, as he raised his glass to Michael, "ever the matchmakers!"

Laughing, Michael emptied his glass and, changing the subject, asked, "Do we have any recent news from Ernst, Richard? Is there anything you can tell us?"

"Speaking very generally, of course," he began, "I can say this: Ernst, with the traveling companion in his care, is making his way toward the Netherlands, with an ultimate destination of London. As I understand it, his companion can pose challenges to those in charge of her care. Ernst has advised me that she has a mind of her own and she rarely hesitates to share it, whether one is interested or not."

"And in London?" Susan asked.

"His companion's student organization in Germany has gained the attention and admiration of the Prime Minister. When she arrives in London, he may or may not request an audience with the young woman to discuss issues yet to be announced. That is as much as I can tell you at the moment."

"The Prime Minister?" Lady Moncrieff said, surprised. "He must be *very* impressed."

"And Ernst?" Susan asked.

"His assignment is to get her there safely," Sir Richard said. "Only a few loose ends remain from his earlier assignment in the Netherlands."

"So, they may encounter Jan Mollenar in London again?" Michael asked.

"I would say that is very likely," Sir Richard nodded.

"It is quite remarkable, isn't it," Lady Moncrieff said, shaking her head in disbelief.

"What?" asked Sir Richard.

"That someone like Ernst, recruited by the Nazis as a youth, commissioned as an officer of the Third Reich, a man who came into our lives as an enemy, is now our ally and is trusted by the Prime Minister to escort an highly-esteemed young woman hundreds of miles across enemy territories and to deliver her safely to his office in London," she said.

The room was silent for a moment before Susan added, "And his mother and his intended have since been entrusted to our care, by miracles only the Almighty could have performed."

Rising and reaching for the bottle of sherry on the tea table, Michael filled each glass and offered a toast.

"To the miracles we have seen together, and to one more—the safe return of Ernst Hoffman to Highfield."

"Hear, hear!" said Sir Richard, as they raised their glasses to salute their absent friend.

Chapter 47

As E.D. had experienced in the past, travel in the Netherlands continued to offer more dangers and more difficulties than he encountered anywhere else in Europe. So many of the Dutch were Nazi sympathizers, some openly, and others who were secretly willing to betray neighbors and friends to ensure their own interests.

With the cities full of uniformed soldiers and the general populace with many who supported them, there was no place where E.D. and Sybil could relax for a moment. Reaching out to contacts E.D. had formerly trusted felt risky, and scheduling meetings with them was even more questionable. While E.D. and Sybil had been able to travel by rail over the last weeks, the depots in Dutch cities crawled with SS and Gestapo who employed thousands of Dutch citizens as their eyes and ears. The two were forced to keep moving, finding shelter on their own, as they could.

While avoiding railways, E.D. and Sybil became practiced bicycle thieves. Small town and village dwellers often left their bicycles unattended on the streets outside markets, bakeries, and cafes. Appropriating those bicycles became routine. Outside the city limits, while pedaling past farms or through villages, the travelers would sometimes appropriate a shovel or a hoe to rest on their handlebars. Farm tools, though part of their disguises, were also ready to serve as weapons, if required. The same tools regularly found another farmer's yard miles away when the pair drew close to the next town.

Eventually, the couple reached The Hague, where E.D. could call on his known and trusted underground allies. He and Sybil remained in hiding for almost a week while E.D. arranged their travel west to the Hoek van Holland waterfront. If all went well, they would soon be meeting Jan Mollenar just off the coast.

Four of the five underground members who aided E.D. on his last visit to The Hague, *Un*, *Deux*, *Trois*, and *Quatre*, led E.D. and Sybil out of the city under the night sky. Typical for the season, the weather was cold, damp, and windy, and traveling by night made their journey even more dismal. While two of the men led E.D. and Sybil, two others remained at varied short distances behind in case the group was followed. When a cold, spring rain began to fall, the group could travel more closely together. Members of the Gestapo were known to enjoy their comforts. A cold, rainy night would likely keep them indoors, where it was warm and dry.

Two nights of travel brought E.D. and Sybil to a beach at Hoek van Holland where the wind was at their backs. Although the east wind drenched them with rain as they made their way toward the beach, it also helped to drive their skiff and its rowers out to sea toward the flat-bottom Dutch boat waiting just offshore in the darkness. Once aboard, E.D. and Sybil were happy to find a dry corner in the cabin.

"So, your friend," Sybil asked, "the one we're meeting, is called 'Jan', right?"

"That's right," E.D. answered, yawning.

"He will meet us somewhere mid-Channel?" she asked.

"Correct," E.D. said, as he pulled a blanket close around his neck.

"And, you said he was Dutch, right?" she asked.

"How long will this interrogation last?" E.D. asked. "We have four hours or more at sea before we meet the next boat. There may be two more boats after that. Now would be a good time to catch up on the sleep you've missed over the past two nights."

"All right," she said, "but you told me he was a student studying in Leiden, and I met some Dutch students in Munich last year, so I was wondering. . ."

Heaving an annoyed sigh, E.D. said, "Wondering what? This is the last question I will answer for the night."

"I was wondering what he was studying, that's all," she said.

"Architecture in Leiden, art in London," E.D. grunted. "Good night."

"Oh, that's interesting," she said. "I was studying architecture at the Technical University in Munich."

Turning her head toward E.D., Sybil noticed he wasn't moving. Pulling her blanket away from her ear, she heard his long, exhausted snore.

Nearly five hours later, the cabin door opened, sending a cold, stiff wind over E.D.'s face. When he looked up, he saw the boat's first mate with a lantern in his hand.

"We're coming up on the *Channel Queen* soon. Best be getting ready to board," he said.

Twenty minutes later, E.D. happily shook Jan's hand and introduced Sybil.

"We need to get her to London once we land," E.D. said. "She may have business there."

"Understood," Jan said. "Thankfully, Hyde Park escaped the last of the bombings. Of course, we never know what might be coming out of the sky today."

Sybil remained surprisingly quiet, to E.D.'s satisfaction. While he and Jan talked in one corner of the cabin, she was content to doze in another.

"I've heard from SIS twice over the last three days. It seems the PM wants something the young lady can deliver," Jan said. "Is that correct?"

"Yes," E.D. answered. "She was with White Rose in Munich. She has quite a story to tell."

"White Rose is the group that distributed anti-Nazi literature, right?" Jan asked. "And some of their leaders were captured. . ."

"And tried in a mock trial, and guillotined within days," E.D. finished. "Sybil has copies of some of their leaflets. The P.M. has plans for them."

"That was at Ludwig Maximilian University, right?" Jan asked.

"That's right," E.D. said.

"And she studied there?" he asked.

"I'm not sure," E.D. answered. "We know she spent a lot of time there and worked with the founders of the group. Oh, that's right," he said, as he recalled his conversation with Sybil before he fell asleep the previous night. "I heard her mumble something last night about studying architecture at the Technical University."

"Architecture?" Jan brightened. "I was studying architecture in Leiden before I left for London."

E.D. said nothing. He just looked at Jan, then at Sybil sleeping in the corner, and back at Jan.

"Is something wrong?" Jan asked.

"I think we'll find out soon enough," E.D. said, "soon enough."

Chapter 48

"You called for me, Sir Richard?" Brenda asked as she looked through the open door of his study.

"Yes, Brenda. Come in, please," he said as he opened his newspaper and covered the open folders on his desk. "Please, have a seat. I have some news for you."

From his smile, Brenda knew the news must be good.

"It concerns Ernst, of course. I'm sure you'll be happy to learn that he landed in England and should be arriving in London today. He accomplished an earlier mission that took him to Munich, then Switzerland, and across Germany to the Netherlands and finally across the Channel to England. He brought with him a student whose life was in peril in Munich, but whose work for the Allied cause brought her to the attention of the British high command," he said.

"Her?" Brenda reacted. "Ernst was rescuing a woman, then?" she asked.

"Yes," he answered, "a rather difficult young woman, willful at times, from all reports. He seemed quite relieved when their travel on the continent was finished. He is presently in London with a Dutch associate we've known for several years."

"Thank you, Sir Richard," she said. "I apologize for the question about the young woman. "It's just that. . ." she began before he interrupted.

"Not to worry, Brenda," he said. "Your reaction is perfectly understandable. This may help," he said as he reached out to hand her a folded note. "This message came to you through my office in London. It was decoded just this morning."

Wide-eyed, Brenda reached for the note and was about to open it when Sir Richard spoke.

"Please," he said, "feel free to read it at your leisure over a cup of tea, somewhere where you can savor it. I'll let you know if any further communications arrive."

With a smile, he stood to excuse her. Offering him a parting smile and a nod of thanks when she got to the door, she turned and ran down the hall to the kitchen to open Ernst's note. When she did, she read,

My Darling Brenda,

Please forgive the long silence between my communications. In Axis territories, secure radio frequencies are impossible, and the post poses even greater risks. I dare not endanger you or our benefactors with those risks simply to satisfy my cravings. I am safe at an Allied location at present and have been granted permission to make this contact. I have no indication of how long I will be here. I expect new orders soon.

Brenda, I would gladly starve a week for one moment to look into your eyes and to hold your hand; a month to hold you in my arms. You know the passion I have for my work, a constant incentive to do whatever I can to end the indescribable Nazi evil that pervades so much of Europe. Only my passion to complete this work and return to you to spend our lives together is stronger.

I rely on your prayers. So many horrors that I have seen confirm my belief that only God can heal what Hell has brought to Europe and beyond. I am also confident that what God begins, He finishes. He brought us together, Brenda. He will do so again. I will continue to pray that the day will be soon.

Your adoring,

Ernst.

As Brenda sat at Highfield's kitchen table with tears on her cheeks, Elke arrived carrying a breakfast tea tray from the dining room. As she placed the tray on the counter next to the sink, she saw the note in Brenda's hands and tears on her face.

"Please tell me those tears are good tears, Brenda," she asked quietly.

Suddenly aware of Elke's presence, Brenda said, "Yes, very good tears. Please, come and sit with me. I'll tell you the news I've had from Sir Richard."

A few minutes later, when Brenda was able to assure Elke that Ernst was not on the continent and in danger from Axis enemies, Elke was delighted.

"Thank God, Brenda, that he's safe in London. Thank God."

"As long as the bombs aren't dropping," Brenda sighed, "as long as the bombs aren't dropping."

Brenda spent the next hour in the kitchen with Elke, helping to prepare lunch for the Moncrieffs and the Morelands. She had the dining room table set when the Morelands arrived, and she spirited the boys away while Michael, Susan, and Christine joined Lady Moncrieff and Sir Richard at the table. While Case and Reed enjoyed their lunch with Brenda in the kitchen, the rest of the family enjoyed their tuna salad sandwiches, a hearty clam chowder, and a rich apple strudel for dessert.

Once the table was cleared, Lady Moncrieff handed Susan Millie's latest letter while Elke poured coffee and tea.

"That letter arrived in this morning's post," Lady Moncrieff began. "It seems the United States Eighth Air Force is flying regularly from airfields in Suffolk—Framingham, Bungay, and Horham. The aircraft are all heavy bombers, from what she writes, noisy, but reassuring."

"Yes," Sir Richard agreed, "B-17's and B-24's, their largest."

Susan was still reading when Michael said, "We're blessed to be sending the bombs to Germany after they've sent so many our way."

Surprised by what she found in Millie's letter, Susan looked up to say, "Mother, is this correct? Myrna Wright is working with Millie at Clifton Manor now?"

"Yes," Lady Moncrieff nodded. Then, noting the surprise on Susan's face, she added, "Oh, perhaps I forgot to tell you. Last month, Millie wrote to say her daughter, Agnes, was concerned for her. Millie had celebrated her sixty-eighth birthday, and Agnes asked her to consider retiring and joining her and Millie's grandchildren in Cambridge."

"But, where does Myrna come into this, Mother?" Susan asked.

"Well, I knew if Millie was to retire, Clifton Manor would need someone to take her place," Lady Moncrieff began. "I thought immediately of Myrna and her children—without a father now—and I hoped Myrna might enjoy secure employment and a place for her family to live at Clifton Manor. I wrote to her, and she agreed right away. They're moving in within a few weeks. At only twenty-six years of age, she may be with us for decades."

"What a capital thought, Mother," Michael said. "Claude must be smiling in heaven."

"I'm sure he is," Sir Richard agreed.

Looking again at the letter, Susan said, "And here's something about another visit from Mr. Fenton. Millie writes, 'He stopped by to thank me for sending his message along to you, and to say that he appreciates his new benefactor.' Do you know what that means?" Susan asked.

"Oh, I think I may have a clue about that," Sir Richard said, as he leaned back in his chair. "It was after you spoke with Joseph about the letter you received from Mr. Fenton, Susan. Joseph was interested in seeing the evidence I had discovered concerning his family line. He was thrilled to find that Mr. Fenton was his cousin. Acquainted with no other relatives, however distant, Joseph was happy to discover a way to help a relative. When we last spoke, Joseph had asked his solicitor to suggest an appropriate monthly allowance to help Mr. Fenton, whose veteran's benefits might prove insufficient for his needs."

Susan smiled as she said, "From orphan to benefactor, Joseph. When will you cease to amaze us?"

Chapter 49

The sun was low in the sky as E.D. and Sybil followed Jan Mollenar to the Abram's London townhouse in Hyde Park. Their walk from the underground stop at Hyde Park Corner was not a long one, but weary from so many days and nights of travel and tension, the trio could hardly wait to enjoy a hot bath, a change of clothes, a warm meal, and a soft bed. Thankfully, Jan was ready to provide for all those needs.

As they approached their destination, Sybil was impressed at the condition of the buildings in the neighborhood, unharmed by the Blitz.

"I expected so much more destruction from the bombings here. The newspapers in Munich reported that London had faced much more intense destruction than we did there, but," she said as she turned to Jan, "your neighborhood looks virtually untouched."

"Hyde Park has been fortunate, but other parts of the city, especially the East End, have been harder hit," he said.

"And please don't forget that the Nazis tell the press in Germany what to report," E.D. reminded them, "so the truth remains unavailable on the continent. What they report of Nazi successes during the war are gross exaggerations." Then, recognizing their destination, he said, "Ah, and here we are."

"I'm impressed," Sybil said. "You have a very nice home, Jan."

"Oh, it's not mine," Jan laughed. "I remain a tenant, and a very grateful one. I could never afford anything this nice."

As Jan opened the front door for his guests, E.D. asked, "Same room upstairs, Jan?"

"Yes," Jan answered, "it should be as you left it."

After thanking Jan, E.D. mounted the stairs, leaving Sybil and Jan behind.

"You have a choice of rooms," Jan said as he led Sybil toward a room at the rear of the house. "This room, once the Abram's study, is now used as a bedroom. There is a bath just down the hall. Your other option is a third bedroom on the second floor where E.D. and I are sleeping."

Taking a quick glance into the room, Sybil smiled and said, "I think I'd be quite comfortable right here, thank you."

"Deborah left a closet full of clothes when she and Jacob left for Canada. If anything there suits your fancy," he said, "feel free to appropriate it."

"I would be delighted with a change of clothes," she said, "but first I'd love to see the bathroom and draw a tub."

"Right this way," Jan said as he led her down the hall. As Sybil stepped into the bathroom, Jan continued, "I'll see about something to eat after we've all had a chance to settle in."

As he turned to walk back to the front hall, Sybil had a question.

"Jan, you mentioned the name, 'Abrams,' didn't you?"

"Yes," Jan answered, "Deborah and Daniel Abrams."

"That name sounds so familiar, but I can't recall why. Perhaps it will come to me," she said as she turned toward her bedroom. "Again, thank you, Jan," she added, looking intently over her shoulder toward him as he turned to walk away.

On his way toward the front hall, he found himself walking slowly and pondering what had just happened. Something about her eyes, so intent, and that long look over her shoulder was saying something to him, but it was in a language he didn't understand.

"I don't know what's up," he said to himself, "but I'd like to find out."

After a trip to Harrods for groceries, Jan served a lamb stew with warm slices of National Loaf and cheddar. To everyone's delight, the Abrams had left a stock of red wine in the basement. The smells from the kitchen brought Sybil and E.D. to the table.

"Rationing makes things simple, but adequate," Jan said, "keeping us thankful. Would you open the wine, E.D.? You'll find a corkscrew and some glasses on the sideboard."

As E.D. was filling three wine glasses, Sybil joined the men and helped set the table. When she had filled the last water glass and put the pitcher in the center of the table, she sat and started the dinner conversation.

"It came to me in the midst of my bath why the name 'Abrams' seemed so familiar to me," she began. "When my grandparents left Germany before the war, they first spent some time in England and then emigrated to Canada, where they were not allowed entry at Halifax. Eventually, they were able to enter the United States at New York City and made their home in Washington Heights. They often spoke about a family named Abrams who arrived in New York at the same time but eventually made their home in, I believe, Connecticut. Because they lived less than a day's drive apart, they saw each other several times a year."

"This is remarkable," Jan said as he stepped into the kitchen and returned with an envelope. "Waiting in the post when we arrived this afternoon was a letter from Daniel and Deborah," he said. Handing the letter to E.D., he continued, "Look at the return address and the postmark."

"I see," E.D. remarked. "The same family, do you think?"

"Perhaps," Jan answered.

Frustrated, Sybil asked, "Would one of you inform me, please?"

"Of course," E.D. said. As he handed her the envelope, Jan explained.

"Daniel and Deborah Abrams lived in Canada for a short time after leaving the Netherlands. They later moved to Connecticut to make their home with Daniel's uncle, who had moved there with his wife and their children some years previously."

"Then your Abrams may be. . ." Sybil said.

"Related to *your* Abrams, but probably a generation removed," Jan said.

"And what did they do here in London?" she asked.

"Daniel taught art at the Royal College of Art. He met Deborah there when she was a student," Jan said.

"And how did you first encounter them?" Sybil asked.

"That's a long story," Jan hesitated, "but they were grateful for some help I was able to provide them while I was studying architecture at Leiden University. I helped them travel to London, and when they left, I became the keeper of their castle, so to speak," he smiled, hiding his wink to E.D.

"You were studying architecture?" she asked.

"Yes," he answered, "but my real passion is in art."

"How interesting," she said, turning her chair toward his, "because I was studying architecture in Munich, but I found myself spending more time with students from Ludwig Maximilian and leaving architecture behind."

The conversation continued through dinner, although it became more of a twosome than a threesome. E.D., having little to add to the dialogue for two, poured a second glass of wine and excused himself to his room to prepare for his debriefing at SIS headquarters in the morning. When he went downstairs to return his wine glass an hour later, Jan and Sybil were still talking, but they had moved to the sofa in the parlor. Interrupting them with only a wave to say, “Good night,” E.D. started up the stairs to his bedroom. On the way up, he found himself shaking his head, not in disbelief, but in confirmation of what he had seen developing in the cabin of a fishing boat only a day or two before.

Chapter 50

E.D. rose early the following morning, planning to be the first in the kitchen. To his surprise, though, when he was halfway down the stairs, he heard Sybil and Jan engaged in an animated conversation about the remarkable ability of French impressionist artists to capture so much life in their paintings, especially when they were away from their studios, *en plein air*. E.D.'s arrival at the kitchen didn't interrupt or slow the couple's conversation. When he finished his coffee and his hard-boiled egg, he wasn't entirely sure they had noticed him enter the room half an hour earlier. Interrupting them again, he reminded Sybil that they needed to leave for her meeting at the Cabinet Rooms in Whitehall shortly.

When E.D. and Sybil arrived at Whitehall at 9:45, they were greeted by uniformed security personnel at the door. Their meeting with the Secretary to the Deputy Prime Minister was scheduled for ten o'clock. Sybil and E.D. were ushered into the Secretary's office promptly on the hour.

Rising from his desk chair, the Secretary introduced himself. "Alden Saunders, Secretary to the Deputy Prime Minister. May I offer you some tea?" he asked as he indicated a tea tray sitting on a side table near his desk.

Deferring to Sybil, E.D. said, "Miss Lytle?"

"No, thank you," she said.

No, thank you," E.D. added.

"Then, let us get down to business," Saunders said as he took his seat. "The Prime Minister has been deeply impressed by the work of White Rose for some time, and, I might add, deeply saddened and distressed over the sudden loss of your comrades for whom he maintains profound respect. It is he who directed the Deputy Prime Minister to arrange this meeting."

"Thank you," Sybil said. "I appreciate the Prime Minister's understanding and kind regards."

"He would be addressing you personally, but he is presently unavailable to us. He has asked me, on his behalf, to request your permission and assistance in distributing many thousands of copies of White Rose's Sixth Manifesto," Saunders said.

Looking at her purse which contained several of the last copies she possessed, she asked, "Many thousands? I am honored to receive such a request, Mr. Secretary, but our network has been trying to distribute large numbers in the past and we've been thwarted at every turn. With all due respect, can you tell me how such a task could be accomplished?"

"By all means, Miss Lytle," he replied. "The Prime Minister plans to engage the assistance of the RAF to distribute them from the air all over Germany and beyond."

Overwhelmed by the thought of RAF bombers showering thousands of White Rose leaflets over Germany from the sky, Sybil looked at E.D. with wide eyes as he offered her a knowing smile and a nod. Turning to Secretary Saunders, Sybil took a moment to compose herself before responding.

"Mr. Saunders, please inform the Prime Minister that I am delighted to pledge my assistance in any way it may be required to achieve such a lofty and worthy goal for those who died for White Rose, Sophie and Hans Scholl, and Christoph Probst."

"Splendid," Saunders smiled. "A report of this meeting will await the Prime Minister upon his return to this office."

Sybil's walk back to the Abrams' townhouse with E.D. was filled with tears of joy, tears of mourning, and, in the end, moments of elation. The goals her friends had worked so long and so hard to achieve would soon be realized, but not among a few hundred, or a few thousand, but among hundreds of thousands in every part of Germany and beyond. Her mourning tears flowed because Sophie, Hans, and Christoph would not see the rewards of their convictions and dedication to their cause. Amidst her moments of tearful elation, E.D. offered a thought.

In a quiet voice, he said, "I believe in a hereafter, Sybil, one where all we've done in good faith and entrusted to God does not end. Your friends were good people who, I believe, entrusted themselves and their passion for the truth to God. In time, He relieved them of their angst and the burdens they shared when they could not see an end to the evil before them. He took them home. They suffer no more, and where they are, they will see and rejoice in the work you are helping to complete. I am convinced the world will not forget them."

"Thank you, E.D.," she said through her tears. "I know I will not forget, and I am glad to give many thousands of others a reason to remember them. Thank you."

Half an hour later, E.D. delivered Sybil to Jan in Hyde Park. As the townhouse door opened, Sybil, still somewhere between tears and laughter, rushed to Jan and, pulling him toward the parlor, said, "Jan, you won't believe it. I need to tell you *everything*."

E.D. could only shake his head and smile. After gathering his attaché, he set out for the SIS headquarters at 54 Broadway for his debriefing.

As with other debriefings upon his return from the field, a stenographer recorded every word. E.D. sat before three men who alternated their questions while E.D. responded. For E.D., the only tension he felt came from his desire to give the committee the best information possible.

At the close of the 60-minute interview, the chairman thanked him, shook his hand, and handed him a sealed SIS envelope, followed by three words, "You've earned it."

Unsure of what the chairman meant, E.D. thanked him, put the envelope safely in his attaché, and waited to open it until he was seated in the back seat of a cab on his way to Hyde Park. When he opened the envelope, he found a fresh set of orders indicating an immediate eight-week leave, complete with RAF air transport between London and Prince Edward Island. His flight west from RAF Northolt was scheduled for take-off at 17:00 hours that afternoon. The orders bore the signature and seal of Sir Stewart Menzies, Chief of SIS, known by many at SIS as "C."

Relaxing into the back seat of the cab and leaving the man called "E.D." behind for the moment, Ernst Hoffman let a daydream carry him across the ocean.

"Eight weeks," he whispered to himself. "Let me see. Four days, perhaps fewer, to fly from London to Charlottetown. Four more to return. That leaves almost seven full weeks."

Smiling broadly as he looked out the cab window, he asked aloud, "How long do honeymoons generally last during wartime?"

Terms and abbreviations

Allies—those countries that fought against the Axis powers in World War II, chiefly the United Kingdom, the United States, France, the Soviet Union, and China

Asamkirche—an early eighteenth-century Baroque church in Munich, Germany

Astra 300—a small semi-automatic pistol manufactured by Astra Unceta in Spain from 1922 to 1946

Axis—those countries that fought against the Allied powers in World War II, primarily Germany, Italy, and Japan

Badischer Bahnhof—a railway station in Basel, Switzerland, near the German-Switzerland border

Botter boat—A flat-bottomed boat with a round, wide, high-rising bow, a cabin, a lower, open stern, often used in shallow waters in the Netherlands.

Cafe Luitpold—a well-known high-end café in Munich during World War II

Clerical stole—a long, narrow band of fabric worn around the neck by ordained ministers and priests

Dallmayr—a notable delicatessen in Munich

En plein air—"In the open air," the practice of painting entire works outdoors

Epinephrine inhaler—a therapy used to treat asthma

Fleet Air Arm—the Royal Navy's aircraft division operating from Royal Navy ships

Gestapo—the official secret police of Nazi Germany and German-occupied Europe

Hirohito—the Emperor of Japan during World War II

Hitlerjugend—Hitler Youth, the youth wing of the Nazi party

HMS—His Majesty's Ship

Kriegsmarine—the navy of Nazi Germany from 1935 to 1945

Leutnant—the lowest junior officer rank in the armed forces of Germany

Low Countries—Belgium, the Netherlands, and Luxembourg

Luftwaffe—the air force of Nazi Germany from 1935 to 1945

Mussolini—the fascist dictator of Italy during World War II

National Loaf—a whole-meal bread rationed by the British government during World War II

Nazi—the National Socialist Party led by Adolf Hitler that ruled Germany from 1933 to 1945

Oberleutnant—and Upper Lieutenant, the highest lieutenant rank in the German armed forces

Odeonsplatz—a large square in central Munich

OSS—the United States Office of Strategic Services, later renamed the CIA

PEI—Prince Edward Island

PTO—Power take-off, a mechanical system that transfers an engine's power to external implements or machinery

Quinacrine—a WWII-era antimalarial drug

RAF—Royal Air Force

RCAF—Royal Canadian Air Force

RCN—Royal Canadian Navy

RN—Royal Navy

SIS—the Secret Intelligence Service in the UK, later commonly known as MI6

SS—Schutzstaffel, a major paramilitary organization under Hitler's Nazi Party

The Abwehr - the German military intelligence service from 1920 to 1944

U-boat—Unterseeboot (under-sea-boat), German submarines used during World War II

Walther PPK—a small, easily concealed semi-automatic pistol often used by SIS personnel

Wehrmacht—the unified armed forces of Nazi Germany from 1935 to 1945

WRNS—the Women's Royal Naval Service, commonly known as Wrens

Zwart mijn vriend—Black, my friend

www.ingramcontent.com/pod-product-compliance
Lightning Source LLC
LaVergne TN
LVHW050634100826
845148LV00011B/1856

* 9 7 9 8 3 8 5 2 8 2 0 3 6 *